THE RIFT

RACHAEL CRAW

CANDLEWICK PRESS

First U.S. edition 2019
First published by Walker Books (Australia) 2018

Library of Congress Catalog Card Number 2019939259
ISBN 978-1-5362-1128-3

19 20 21 22 23 24 LBM 10 9 8 7 6 5 4 3 2 1

Printed in Melrose Park, IL, U.S.A.

This book was typeset in Adobe Caslon Pro.

Candlewick Press
99 Dover Street
Somerville, Massachusetts 02144

visit us at www.candlewick.com

For Ian

WARNING NOTES

Cal's too late. He knows it even as he leaps down the thickly treed slope, knees jarring with the impact of each footstep. Certainty like an iron clamp fastens at the top of his throat, making his breath short. The long oilskin hampers his stride. His rifle thumps, bruising his hip. Heavy rain slicks his hair to his face, and he mops it back, hot with frustration and fear. Everything's working against him — weather, terrain, gear, the thunder of his pulse — obscuring the Voice of the Herd.

Clinging to the initial flare of instinct, Cal makes for the Western Spit. He strains to hear past the torrential rain. There's no howling. Not yet. Maybe it's too far from the Rift for the animal's distress signal to draw the Hounds. Or maybe that's wishful thinking. There are only four days until the moon grows full; the timing couldn't be worse.

Reeva's frantic cawing echoes above the treetops, and he curses her — *useless bird*. He could have used the aerial support to boost his night vision. His boots slide in the wet, mud and leaf mold threatening to wrench his ankles.

It must be a full five minutes since he first felt the alarm up on the Ridgeway. Perhaps he should be grateful he's too agitated to tap into it now—the signal must be roaring with grief. That first sign of distress had been a shock vibration in his mind—like the string of a fragile instrument, viciously plucked. If he'd been concentrating, he'd have caught the earlier warning notes of danger and deployed his raven to scout. But he hadn't been paying attention, too self-absorbed, obsessing over the news he'd heard in the mess hall this morning. Meg Archer is coming home.

Meg Archer.

When the signal from the Old Herd finally broke into his consciousness, panic cost him precious seconds *and* his link with Reeva.

Cal curses himself. *This proves everything they've ever said about you, you worthless piece of—*

An image flashes into his mind. A doe, tall, slender, strong. A sable coat with silver markings on her chest and flanks. Deep, brown, fathomless eyes. Ancient, knowing, wild. His gut plummets. *What if it's Fallon? What if it's Fallon and she's been killed by a trapper's snare?*

The unthinkable shame of losing the matriarch of the Old Herd . . . it scrambles his brain. He pictures himself denounced by the head ranger before the whole community, cast out under the full weight of his failure, heralding the total collapse of everything the Black Water Rangers stand for. Thousands

2

of years of toil, trials, and tradition passed from parent to child, nullified in a single night's screwup by a kid who never deserved to be counted among their ranks.

God. God. Please don't let it be Fallon.

As if her name in his thoughts summons it, the Voice of the Herd flickers in his mind. He gasps—or sobs—and skids to a stop. His chest heaves, and his quads and calves burn, but the momentary relief of connection fills him, centers him. Oneness, wonder, and longing for the mountain. Longing for the veins of living energy pulsing in the ley lines. He listens. Even that small flicker thrums with oppressive grief. Knowing fills him, confirming the location like an internal GPS. There, in the deep shadow, forty feet below where the narrow track twists back on itself, a light gray smudge swings from a noose. His skin contracts with goose bumps; if his hair wasn't slicked to his head, tendrils would rise at the nape of his neck.

He sees the antlers, and his heart beats. *It's not Fallon. It's not Fallon.*

UNSPOKEN MESSAGES

The gloves are a polymer-based microfiber blended with Tibetan yak fur. Better than her rock-climbing gloves. Better than her hiking gloves. Better than any of her kayaking, water sports, or orienteering gloves. Meg slides them out of the fabric drawstring bag like she's handling a booby trap and lays them beside her on the bed. Even the ethically sourced eco-packaging is hipster nonsense.

There's no way Sargent bought them on Black Water Island, that's for sure. The knot in her gut gives a nauseating little tug. Two hundred and forty-seven dollars—the price tag left on the gift. Her mother's jaw clicked with the grinding of her teeth when Meg unwrapped them in the kitchen yesterday morning.

That man.

Meg had stuffed them in her dresser drawer, an odd mix of giddy and bitter and aware. So many unspoken messages. But how to read the meaning? Meg fixates on the unlikely logistics of Sargent selecting the gloves from a catalog, posting an order at Leaman's General Store, explaining to Mrs. Leaman who they're for and the occasion. Maybe Mrs. Leaman helped him choose. It's the first gift Sargent has bothered to send her since he became head ranger. It may have arrived a few days early but still well within the week of her eighteenth birthday. Blue wrapping paper decorated with gray antlers. No card, of course, just her name and address and a Black Water postage stamp.

He could have waited and given them to her in person.

An alert pings on her phone, and she bounces with a pulse of nervous energy. Eleven fifteen. The taxi for the Midnight Ferry will be here soon. Rain thunders on the roof. She can hear her mother moving through the house checking windows and locks. Meg blows through her lips; she's been packed for days. Passport and ticket secure beneath the old troop leader trophy on her dresser. Now only minutes to fill. She dabs tiny drops of Bio-Oil on her palms, massaging it into the rough lattice of scars. The webbing of melted skin is numb, a hash of dead nerve endings in raw pinks and mottled whites.

Bio-Oil is supposed to be good for scars; pregnant women rub it on their stretch marks. She's been religious about smearing it on her hands morning and night for almost nine years, though she doubts the manufacturer had campfire burns in mind for its application. She ignores the tremor in her fingers and blows on her palms, rubbing them on the smooth unmarked tops of her hands, testing for residue. Once she's sure they're dry, she slips on the gloves.

Slim fitting, lightweight yet tough, water-repellent, perfect for outdoor pursuits and light rock-climbing. Breathable fabric to keep her cool in the heat and warm in the cold. An invitation to explore the island? A practical solution to hide her scars from prying eyes and annoying questions? Maybe it's a warning. *Cover your hands.*

Somewhere a Tibetan yak herder is keeping his family warm and fed because of these gloves. It says so on the package.

Footsteps in the hall and her mother opens the door. Meg squeezes her hands between her knees. Cora leans on the threshold, narrowing her eyes at the glove packaging. She sucks the corner of her lower lip and tucks her hair beneath her beanie. It used to be dark like Meg's, but after the final round of chemo, it grew back silver, and her mother refuses to dye it. Usually she looks badass with it styled into an architectural quiff, but tonight's about warmth not fashion. Otherwise, Cora's coloring, sharp brow line, yellow-green eyes, and expressive mouth provide a middle-age glimpse of Meg's future. Right now the future looks tired and irritable.

Her mother zips her thick jacket with a quick, sharp yank. She has her cane hooked over her arm, her expression resigned. Cora's cancer was a tumor on her femur. The surgery required removal of part of the bone. Surgical splints let her walk and run for the most part with ease, and she keeps herself fit, but after a long day on her feet, her leg gets weak and tired. The cane eases the load. Sometimes it annoys her, while other times, she wields it like a scepter. "You have everything?"

Meg nods.

Lines pull at the corners of Cora's mouth. "It's not too late to change your mind."

"I'm not bailing now; this is a united front."

"You could be home with the Wi-Fi."

"*You're* the one who'll miss the Wi-Fi."

"Sooo much." Cora groans, and Meg grins, then her mother grows serious. "He won't make it easy."

"Fine, I'll take my bow." Meg gets to her feet and acts like she's going to get it from her closet. "I'll take the arrows with the short fletching. That way if he gives us any grief, I can shoot from a distance."

Cora yields a weary smile. "As much as I love that idea, this is a no-weapons scenario."

"That's not really fair, given the island could be crawling with Fortune Hunters. *And* it's my birthday; I should get to shoot *someone*."

"Fine, but you're not officially eighteen for another forty-eight hours, and I'm pretty sure there's something in the scout oath about not killing people." Cora glances at her daughter's hands. The humor fades, and Meg pulls on her jacket, jamming her arms through the sleeves.

"It's not a big deal; I would have worn gloves anyway."

"He'll think he's won."

"Let him."

"You know it's manipulation, sending you a birthday present."

The knot tugs hard in Meg's gut, and she shrugs, gaze dropping to her hiking boots. "Probably."

Cora steps in the room and brushes Meg's bangs back behind her ear, the gesture achingly tender. Her expression shifts back and forth from fierce to fearful. "Don't pin your hopes on Sargent."

Outside, the sound of a car pulling into the driveway. The taxi's here.

"All I want is what he owes me." Meg swallows a sharp lump and hoists her pack onto her shoulder. "We get the deed. Sell the house. Pay the bills. Get on with our lives."

SUDDEN FROST

Cal pauses to scent the air. Moss, leaf mold, old scat, boot rubber, something plastic, animal-panic sweat . . . fear. No distinct human scent. No whiff of deodorant or soap or the lingering trace of cleaning supplies. How is that possible? He pivots and drops, cutting the corner of the track. He lands noiselessly on a mossy outcropping and releases a long, shaky breath. *It's not Fallon.* Crouching brings him face-to-face with a young buck from the Old Herd; its blank eyes bulge from the pressure of the noose.

He shudders, his initial relief swallowed by the chilling presence of death. Awareness prickles his skin, feathering behind his ears. He presses the back of his hand to his nose, and his breath turns white in the cold night air. A soft snapping draws his gaze to his feet where, despite the rain, an inch of moss around his boots crackles with sudden frost. He waits a beat or two for his head to stop swimming.

"This isn't my kill," he whispers, as though he might convince death, as though he might convince himself, or at least keep from passing out. The downpour doesn't cloak the stench of freshly voided bowel and bladder. He rubs the mint leaves through his shirt pocket and ducks his head to draw a cleansing breath. It barely helps.

The snare didn't break the buck's neck; it was death by strangulation. Not the quick release of life in a single snap. Incompetence or cruelty? Cal can't help but imagine the beast's terror, the panicked flailing of its legs. The pain it must have suffered. The swelling horror of the Old Herd sensing that pain.

What was a buck from the Old Herd doing on this side of the ley line? This is Lower Herd territory. Old Herd deer stay above the electromagnetic surges that ripple along the borders. He shivers at the thought of what would drive the beast to leave its protected territory and shuts his mind against the dark rush of possibility. Maybe his chief concern shouldn't be that the animal's distress signal will *draw* the Hounds from the Rift. Maybe the growing moon has *already* made the Rift so unstable, a Hound broke through and terrified the young buck, causing it to bolt. No. He's letting fear scramble his thoughts. There is nothing to suggest the Rift is active. No howling. No dogs. Not yet.

He sighs and tips his head back to catch rainwater in his mouth—rinse and spit—before steadying himself to recite the crossing prayer. Barely moving his lips, he speaks in the old tongue. Something like a sigh vibrates back to him, the ancient soul, separating from the animus, lifting away. The chill lifts with it. The frost melts. His breath no longer mists the air. Rubbing the goose bumps from his arms and behind his ears, he sighs at the poor buck. All that remains is the vessel. Meat, mainlanders would say. The thought brings a sour taste to his mouth.

Finally the Voice of the Herd lifts. His mind clears and the heaviness too. The sense of sudden emptiness almost brings another sob. He reminds himself the rush of grief is a good thing; *real* rangers value their connection with the Old Herd. Sargent says so all the time. Apprentices are careful not to moan about headaches or complain about the Voice of the Herd keeping them awake when Sargent is around. Cal never complains. Admittedly he can tune in and out with ease, but he doesn't let on about it; he's unpopular enough as it is.

Whatever the case, Cal's extra bells and whistles won't save him from punishment. Sargent may lack the flashy gifts that traditionally reveal themselves in head rangers, but his sensitivity to the Voice of the Herd is second to none. He'll know already about the buck. Cal will be stuck on latrine duty for the rest of the month. Worse if the Hounds come after his screwup.

Shit.

Exactly.

The rain is louder than he realized and the forest muted beneath it as though the shoulders of the mountain are hunkering down to wait it out. Cal doesn't touch the deer, not with the death so fresh and vicious. Though it grates him to leave the buck hanging, if the poacher intends to claim his prize, Cal needs the bait to remain like the surrounding area—untouched.

The snare is attached to the stripped trunk of a sturdy sapling, and the knot is crude, no ranger's finesse. Whoever tied it will have to cut the line, and a ranger would despise the waste. He frowns. Ranger's hemp. Poacher's knot. He calculates the length of rope, the angle of the branch, the trigger. Everything looks roughly coordinated.

He sniffs the air again, but the rain has obliterated any lingering scent of the poachers. Scanning the dirt and leaf mold, he notes fresh boot prints hastily covered and a yellow lighter discarded below the rock face. Near it are a couple of crushed beer cans and a crumpled package of vending machine candy. Mainlanders and a blatant *screw you* to the rangers who guard the island.

For most poachers, the antlers alone would be worth risking a ranger's bullet to the back of the head. With Nutris Pharmaceuticals maintaining a stranglehold on the island's cull tenders, a volatile black-market trade in Actaeon's Bane keeps the island's protectors on high alert. Not even the rangers' shoot-first policy fully discourages poachers from trying their luck in the off-season. Sargent warned them to be on guard, but the boldness of such an attempt so close to the cull shocks him.

He shakes his head and hoists himself onto the lower branches of the nearest tree. His shoulders tighten, and the echo of last month's fractured rib twinges with the effort of hauling his body weight. He makes a quick, careful crossing to the upper track for one last look. He'll take cover in the thick scrub above the path and wait. If there's no sign of the poacher by sunrise, he'll have to shift the carcass before it attracts predators. Or something worse.

He doesn't want to think about returning to camp and breaking the news without catching the guilty party first, and he sure as hell doesn't want another broken rib or black eye, not with Meg about to arrive. Any mistake would make him wary, but to lose one of the Old Herd on the Northwest Loop is more than unsettling. It feels loaded with meaning. A message or threat. He rubs his face, unconsciously tracing the half-moon scar on his jaw. Meg coming now, with the cull so close and the full moon too . . .

A distant cawing reaches him through the noise of the rain. Reeva, her panic turned to lament.

FORTUNE HUNTER

There are only a handful of protesters at the port. It doesn't make Meg any less nervous. Two small groups huddle behind protective bollards at either side of the security gate, illuminated by the cordon floodlights, wilted by the rain. Meg reads their picket signs through the darkened window of the taxi. On the left, signs from the Voice of Saint Francis: ONLY KILLERS CULL. STOP THE SLAUGHTER. SAVE BLACK WATER. On the right, signs from their opponent, Heal Our Kids: ACTAEON'S BANE = MY CURE. DEREGULATE! MAKE MEDICINE NOW!

Her whole body trembles, and Cora squeezes her arm.

Meg remembers when she first arrived on the mainland at eight years old. *A frightening press of people and flashing lights. Her burned hands cradled in ice packs and medical gauze. The bloodied back of her neck thickly bandaged. More people than the entire population of Black Water pack the wharf—furious, hungry, and wild-eyed—banners and pickets waving. Paramedics lift her from the ferry onto an ambulance gurney, shouting for people to move back—make some room. Her mother, pale and breathless beside her, murmurs assurances she can't hear above the crowd. In the back of the ambulance, traffic lights blink through the window, a world so huge and treeless it frightens her.*

She wonders if any of the same protesters are here tonight.

Many of the usual groups are well-coordinated. Sure enough, some of them pull phones from their pockets as the taxi pulls up to the cordon. Meg guesses they'll live-stream each arrival or log commentary on social media. A drum rolls fast and hard in her chest. She tugs the hood of her jacket low over her eyes, and Cora does the same; neither of them want to see their faces splashed on VoSF's anti–Actaeon's Bane websites. Nor do they want to become targets for black-market recruitment.

Two armed Ministry for Primary Industries workers stalk toward the taxi, but Meg's eyes are on the protesters. "Can't we just tell them we're not here for the cull?"

Cora gives her a look that says *We've had this conversation.* "Don't engage."

They pay the driver and show the men their ferry tickets and passports. The men frown but nod and grunt and lead the way to the registration office. A long walk. The air is cold and briny. Meg blinks against the floodlights. Her joints are mud-packed, and she struggles to keep step with Cora.

Though she braces for it, no one shouts or throws things from the picket line. She doesn't risk lifting her head to check faces for curiosity or judgment. There's still a week before the official start of the cull. Things will heat up between now and then with more Hunters, sponsors, and corporate officials arriving from all over the country. The numbers of protesters will grow, and it won't be silent. The news has been running clips from old protests, noisy, volatile clashes.

Meg wants to call out, *This isn't what it looks like! We're not Fortune Hunters!*

The registration "office" is a windowless freezer. Three white counters sit in parallel lines. Soaring steel beams crisscross the ceiling. Droplights divide the shadows with shafts of cold light. A Fortune Hunter is being processed for the cull. A man with a jagged scar on the back of his head, carving a path through his short blond hair. He gives a brief gravelly reply to the officials, shifting his shoulders beneath an expensive-looking coat. Meg squints for a sign of a Nutris Pharmaceuticals logo on his pack. They tend to arrive closer to the start of the cull—they don't have to fight for a place to stay, and they get to drive the Lower Herd down the mountain, guaranteed kills.

She follows her mother to the first counter, watching the Fortune Hunter's back while Cora answers the customs official's questions. Former residents. Not Hunters. Not Nutris reps. Not Mobile Freezing Works processors or cull vendors or temporary infrastructure service workers. The island gets busy during the cull. The official scans their Black Water passports. Another checklist of questions. Declarations. Intended length of stay? Three or four days—if Sargent cooperates.

Meanwhile, at the next counter, the Fortune Hunter is

having his weapons processed. Rifles, handguns, knives, and a crossbow. He hands over paperwork as the official asks for his gun license, medical certificate, police vetting form, psychological test results, and verification of affiliations. Everything confirms he is legal and healthy. Meg shivers, picturing her own longbow hanging in her closet. Culls are notoriously chaotic. Rangers won't hesitate to put down a trigger-happy weekend warrior.

Cora tugs her sleeve, and they move toward the final counter. As they pass, Meg stares at the side of the Fortune Hunter's face. He has the look of an aged soap star, heavily tanned with fans of pale lines around his eyes indicating an outdoorsy life and lots of manly squinting. He looks up and smirks at her. Meg coldly cuts her gaze away, surprising herself with her own boldness. Is it that ingrained, even nine years on, the instinctual suspicion of Fortune Hunters?

They reach the final counter, and their packs are processed through a security scanner. A woman waves a paddle over her body.

The weight of her gear seems heavier than she remembers from her bedroom. Now her face feels as numb as her feet. "Thanks," she mutters and heads for the exit to the dock, trying hard not to wobble as she walks. Cora offers a bolstering smile, but she looks as grim and uncertain as Meg feels.

It's dark on the dockside, broad strokes of layered black, wharf and buildings hunkered beneath an ominously bowed sky. Meg tastes ozone in the air. Offshore, the sea will be rough. At least she was too nervous to eat before she came, though she doubts it will keep her stomach from folding itself inside out once they're on the water.

It's a jittery walk from the registry building all the way down the wharf to where the Midnight Ferry boards passengers. The well-lit cordon at the front gate seems a long way behind them. There are no officials to be seen except the ones in reflective vests beneath a single lamppost at the far end of the dock. It's dark, and the rain is loud. The spider-crawl sensation up her spine doesn't help. Shadows left and right cloak a corridor of shipping containers stacked in tiers of three. Graffiti splashes the sides like spilled blood. NUTRIS PHARMACEUTICALS = NATURE RAPISTS.

"Misses?"

Meg swears, a skittering two-step almost taking her off balance beneath the weight of her pack. Cora steadies her.

"Excuse me, misses," a man calls, a stage whisper from a gap between containers.

"We can't help you," Cora says, pulling Meg behind her.

A shadowy form takes a step toward them. "Please, misses."

"Stay there." Cora extends her hand like she can shoot laser beams from her palm.

"I'm not going to hurt you. *Please.*"

"I'm not—we're not—"

"My boy needs help . . ." He shuffles forward, brushing his hands over a creased gray suit between the flaps of his overcoat. The desperation in his face is harrowing. "My boy, he's—he's very sick."

Meg's gut sinks. How did he get past the cordon? He could be shot on sight.

"We can't help you," Cora says, pleading in her voice. "We're not Hunters."

"I can pay—"

"We can't take your money. You know we can't."

His Adam's apple bobs above the yellowing collar of his shirt. "I can pay you." He digs inside his overcoat, drawing out a wallet. The silver clasp winks in the low light, a Chinese dragon.

"Stop," she hisses. "We're not Hunters. Even if we were, you know what happens to smugglers."

"Please." His face screws up, and he digs in his other pocket, retrieving a photograph, lined from folding. "Mika is six years old. He has a tumor. On his heart . . ." He presses it into her hands. "Please, just look at him."

The boy wears a Batman T-shirt. He grins at the camera, nose wrinkled in delight. Meg wants to howl. Cora blinks and her hands shake. "He's beautiful. I'm sorry. There's nothing I can do."

The man groans and lunges at Cora, grabbing her coat. Cora gasps, and Meg yelps.

"Please. Please. I have money."

"I can't help you!"

"Let her go!" Meg yanks at his sleeve.

Trying to pull herself free, Cora drops her cane and overbalances beneath the weight of her pack, bringing him with her as she topples. Meg shouts, but panic takes the punch from her voice—she doesn't want to get the man killed. Her mother thrashes beneath him like an upended turtle, helpless to right herself.

A pounding of boots and the blond Fortune Hunter is there, his gear dropped on the dock. Grunting, he grabs the man off her mother with an upward *whoosh*.

The man in the suit cries out, flailing his arms and legs, but the blond man is bigger and stronger. "Go!" he barks at Cora and Meg, jerking his head in the direction of the ferry. "And keep your mouths shut. I'm not missing this boat for a police interview."

Meg helps her mother up, and Cora grabs her cane. For a moment, they stand frozen as he drags the man back between the containers. A dull thud precedes a gasp and a whimper. The sounds bring Cora back to life, and she hauls Meg away, walking so fast she almost breaks into a run. Meg stumbles along beside her, heart thumping.

"What if he hurts him?"

Cora shakes her head. "He won't hurt him."

"It sounded like he was hurting him."

"Meg, we're not getting involved."

"We're *already* involved."

Cora swings her to a stop, lips pale, eyes wide and glassy. "There's no way they'll let us board if we report it. The slightest whiff of smuggling . . ." She shakes her head tightly. "We'd never set foot on Black Water again, and there goes your inheritance."

Blinking away the sting of tears, Meg gives a small nod at the crumpled photo still clutched in her mother's hand. "Then you better hide that."

Cora swallows and stares at the little dark-haired boy, a quiver in her lip. She glances at the edge of the wharf but can't seem to bring herself to drop the photo into the water.

Meg snatches it and stuffs it in her pocket. By the time they board the Midnight Ferry, her gut is tied in double knots.

LARGELY RESPONSIBLE

Howls tear the night, long ragged ribbons of sound, amplified by the arms of the mountain. Involuntary shudders ripple from Cal's nape to his tailbone. Meg shivers beside him, hugging her little bow, quiver at her feet. She scans the cave as though feral dogs might slink from the shadows, dancing in the light of their campfire. Her yellow-green eyes are huge behind her thick glasses. "There must be a mistake," she whispers.

Cal gives a sharp shake of his head. "They're getting close."

"Sargent says—he says they only leave their hunting ground at full moon."

"Meg—"

"I checked the calendar. We're supposed to be safe."

"I don't think they care about the calendar."

Her bottom lip wobbles. "We're supposed to be safe."

A single howl rises.

Meg winces. Breathless with terror, Cal can't think of a single reassuring thing to say. Even non-ranger kids know about the dangers of feral dogs. Nightmare stories of Hunters caught by surprise. Bodies found in ribbons. "One of us should guard the entrance."

She squares her shoulders. "I'm the oldest."

"Only by six months," he says.

Meg holds up her little bow. "I have a weapon."

"So do I," Cal hisses, brandishing his pocketknife.

Meg screws up her freckled nose. "I'm a ranger's kid. You're a fisherman's son."

He leans away from her, and his back hits a boulder made warm by geothermal fissures. Instantly, he knows he's dreaming. For some reason the sensation of warm rock at his back is fused with the visceral memory. He notes how small his body feels, the knobs on his spine, sharp and uncomfortable scraping against the boulder. Divided within, dreamer and dream, he's incapable of waking himself from the horror he knows is coming. His clueless dream-self glowers at Meg, the weight of terrible truths hanging in the air between them.

Fat tears slip down Meg's pale cheeks. "I shouldn't have said that. Cal, I didn't mean it. Your dad was great."

It's the quaver in her voice when she lands on "was" that triggers it, a rush of raw grief hollowing his chest, and he remembers why they're hiding.

When he doesn't reply, she fills the silence, giving a watery sniff. "You know, Mom wants to send me to boarding school; she thinks becoming a ranger is too dangerous and that I have more to offer the world."

He hesitates, then says, *"Who wants to be a ranger, anyway? They're so full of themselves."*

She produces a small hiccupping laugh. *"So full of themselves . . . 'cept Sargent."*

"Except Sargent."

The howls rise again, so close this time Meg and Cal cling to each other without thinking. Eyes closed tight, he prays, Don't let them find me, don't let them find me. *Whether he means the feral dogs or Social Services, he can't tell.*

Meg squeezes him. *"I won't let them, Cal."*

His face burns as he realizes he's spoken aloud.

"You're staying on Black Water," she says.

The detached part of his brain supplies the missing pieces in snapshots. His father signing a Nutris Pharmaceuticals contract to command his own trawler in the temporary coast guard for the duration of the cull. Later that same night, his father brushing his hair back from his forehead, soothing Cal's fears, making him laugh with the promise of LEGOs and a stack of X-Men comics for Christmas. Cull money is too good to pass up. Cal knows that.

Three days later, his father's body laid out on the dock. Killed by unlicensed Fortune Hunters attempting to land on the east coast of Black Water. A sensation like Cal's lungs are disintegrating behind his ribs. His screams attract rangers and cull officials to the wharf. No one can calm him. Sargent arrives and scoops him up, carrying him away from the crowd.

When Cal stops screaming, he finds himself seated at Meg Archer's kitchen table, her hand patting his, her eyes wet with tears steaming up her glasses. Sargent is gone. Meg's mother stands at

their potbellied stove, heating soup from a can in a butter-yellow
saucepan. The spoon scrapes softly on the bottom of the pan. Around
and around. Flecks in the Formica tabletop spiral and loop.

At some point, Mrs. Leaman arrives with chocolate from the
high shelf behind her counter at the general store. She explains that
everything will be all right. Social Services has been notified. He
locks eyes with Meg, and the horror in her face confirms what his
brain struggles to comprehend. His father is gone. He has no other
family. He is eight years old. They will never let him stay by himself.
Social Services will take him away. To the mainland. Forever. He
passes out and wakes later in the night bundled in a sleeping bag
on a camp cot beside Meg's bed. She sits there watching him in the
dark, hugging her knees, her Rainbow Dash nightie pulled to her
ankles like a tent. She's holding a flashlight, and she clicks it on.
"I have an idea."

Water splashes Cal's face, and he jerks awake. The roof of
his shelter has slipped in the rough weather. Rain drips freely
onto his head, and he pulls his hood back into place. Judging
by the light, he hasn't slept long, but he still feels guilty. He
quiets himself and listens. No howling. With a shaky sigh, he
exhales. It must be only an hour or so till dawn and no sign of
poachers. He decides he might as well cut the noose and take
the buck down. No point delaying the inevitable. Getting to
his feet, he takes a moment to stretch stiff muscles and shake
the weight of the dream from his thoughts.

Even though he didn't get to the part of the dream where
Fergus Welsh, the former head ranger of Black Water Island,
and Sargent found their cave, the part where screaming and

25

bleeding and burning begin, the impression of the man lingers like an echo. It hurts his chest to think of Fergus. He had a gift like Cal's—one of them. An amplified sense of smell. Sensory gifts aren't that rare among Rift Hound bite survivors, but it's always been a comfort to him, sharing the same gift as Fergus. Evidence to hold up in a court of his peers. Not that he would *ever* bring it up. The apprentices would balk and accuse him of delusions of grandeur. Plus, Fergus was well-liked, and Cal doesn't like to remind people he's largely responsible for the man's death . . . or Sargent's untimely promotion. Right now, he has more than enough to feel bad about.

MIDNIGHT FERRY

Meg grips the rail as the boat heaves and pitches, her innards rolling against the sea and the faint reek of fish guts. Her hands are numb with cold, even with yak fur gloves, and she hunches against the rain, searching for a jagged blot on the horizon. No sign of Black Water. Just needles of lightning stitching the seam between sky and sea. She doubts they'll beat the storm to harbor, but still, she feels better out here under the veranda than sitting in the cabin where she was close to puking all over her boots.

She glances back at the window. Her mother's expression is carefully composed as she sits pretending not to hear the conversation of the three Nutris Fortune Hunters traveling alongside her. Three young men, built like bodybuilders, dressed in black like special-ops marines. It's their job to audit the Lower Slopes before the cull.

Before Meg came out on deck, she'd heard the one man

boasting that he'd bought and paid for a beach house on the profits of a single adult buck's antlers when he was only nineteen. He's back again hoping to cover the cost of a yacht and his girlfriend's plastic surgery. Meg wonders if he's on a protesters watch list.

It wasn't until her mother brought her to live on the mainland that Meg became aware of the seething unrest surrounding the four-yearly cull. Growing up on Black Water, there had been no television, radio, or Internet access to inform her otherwise. The locals considered it a necessary evil to protect the fragile ecosystem. The wider ethical ramifications of Actaeon's Bane as a consumable product had escaped her. Truth is, the treaty with Nutris Pharmaceuticals is sketchy at best, and thinking about it makes her uncomfortable. All those protesters on the wharf. The desperate father on the dock. The blond Fortune Hunter and his meaty fists. Meg and Cora's silence — their motivation in returning to the island at all. Her moral high ground is a swamp.

It crosses her mind that if her mother had let her stay on Black Water, let her train as a ranger, she'd be getting ready for this audit. Perhaps she would have been assigned as a cull guide for some clueless mainlander. Dealing with Fortune Hunters was always Sargent's least favorite part of the job. Glancing back at the intimidating men in the cabin, she wonders how she would have coped, though a couple of them don't look too much older than her.

Her mother had tried to compensate for wrenching Meg from the island by encouraging her endless pursuit of outdoor activities. Meg became a scout, took up archery, rock-climbing, and orienteering. Rather than broadening her horizons about the possibilities of a mainland life, Meg took it as an opportunity to train and prepare while biding her time. She lived those first three years after the attack in bated-breath expectation of a letter from Sargent forgiving her, begging her to return to Black Water, and, ultimately, inviting her to take her place among the rangers.

Pathetic really. Poor Cora's attempts to deal with Meg's delusion were met with volcanic resistance, fiery tears, and door slamming until the age of twelve, when one day she simply stopped checking the mail. Twelve was the age ranger kids left the village school and joined the junior barracks on Little Peak. Her letter never came, and the secret lore of the ranger community seemed lost to her forever. However, the hunger for mountains and forests, rivers and star-filled skies, never left.

Movement to her right and Meg stiffens. The blond man, undaunted by the weather, steps out of the skipper's cabin and crosses to the rail, pulling a black rectangular object from his pocket. A flash of silver in the darkness—the Chinese dragon clasp. Meg considers bolting back inside, but if she moves, he'll see her. She stands as still as she can. He removes a thick wad of notes that he folds in half and slides inside his coat pocket. Unhurried, he searches the remaining compartments of the wallet before closing it and turning his head. Meg snaps her mouth shut, but she can't look away. He cocks his head, a slow smile stretching his lips, and her gut plummets; he knew she was there. With a lazy flick of his wrist, he tosses the wallet into the water and strolls back to the main cabin.

The ferry dips on a plunging wave, and Meg wraps her arm around the support beam of the veranda, pulse hammering in her ears. What is she supposed to think? He mugged the guy? Agreed to smuggle for him? Killed him?

The click of the cabin door makes her jump but it's her mother, and Meg wilts with relief.

"Have you been sick, honey? You look dreadful."

In a breathless rush, Meg explains what she just saw, darting nervous glances over her shoulder. The blond man sits with his back to the window, talking and laughing with the younger Fortune Hunters. He pulls something from his coat, and the other three men lean in, faces keen with interest. Meg yanks on her mother's sleeve. "What's he showing them? The money? Is he paying them off?"

"Stop looking." Cora squeezes her arm.

"What are we going to do?"

"We're not going to do anything."

"But—"

"He *let* you see because he's untouchable. He wants you to *know* he's untouchable."

"Sargent can kick him off the island."

"The man is clearly sponsored. If Nutris is paying him to be here, he *is* untouchable. Besides, Sargent has no jurisdiction over anything beyond the coast of Black Water. The wallet was taken on the mainland."

"It's not just a theft, is it? The guy, the dad, was looking to pay for smuggled Bane." She nods sharply toward the cabin. "*He* knew that and took the money. We have to warn Sargent he might be intending to smuggle ground horn from the island."

Cora closes her eyes and rubs her brow. "These Fortune Hunters are serious people, Meg. They're not conservationists or rangers or anything good. If you tell Sargent, and if Sargent acts on that knowledge, you make yourself a target. You make *us* a target. Think it through. How will we sell the house? The only buyer will be Nutris. If we aggravate them by landing one of their Fortune Hunters in trouble, why would they help us? They can refuse to buy it and leave us hanging with an unusable asset. Or they could offer us peanuts, and there goes your inheritance."

"What about the man at the port?" She can't bring herself to complete the thought, the photo of the man's son almost throbbing in her pocket.

"Someone would have found him, helped him. Probably arrested him — he was breaking the law."

"That's cold."

"I have forty thousand dollars in hospital bills, and I'm about to rob my daughter's inheritance to pay for it. I have no conscience." Cora's eyes glisten, and Meg's chest aches. The wind howls, the ferry rocks, and neither of them can speak.

Finally, Meg swallows and says softly, "Well, it was very selfish of you to get cancer and fight so hard to live. What kind of mother does that?"

Moisture gleams on Cora's lashes, but she produces an amused snort.

Meg leans her head on Cora's shoulder, swamping her mother's narrow frame. "I don't like this."

"Neither do I."

They stare at the rough sea.

Meg's stomach churns with nausea and worry. The night seems bruised with the colors and sounds of her old nightmares, horrors made of smoke, shadow, and flashing fangs, a biting wind that howls. "We could hide a steak in his pack, let the hellhounds take care of him."

Cora gives her a warning look. "Calling them hellhounds gives power to an ignorant fear."

"If anyone deserves a good shredding, it's that guy."

"You don't mean that."

Meg doesn't argue, her thoughts tumbling into a thorny patch of memory. She rubs the scars, hidden in the hairline at the nape of her neck, puncture wounds from being bitten. Her gloves are wet, and she shivers, trying not to picture the night her life on Black Water came to an end. She finally murmurs, "Do you ever think about Cal?"

Cora doesn't answer right away, her expression closing in. "Every now and then, more since we started planning this trip."

"Same."

In the early days after they left the island, Meg used to cry herself to sleep wondering about the boy, hating the thought of him taken into the custody of Social Services, forced from the island. Despite Cora's repeated inquiries, the agency refused to disclose any information about the orphaned boy. Not knowing had eaten Meg up. It became a mournful sort of game, inventing a best-case scenario for him.

"What do you think he's doing?" Meg asks.

Another prolonged pause. "Sleeping. I suppose."

Meg gives Cora a chiding nudge. "Not living with a nice mainland family, wasting his college tuition on video games and basketball shoes?"

Cora huffs softly through her nose and frowns at the dark horizon.

NUTRIS PHARMACEUTICALS

Soaked and reeking, Cal trudges down the track. By the time he reaches the village, dawn is near, and his knees are almost shot. A single road carves the base of the mountain, tracing the downturned mouth of the bay. Business premises lean away from the bedrock like graying, misshapen teeth, most with living quarters stacked two and three stories above with a view across the road to the measly pebble beach.

Cal pauses between buildings to give himself a moment to catch his breath. He mops his face with the back of his hand and rebalances the weight of the buck on his shoulders. From habit, he tucks his hair behind his right ear, leaving it long to cover his face on the left. Hooking one arm behind the buck's antlers and the other around its hind legs, he strides out into the road, willing his knees not to give out before he reaches Nero's Palace.

Fog sits low in the bay, a hangover from last night's squall.

The tide laps weakly at the shore, as though reluctant and muscle sore. Torn branches and debris litter the tiny beach. Cal takes in the upheaval, eyes tracing to the wharf where three battered trawlers huddle against the dock. Out in the bay, a dinghy rocks facedown in the black water. Steam rises from the fishing plant, reaching from the end of the wharf into the sea. It's too dark to recognize any of the workers checking boats and moorings for damage, too early to call out even if he did.

The street is awake but quiet. First pots of coffee still brewing in upstairs kitchens, potbelly stoves spooling wreaths of white smoke to pearl in the overhanging forest. Cal keeps an even pace up the middle of the road, no vehicles to worry about at this hour—not many to worry about in general. Nowhere to drive in a one-road town.

He pants up the gentle rise of the road, passing Millers Workshop. When he reaches the long flat, he spots three bulky figures striding up from the opposite side of the bay. Cal debates ducking between buildings to wait until they pass, but it's too late. They've seen him. Through the mist, he glimpses the Midnight Ferry docked at the end of the jetty by Nero's Palace—lanterns on in the cabin. He notes the approaching men's duffel bags, rifles, packs, and black clothes. Nutris Fortune Hunters arriving early to audit the Lower Slopes.

Immediately his heart belts in his chest, a flare of adrenaline unrelated to physical exertion, long years of hate turned toxic. He grinds his teeth at being caught carrying unsanctioned kill. He wants to bark, *This isn't what it looks like,* but the covenants protecting the island are well known. The rangers who protect those covenants, infamous. *Feral greenies with guns.* Even through the filth, his oilskin is identifiable; they'll recognize his gear.

They reach the boardinghouse where most of the seasonal workers stay. They look pale and worn out, and he tries not to smile at the thought of how rough it must have been on the crossing from the mainland. Cal drifts casually to the left side of the road, hugging the seawall. The men pause, watchful and expectant as he passes beneath the street lantern, but when Cal makes no eye contact and offers no greeting, one of the men calls out. "You need a hand, friend? Big fella you got there."

Cal grunts a negative and keeps on walking. *Friend.*

"The size of that thing."

"Not even fully grown, judging by the antlers."

"Still. You're looking at fourteen, fifteen pounds in ground horn on a buck that size."

"What's that sell for? Eighty, ninety K?"

"Depends on the potency of Actaeon's Bane."

"Black market you could double it. Rich dads with cancer kids pay through the nose."

"Only certain kinds of cancer."

"You think that's sanctioned kill?"

"Ask him."

"I'm not asking him."

"Thinks we're mercenary garbage."

"We *are* mercenary garbage." More chuckling.

Beyond their line of sight, Cal scowls so hard his face aches. He understands the two-hundred-year-old treaty *allows*

Nutris legal access to the island, but he doesn't have to like it.

In his opinion, Colm Lennox, head ranger at the time of the treaty—a rare telepath with a gift for healing, according to the chronicles—must have been a gutless fool, capitulating to mainland pressure. Mainland greed. The Old Herd might have been on the verge of extinction two hundred years ago, depleted by relentless poaching, but the "mutually beneficial" compromise proposed by Nutris forebears was little better.

The treaty simply legalized their pillaging and ensured the longevity of their profit margin. Never mind it was *their* fault in the first place that the demand for Actaeon's Bane exceeded natural production of the compound. Cal read the damning accounts—devoured them when he became an apprentice. Nutris tried plenty of sinister avenues before getting lawyers involved. Attempts to steal breeding pairs and replicate the Herd off the island failed miserably. Even by early science, they deduced a link between the Old Herd and its unique environment. Later science identified the high levels of electromagnetism and rare mineral deposits formed by the geothermal springs as a central contributor to the production of Actaeon's Bane. The source of those unique elements proved to be a "dimensional peculiarity" best handled by the rangers themselves.

Cal wonders if he would care less if he hadn't been bitten—if he hadn't developed his gifts. Sensitivity to the presence of death is a pretty bloody inconvenient skill set in an environment where slaughter is par for the course every four years. As far as he's concerned, Colm Lennox was a traitor. He *agreed* to the introduction of mainland deer to the Lower Slopes and *allowed* the "regulated" interbreeding with the Old Herd. Nutris weren't fazed by the less potent deposits of Actaeon's Bane in the offspring. Not when they flourished on the Lower Slopes and quickly overwhelmed the ecosystem with almost catastrophic browsing. Cull rights meant Nutris could harvest their product while appearing to conserve the environment, benefiting humanity with their grossly overpriced medicinal supplements.

Cal's supposed to be grateful for a treaty that allows rangers to maintain total rule of law over the island and absolute protection for the Old Herd. Grateful for the mainland *overlooking* the *dimensional peculiarity* rangers call the Rift. Grateful for the financial subsidies for business owners and operators on Black Water. Funding, infrastructure, health care, insurance, education, and pensions for the ranger community and their families. At what cost? Just his soul.

Sargent calls it a marriage of need and greed.

Cal calls it prostitution.

Extortion.

Bullshit.

His bitter thoughts are interrupted by a figure emerging from the mist. Big and heavily laden. A blond man with a face like someone you might find on one of Mrs. Leaman's pointless TV guides.

The man's teeth flash white in the gloom, squint lines creasing the corners of his eyes. "Fine beast you have there. Old Herd?"

Cal says nothing. He guesses he wouldn't like the scent of this guy, even if he could smell past his own reek.

Unperturbed, the blond man walks right up to him. Cal steels himself not to sidestep. Unlike the other three Hunters, this man isn't intimidated by ranger urban legend or Cal's fierce expression. He reaches for the antlers, running his fingers over the tips. He digs in his pocket for a little metal vernier and then grabs at the buck's mouth, pulling back its lips, running his fingers over the teeth, measuring the incisors. A weird chemical waft cuts through the stench of death and feces. "Nutris will take these, this year," the man says, his accent making odd vowels and dips. "The molars carry deep deposits. They can separate the Bane from the calcium in their laboratories."

"You're sponsored." Cal makes it sound like an accusation.

The blond man arches a golden eyebrow. "Proxy for Franklin Abel."

Franklin Abel. CEO of Nutris Pharmaceuticals. His own personal Hunter. Cal keeps his face blank, but his pulse takes a tumble. This isn't someone to mess with. Sargent has to deal with these money-grubbers, and if Cal messes things up—

"Jackson Spear." The man offers his hand to shake.

Cal is glad he's in no position to take it, balancing a buck on his shoulders.

Unfazed by the cold silence, Spear hooks his thumbs into the straps of his hiking pack, and his eyes hitch on the buck's wounded neck. "Snare, was it?"

"Poachers."

Spear's eyes light up. "Slow death pollutes the Bane. Chemical panic."

"Whoever did this deserves a slow death."

"Then I hope you find him."

Unable to think of a reply, Cal nods and walks on, jumpy in his skin. That weird chemical waft seems to have gotten stuck up his nose. The road dips and curves, and he can see movement on the jetty. Cal considers changing course, dropping the carcass at Bertrum's, which is where it will end up anyway, and coming back later to explain. But Cal likes Abigail Bertrum and doesn't want to give the woman a morning of panic. Butchering, processing, and selling unsanctioned kill is illegal and will get you kicked off the island faster than you can blink. Abigail will take one look at the natural markings of the buck, its grazed neck and bulging eyes, and choke.

Bracing for another Fortune Hunter encounter, he presses on to Nero's Palace, eyes skipping back and forth from the jetty to the road. A milky yellow gaslight glows through the fog, and Nero's fully emerges like an apparition through the gloom.

ANGRY ENUNCIATOR

Meg locks her knees and glues her feet to the jetty, eyes fixed, unblinking, on the dark forest above the fishing village and the mountains beyond. The pressure in her chest makes her throat ache. It started maybe a mile from the coast, the hitch in her breath, the inexorable drawing, as though she were being reeled to shore by a tether to her heart. Faint tingling races from her sternum to the back of her neck, fanning up and over her scalp. Little surges of electricity that bring inexplicable tears to her eyes. She can't tell if she wants to laugh or sob.

It must be fatigue. Fatigue and dehydration. A dip in blood glucose? When was the last time she ate? Add a backlog of poorly processed emotional baggage and of course she's freaking out. Did she expect to skip from the Midnight Ferry without a flinch?

"Can you see the apartment?" Her mother gestures across

the bay. Meg notes the half-strangled quality of Cora's voice, the stiffness of her posture.

Meg squints, but she can't make out the post office or the apartment above it. It's too dark and foggy. What she *can* make out, from Leaman's General Store to the boardinghouse, takes some jarring recalibration. Her florid childhood memories give way to the shrunken, colder, and more derelict reality of Black Water. It makes no difference; the sense of homecoming is a marrow-deep ache. Years of resentment were supposed to dilute the pull — make her immune — but she still loves it. She *loves* Black Water. Utterly. Bitterly.

Gaslight casts a grimy yellow halo above her head. Four signs are nailed to the lamppost. The first reads: CAUTION. ELECTROMAGNETIC INTERFERENCE. TURN OFF ALL ELECTRONIC DEVICES. The sign beneath that reads: ACCESS TO FLINT'S GULLY IS STRICTLY FORBIDDEN DUE TO FERAL DOGS. A third sign warns: BEWARE OF THERMAL FISSURES AND EMISSIONS. OXYGEN FILTERS RECOMMENDED FOR HIKING AND LEGAL HUNTS. Finally, a sign at the bottom, printed in bold script, reads: LEAMAN'S GENERAL STORE. SUPPLIERS OF QUALITY BLACK WATER–COMPATIBLE HOUSEHOLD, SPORTING & CAMPING GOODS. Well played, Mrs. Leaman.

Thankfully the Fortune Hunters cleared out with their high-performance lanterns as soon as the ferry docked, the blond man close behind them with his multiple bags of weapons. Cora and Meg pretended to reorganize their packs to avoid any parting interactions. It didn't stop him pausing beside them, cocking his head to offer a smarmy farewell. "Ladies."

Now Cora stands apart, quietly taking in the sight of Nero's Palace rising at the end of the jetty, hulking and shadowy in the predawn. Above it, the tapering arm of headland and primeval forest thrusts toward the northern sea. The two-story building houses a restaurant below and proprietor's lodgings above. The veranda sags, and a weathered sign with grand lettering leans drunkenly on the gables. She sighs. "I miss this place."

Meg crouches beside her pack and digs out her gas lantern.

Cora gives her a wavering smile. "Are you freaking out? I'm completely freaking out."

"My hands are shaking. Can you attach this?"

Cora takes the lantern and attaches the cylinder for her, then cups Meg's face. "We'll be all right."

Meg doesn't trust herself to speak. She toggles the ignition and a *swoosh* precedes the flame. Settling her pack on her shoulders, she carries the lantern before her and takes short steps toward Nero's, uncertain on her land legs.

Cora taps her shoulder and gestures toward a man-shaped shadow, big and cumbersome, displacing the mist up on the main road. *Sasquatch*, Meg thinks.

"Sasquatch," Cora says.

"Stranger things in the Black Water mountains than oddly shaped yeti-men."

"Don't start," Cora warns, that same tender smile touching her pale lips. Meg studies her face. Cora lived here much longer than Meg, was a part of the fabric of the community.

How surreal must it be, for her, returning after all this time?

The Sasquatch strides in the direction of Nero's Palace. A cold thought chills Meg. *What if it's a ranger? What if it's Sargent?* She's not ready for an immediate face-to-face. She needs a hot shower, actual sleep, and possibly some horse tranquilizers before she'll be capable of saying anything coherent.

They mount the yellowing stairs to the veranda of Nero's Palace and cross the porch to the double doors of the restaurant. As she peers through the frosted design etched on the glass, it's hard to make out much of the dining room, still sitting in shadows. As a kid, Meg thought it looked like a fancy saloon. The light comes through the swing doors behind the bar. Someone is working in the kitchen, but the sign in the window says CLOSED.

Heavy boots clomp up the veranda steps. The Sasquatch proves to be a large man in a filthy oilskin coat, face obscured by dark chin-length hair, a dead deer slung across his broad shoulders.

Definitely a ranger.

A rush of breathtaking panic tips Meg's thoughts into chaos. This is real. It isn't like she fantasized, acting cool and calm and holding it all together. Why did she think she could come back here and not flip out?

The ranger disappears around the side of the building. Meg exchanges a look with her mother, but Cora appears frozen. A thump rattles the porch boards, making them jump, the deer deposited by a service entrance. Meg mouths, "What shall we do?" Cora responds with a grimace. Perhaps a rip-off-the-

Band-Aid approach is the healthiest option. Meg squares her shoulders and takes the lead.

Don't be Sargent. Don't be Sargent.

She rounds the corner and finds the man doubled over, hands on thighs, wheezing as he tries to catch his breath. And no wonder—the deer looks huge lying on the porch, antlers propping its head on an awkward angle.

"Excuse me," Meg says, holding her lantern out between them.

The man snaps upright, and the panting stops. He swipes his hair back behind his right ear so he can glower at her with one eye. *Not Sargent.* Giddy relief slows Meg's mental adjustment from man to boy. Large boy. Reeking and dirty and hostile. She notes the rifle and machete and the curtain of matted hair still covering half of his face. He doesn't speak, but his expression demands, *What?*

"Are you—" She cuts off, eyes watering with the stench. "Do you work here?"

The glower becomes a scowl—dark eyebrow bearing low. "Do I look like I work here?" He turns his arms out, showing the spectacular filthy length of him.

Irritation makes her hot in her coat. "Is the owner around?"

The boy's expression sours further, lower lip tucking back in the corners, before he thumps the side of his fist three times on the door to the service entrance. He takes a couple of steps back and turns away from her, his back and shoulders expanding.

Meg can't decide if he's shutting her out, embarrassed

by his stench, or trying to hide how breathless he is. Maybe all three. The idea that she is one degree of separation from Sargent makes her skin prickle, and the knot in her chest burns again. *Rangers.* If she says who she is, how long would it take for the news to get back to Sargent? Would he march down the mountain, smug or indifferent? Picturing him either way gets her hackles up. She widens her eyes and asks blandly, "Is this your kill?"

He satisfies her with a vicious look, muscle knotting the hard edge of his jaw. "The cull hasn't started, and unsanctioned kill is illegal."

She keeps her expression impassive; he's an angry enunciator. When he fails to offer any further explanation, she lifts her eyebrows. "So, that's a no."

Cora steps up beside her, giving her a nudge with her elbow. "Don't be rude, Meg."

The boy freezes.

The restaurant door opens.

Antonia steps out into the glow of the lantern, ready delight on her face—Meg recognizes her like a snapshot in time, triggering an achy rush of nostalgia.

"Here's a sight for sore eyes. Cora! Meg!" Tall and broad with a thick waist, she must be somewhere north of fifty by now. Tight black curls and silver tendrils secured by a bright red bandana. She wears a crisp white shirt—striking against her dark skin—sleeves rolled to the elbows, belted into cheery patterned cobalt pants. Thick black military boots, polished to gleaming, lace halfway up her calves. A slash of red lipstick and flushed cheeks make her face seem to glow in the light. She exudes authority, calm, and a zero tolerance for nonsense. Antonia's smile looks ready to hit full brightness when the sight of the Sasquatch and the deer dull the shine. "Son, tell me this isn't what I think it is."

PIPE BOMB

Cal's initial relief when Antonia emerges from the kitchen is shattered by a pipe bomb of comprehension. *Cora! Meg!* His breathing gets shallow. His vision blurs. Pinpricks of light pop in his peripheral vision. Antonia peers at him down a long shimmering tunnel, and her voice is far away. "Oh, no. One of your boys?"

Gripping the veranda railing to keep from toppling, Cal manages a delayed nod.

"Poachers?"

He nods again—he thinks. It's hard to tell; he can't feel his head.

"You watch all night?"

Exhaling sharply through his nose, he swallows.

"And you carried him down from the mountain by yourself?"

He tries to shrug, but his muscles are ninety percent mud, and the gesture comes off weird and ungainly.

"No wonder you look like roadkill." Antonia sighs and wrinkles her nose. "And you smell like hell."

Heat flashes up Cal's neck, and that little surge of adrenaline brings him back to his body. *Cora! Meg!* Here. Now. He didn't recognize her at first. *How* did he not recognize her? He was expecting . . . well, a *girl*. Someone short. Round faced. Thick glasses. This Meg must be almost six feet with—with legs and cheekbones and . . . He realizes something else. Meg doesn't recognize him either.

Cora raises her lantern a little higher and clears her throat. "Antonia, you haven't changed a bit."

"Who even looks like that before six a.m.?" she adds, happy tears in her eyes. "It's not right."

"Don't you start crying." Antonia chuckles, grabbing Cora for a hug and tucking her under one arm. She shakes her head and touches Meg's cheek. "Is that really you? Little Meg? My goodness, look at you."

Meg laughs and covers her stomach. "Am I green?"

"Everybody's a bit green after four hours on the Midnight Ferry," Antonia says.

"Five." Cora groans. "The weather was rough, and the going was slow."

Cal stares at Meg's gloves, and he's remembering things he doesn't want to remember. He clears his throat and gestures at the deer. "If you could record the serial number and sign it over to Bertrum's—" He's husky and red and itching to flee the scene. "I'll come back for the paperwork later."

Antonia's eyes widen, her gaze flitting back and forth from

Meg to him with dawning awareness. Cal gives her a warning look, but before she can say anything, there's a squawk and thick flapping overhead. Meg gasps, and Cora ducks as Reeva swoops to land on the wooden balustrade. Hopping from side to side, she holds her wings out in an awkward dance, with a sound like a creaking door rumbling in her throat. Cal waves to shoo her away, but Reeva shrieks and claps her wings, stabbing her beak at his fingers.

"Don't," Meg cries. "You'll hurt him."

For a second, Cal thinks she's scolding the raven, before he finds her flashing eyes drilling his. "It's a *her* not a *him*," he says, and snaps his fingers. "Reeva."

Meg startles and takes a step back as the bird, chortling, leaps on his arm.

Meg gapes a little, and her gaze moves over his face, snagging on an unexpected detail. Cal's hair has slipped back, exposing the side of his jaw. He is instantly aware and instantly certain that he is not ready for this conversation. Not here . . . not now . . . not like this. Desperate for shadows, he drops his head, spins on his heel, and stalks down the stairs. Then he hears it, that small, sharp intake of breath, the sound of sudden realization. He can't tell if it's Cora or Meg, and he cringes, afraid they'll call him back . . . but they don't, and he doesn't know whether to be relieved or devastated. Though his legs are weak as water, he lengthens his stride, determined to get out of earshot. He's more fully alert than he's been in the last thirty-eight hours, more undone than he's felt in nine years.

Reeva climbs to his shoulder, claws and beak nipping the

sleeve of his oilskin coat, glossy black wings smacking his face as she keeps her balance. She wants his forgiveness, and Cal's too distracted to hold a grudge about last night's mistakes. The bird butts her silky head beneath the corner of his jaw and lets out a worried yodel. She sends images of Meg on the veranda. Cal nudges the raven with the side of his face and mutters an absolution. "I'm sorry too."

Reeva nibbles his ear, then with a flap and caw the bird launches back into the air, her weight lifting from Cal's shoulder. The sensation pierces Cal through the heart, an inexplicable sense of being untethered, leaving him momentarily lost. Suddenly he doesn't want to be alone. He blinks against the sting behind his eyes; he's acting like a child.

OILSKIN COAT

Molasses scents the air, warm wafts of sweetness from beyond the swing doors, a note of something savory on the cross-current. Echoing within, the sound of pots rattling, utensils at work, and low feminine muttering. Meg sits at a table, head in her hands, fatigue and shock making the floorboards spin beneath her boots.

Cora touches her shoulder. "Are you going to be sick?"

"He's here."

"He is."

"*How* is he here?"

Her mother says nothing.

Meg shakes her head. "Why was he dressed like that?"

Cora sighs.

"You think he's visiting?"

"No."

Meg presses her knuckles into her eye sockets, her gloves

damp and prickly. "He looks like he's never left."

Cora rubs soothing circles between her shoulder blades.

"Why didn't he say something?"

"He looked a bit overwhelmed."

"He was dressed like a ranger."

Her mother's hand stops.

Meg pops up her head. "There's no way he can be a ranger."

"Love . . ."

"He *can't* be," she snaps, like her mother was about to suggest otherwise. "There's no way. They'd never allow it."

Her mother withdraws her hand but says nothing.

Meg jabs a finger at the ceiling, indicating the general direction of the mountains and the rangers' headquarters on Little Peak. "*Sargent* would never allow it."

Silence.

"Honey, would it be so bad? If they made a place for him?"

"There is no goddamn way they'd let an outsider—*a fisherman's son*—become a ranger."

"*Meg.*"

"What?" Her voice takes a shrill upward swing.

"*Lower your voice,*" Cora says, warning in her eyes. "Cal is your friend."

"Was my friend."

"*Really?*"

"It was nine years ago. We were kids. I don't know who *this* Cal is." She flicks her hand at the veranda.

"An orphan who nearly got his face ripped off trying to save your life?"

Meg jerks in her chair. "He got to *stay*."

Cora searches Meg's face, deep weariness lining her eyes. She speaks softly, slowly. "He got the oilskin coat. He got Sargent."

"That's not what I was going to say."

"It's what you meant."

Antonia pushes through the swing doors leading a statuesque woman by the hand, their fingers twined together. She is even taller than Antonia, taller than Meg, wearing a black apron over a black shirt-waisted dress, displaying strong, sculpted arms. Her braided hair sits coiled atop her head like a crown, glossy and gold. Curling tendrils map her temples and the nape of her neck. A necklace of thick red beads gleams at her pale throat. Everything about her is striking. Meg and Cora get to their feet.

The woman appears wary as she makes her way around the bar, not meeting their gaze. Antonia chews the inside of her cheek. Meg feels like she's about to meet the principal; together the women look like pirate queen and . . . queen.

The woman fixes her eyes on a spot over Meg's shoulder. "Welcome, Cora and Meg."

Cora sticks out her hand. "It's lovely to meet you, Leira."

There's a pause. The woman squints at the table to Cora's right.

Antonia clears her throat. "Leira's blind."

"But not deliberately rude," the woman says, her thick accent lending the statement an impressive snap.

Antonia smiles, affection crinkling her eyes, and Cora drops her hand.

"Forgive me"—the woman turns up her palms—"I have been chopping onions."

"Oh," Cora blurts. "Is that safe?"

Antonia cringes, and Leira's nostrils pinch, lips growing thin.

"God, sorry," Cora says, her cheeks turning pink.

Meg drops her face into the palm of her scratchy glove.

"Leira took over the kitchen after Hank Hess returned to the mainland, about a year after—after Fergus died."

Instantly Meg's shock and upset over Cal is displaced by a plunging rush of guilt and perspective. *Fergus Welsh.*

"Oh," Cora says again. But this *oh* is too big.

"He thought he could stick it out, but with Fergus gone, he had nothing really to keep him here."

Everything is excruciating, and Meg clears her throat. "Hank gave us toffees on Tuesdays—if we finished our reading assignments."

The little school met in the post office storeroom. Before Meg left, the class was made up of eight to ten students spanning from five- to twelve-year-olds. Cal was there too. Some of the ranger kids, a boy called Joss and Antonia's niece, Rilke. The teaching was shared by Hank Hess, her mother, and Mrs. Leaman, an unpredictable curriculum of reading and writing, mathematics and "health." Mrs. Leaman's "health" lessons were perilous lectures about hygiene and all the germs that would likely kill them before adolescence. And now there's no more school because Hank Hess left . . . because Fergus Welsh died . . . because Sargent asked for help . . . because Meg and Cal were hiding in the mountains . . . because Meg had an "idea."

"They closed the school," Antonia says. "A lot of families left."

Meg says nothing, too crushed to speak.

"Enough." Leira pats Antonia's arm. "You are depressing our guests."

Antonia offers an apologetic smile. "How does a hot bath sound? Followed by something warm to eat and a long nap while the sun comes up?"

Cora sighs. "Sounds like bliss."

Antonia gestures toward the stairs. "We've got some extra hands arriving this afternoon to help prepare for the cull, but I saved you the best room. It overlooks the garden."

"I know it's terrible timing," Cora says. "But it's the only timing that works for having everyone in the same place at the same time."

"We're glad to have you. You know that. And I welcome any opportunity to exercise my lawyering muscle. We'll sort out Sargent *and* those greedy Nutris sons of—"

"Antonia," Leira says, half scolding, half amused.

Lifting her pack, Meg wonders how it doubled in weight. Maybe it's the chemical release of shock that's sapped her strength or the reminder she's ruined more lives than she can bear to think about. Following her mother up the stairs, Meg recalls eight-year-old Cal, grief-stricken at their kitchen table, the animal panic in his eyes at the mention of Social Services. She remembers how she felt his panic in her skin—what could be worse than being torn from your home, torn from the island itself? All she had wanted was to save him.

THE LAMENT

An involuntary *whoosh* slips past Cal's numb lips as he plunges his oilskin into the river. Cold with a bone-deep bite. His knees soak up the wet chill through his canvas pants. Shivering and swearing under his breath, he swishes the coat in the current, brushing at the worst stains.

Meg Archer.

He should have said something. Pretending like he didn't recognize her, bolting like a coward. If there were any heat left in his body, he'd burn red just thinking about how rude he was.

"Well, this looks normal."

Cal jerks upright, almost overbalancing into the river.

Joss Fenchurch yawns as he makes his way down the bank, thick fisherman's rib jersey over fleecy pajama pants and his feet jammed into unlaced boots. He squints one sleep-crusted eye, taking in Cal's mess, and scrubs his hand through his red-blond hair, making it stick up in tufts.

"Bloody hell, man." Cal's heart still belts, on high alert for Sargent.

With a grimace, Joss presses the back of his hand to his nostrils, wrinkling his freckled nose. "So that's how I made it past your radar. Blistering stink."

Everything aches as Cal hauls himself to his feet, shaking off the heavy oilskin.

Joss digs his hands inside the cuffs of his jersey, tucking his chin into the collar as he watches Cal with calculating blue eyes. "You missed Leira's vegetarian curry."

Cal groans.

"You love Leira's vegetarian curry."

Cal holds his coat away from his body while he tries to scrape mud and muck from his boots onto the rocks. "Why are you down here?"

"I could ask the same thing." Joss unfolds his arms and steps to the river's edge.

Cal waits, his teeth clenched hard against chattering. He wants a shower, he wants breakfast, he wants his bed. "Reeva told Otho?"

"Just the image of you, here, thrashing your coat in the river like you're trying to teach it a lesson. Birds gossip."

Some birds. Not Reeva. She can barely tolerate the other bonded scouts. If she shared anything with Joss's small tawny owl, it means she's seriously worried. Cal sighs and slings his coat over his arm, ignoring the flash of shivering and soaking cold. "Great." He scans the trees for sign of either of the birds, but Reeva is almost impossible to spot when she wants to stay hidden, and Otho doesn't travel far, being ancient and mostly blind.

"Are you going to spill or do I have to guess?" Joss demands.

Cal briefly closes his eyes, and the island tilts beneath him. "I lost an Old Herd buck on the Northwest Loop."

Joss's expression shifts gear, hardening with worry. Cal tells him about the distress signal, his panic, the amateur snare that ensured the buck's cruel death, the long night, and the trek down to the village. His throat closes again before mentioning Meg, not wanting to spark an interrogation.

Joss screws up his face. "Why would anyone risk it this close to the cull? Why not wait and take a legal kill?"

Cal lifts his palm. "Mainlanders."

With a slow shake of his head, Joss says, "Doesn't explain why an Old Herd buck would cross the ley line."

It taps at Cal's own dissatisfaction, and he drops his voice. "You think the Rift is active? Something chased him across the border?"

Joss shivers and gives him a wry look. "You're more likely to know if that's the case than me."

"We've still got three days till full moon."

"That's right," Joss says, his tone bolstering. "Last month, the Rift held, and no Hounds came through."

"True." Cal nods but takes no comfort.

Simultaneously, their gazes drift up the valley to the mountain where low-hanging mist clings to the dark and craggy base. Cal skims his fingers over the scar on his jaw as though the mark might confirm it.

Joss looks away first. "Sargent would have sent more of us to the border if there was movement. And there's no indication the Old Herd has scattered. No one mentioned anything at handover."

Handover. Cal sighs. His failure to return from his shift will have been noted. Sargent will be waiting for an explanation — a confession. "I am so royally screwed."

"You so royally are." Joss reaches as though to clap Cal on the shoulder before redirecting the gesture into a poor excuse for a stretch. If he wasn't already pressed down by exhaustion and worry, Cal would feel bad about it. Joss hauled himself from his warm bed to investigate Reeva's sending. Cal knew it was more than curiosity that inspired the effort. He wouldn't stomach the interference from anyone else, but Joss has the knack for slipping past trip wires and defense mechanisms that keep most people at a distance. Joss has never treated him differently from the other apprentices, never called him *the fisherman's son*. Of anyone, he should be able to clap Cal on the shoulder, shake his hand, or hug him or any of the normal things that pass for friendship.

"Trust me. You don't want to get this stink on you," Cal says, forcing lightness into his voice.

Joss covers his nose and takes a sizeable step away from him. "Not with the Southern Gables girls arriving tonight." He bounces his eyebrows and grins behind his hand.

With a snort, Cal turns and makes his way back up the bank, Joss keeping pace beside him. He tries to imagine flirting with one of the Southern Gables girls. Six or seven resort workers take the ferry from the south side of the island on Friday and Saturday afternoons to mix with the rangers at Nero's Palace. Some of the young guys too, depending on their shifts. Cal won't be going to Nero's Palace tonight, not after Sargent is finished with him.

He's not sure what scares him more: the thought of facing Sargent or having to look Meg in the eye the next time he sees her. She saw his clothes and gear and what he was doing; she'll know what it means, what he is. He hopes Meg, at least, is unlikely to break his ribs or give him a black eye.

* * *

The camp is quiet as Cal and Joss reach the saddle of Little Peak. Soft-footed, they skirt the path through the fir trees, alert for sound of movement. With Cal's sense of smell so hampered by his own stench, he can't catch wind of anyone's approach. He listens hard for the tread of boots—the first watch will already be up and patrolling the border—but he trusts his ears less than his nose.

They step out into the clearing. The winter barracks bleed yellow light through cracks in the shutters, and the long wooden cabin with its low tin roof fills him with longing. They make their way into the open ground between the U-formation of buildings. Their meeting place, training ground, and sparring ring—a thick carpet of pine needles. No residual ponds, none of the storm debris that litters the fishing village in the mouth of the bay. Hedged on all sides by the forest, the camp is well protected in the saddle of the mountain.

The murmur of voices rumbles from the summer barracks, on the right, converted at this time of year to a mess hall and meeting room in one. The smell of bacon wafts from the shuttered kitchen, and Cal's stomach growls.

"You should report first," Joss says.

Cal nods.

"He won't be far," Joss says. "Listen — it's not your —"

"It *is* my fault."

Joss knows as well as Cal that the weight of responsibility can't be erased by those four words. Joss points at him. "You weren't even scheduled to take that watch."

Lots had been drawn with the usual tense anticipation. Cal's moan at being allocated the steep, crevasse-filled Flint's Gully attracted Sargent's immediate annoyance. He'd snapped Cal's straw, scowled, and then said, "Northwest Loop."

The other rangers had snickered but avoided meeting Cal's gaze. Northwest Loop was considered the easiest of all watches, being so close to the village with a clear track and regular plateaus against the steep face of the foothills. No Old Herd deer to worry about. No mountain cats or boar. No poachers — theoretically. Not the slightest chance of Rift Hounds stalking in the shadows.

Cal's thoughts are snap-frozen by movement in the camp. Sargent enters the clearing flanked by two master rangers dressed in much the same outfit as Cal's: oilskins, canvas pants, rifles, and machetes. Yet their bulky outfits still don't make them seem as imposing as Sargent—barefoot in his cargo pants and khaki shirt, no sign of the cold causing him discomfort.

Cal brings his arm across his body, shielding his tender ribs.

Sargent's eyes dart toward them, and he stops in his tracks, the rangers on either side stopping with him. "Cal," he calls, the rich timbre of his voice made hard in one syllable. Every follicle on Cal's body contracts. The master rangers turn out to be Antonia's brother, Bren, and Joss's mother, Nellie. They keep their faces even, though on Bren—dark and hulking—it only emphasizes his sternness. Nellie, with her shaggy braid of red-blond hair, only gives away her apprehension with the flick of her gaze to her son and a weary sigh.

Cal forces his legs to move, aware of the sudden horrible awkwardness of his reluctant body. The arm not protecting his ribs doesn't swing with the right rhythm, and his gait is brittle. He imagines his stench wafting before him. When he stops a couple of feet from the senior rangers, he watches the muscles tighten around Sargent's eyes. It crosses his mind—this is where Meg gets her height and her implacable mouth.

Bren presses the back of his hand to his nose, and Nellie tucks her chin down, nostrils pinching.

"I took the carcass to Nero's," Cal says, his voice sticking in his throat. He has to puff the words out. "Antonia will sign the audit. Abigail Bertrum will—"

Sargent scowls and reaches for Cal's forehead.

Cal jerks back. "Let me *tell* you. I can tell you just as well. You don't need to—"

Sargent palms Cal's forehead, thumb and middle finger pressed temple to temple. The jolt comes with a jagged and twisting quality that always confuses Cal. He can't interpret the dark note, and his instinct stirs to shove the man away. Before he can make that mistake, Sargent's authority roars through Cal. An ancient instinct eclipses his revulsion, and Cal obeys the command to yield.

Seconds, that's all it takes for Sargent to dominate Cal's will and leave him wide open. His ears fill with buzzing. The oppressive heaviness that comes over his head isn't the weight of Sargent's hand but the obliterating Voice of the Herd. The lament. The panic. The warning. The pain and terror of loss. Then in rapid montage Cal's movements on the Ridgeway, his sulking, his distraction, and all the humiliating self-aggrandizing fantasies of a seventeen-year-old boy performing duty beneath his station. Sargent suffers only brief glimpses of Cal's repentance watching in the rain all night or his Herculean efforts in carrying the buck down to the village.

Helpless to close the valve, Cal feels his shame pour like water from a running faucet straight into the Old Herd. Sargent may as well have stripped him naked in the yard and whipped him with a switch, but worse is about to follow.

In a dizzying change of gear, the pressure in Cal's head shifts from his forehead to the base of his skull. He barely has time to clench his teeth and brace when the Voice of the Herd surges through him, obliterating everything. His legs buckle, his knees hit the ground, and he sinks back onto his heels. In his mind, he sees Fallon's doe eyes. The matriarch of the Old Herd, her voice like a throbbing silver thread looping through him, binding him to her. Through that silver thread her grief beats at him as though bruising his bone and marrow. A mother's grief, human and wild; raging, inconsolable loss.

Unable to bear it, Cal scrabbles for another focus: Joss at the river, Reeva nipping his ear, Meg and Cora on the veranda at Nero's Palace.

Shock rattles the connection, and Sargent tightens his grasp of Cal's head. He seizes control of the shift in focus and zooms in on Meg's face, her yellow-green eyes, her gloved hands in the lantern light. Recognition. Awareness. Urgency. Cal can't tell if these are his feelings or Sargent's.

Instantly, the surge stops. Sargent releases him. Cal's vision swims as the Voice of the Herd lifts but the oppressive weight remains. He staggers to his feet as though a cinder block rests on the back of his head, his face wet with tears and snot, his throat raw. Did he scream?

Blinking through his hair, he sees the junior barracks have emptied out. Half a dozen apprentices and a handful of senior rangers look on. Taller than the other apprentices, Abbot, Bren's son, looks on with pained concern. His partner Leif, snowy-haired and pale-eyed, shares the same distress, palm pressed to his forehead. They are the only apprentices who show concern for Cal. Rilke, Abbot's sister, looks on tight-lipped. The faces of the other apprentices are ashen, eyes fixed and unblinking.

Like Leif, some of them grip their heads, which means they saw it too.

The yard is silent. Sargent runs his hand up through his thick brown hair, his chest expanding and contracting as though he's exerted himself. His eyes stay fixed on Cal. He doesn't need to raise his voice. *"His end is our shame."*

Cal's seared throat hurts to swallow, but he makes the required confession. *"His end is my shame."*

"Nutris arrives today to begin the audit of the Lower Slopes. We are three days from full moon—a week from the beginning of the cull itself, when the island will be crawling with mainlanders. It's bad enough that the Rift will be unstable, let alone to rattle the bloody gates with the distress signal of a dying stag and *draw* Rift Hounds onto the mountain." Sargent cuts short, balling his fingers into a fist. Cal retreats inward, bracing for impact. Miraculously, the head ranger doesn't swing. "Clean yourself up; you smell like death."

RUBBER GLOVES

Meg dabs the back of her arm to her forehead, the heat and steam emanating from the hot sink misting her face. No industrial dishwashers here in Nero's Palace. The electromagnetic interference on Black Water makes it a living yesterworld. Schools on the mainland book visits in the warmer months so kids can have a glimpse of old-timey living and swim in the thermal springs. The only things missing are corsets, bustles, and bonnets. Leira cooks everything on a ferocious wood stove with a backup gas burner grill, making everything tick. Antonia keeps their supplies in an insulated room, lined with blocks of ice. The same freighters that supply the fish processing plant deposit the blocks on the back step of Nero's twice a week.

Meg plunges her thick rubber gloves into the soapy water, still drowsy from sleeping most of the day. Cora was gone before she woke, headed to the post office and their old apartment to do an inventory check before tomorrow's Team Big Clean. She left a note: *Please stay and help Antonia. Her kitchen hands haven't turned up.* Meg doesn't mind. She's glad for the distraction, and it saves her from awkward alone time with her mother. Neither of them had attempted to discuss the issues raised by the surprise appearance of Cal before climbing into bed. Meg doesn't trust herself to say anything rational.

It looks cold outside in the early evening light, but in the kitchen heat, Meg's tank top clings to her body and her jeans feel too tight. Over her shoulder she sneaks a look at Leira, gleaming with perspiration as she operates the stove. She tries not to stare, but the blind woman's precise, efficient movements are impressive. When Leira pats the counter behind her, missing the wooden spoon, Meg darts over to help.

"Here, let me—"

Leira swipes the utensil before Meg can pick it up. She offers a tight smile, eyes fixed past Meg's shoulder. "You are dripping dishwater."

"Oh." Meg blushes and peels her gloves off to grab a mop. "Sorry."

Leira lifts her chin and turns back to the stove when Antonia breezes into the kitchen, flushed and smiling. "Heaving out there," she says with a wicked grin. "God bless those lusty Southern Gables girls."

The dinner crowd definitely sounds boisterous—a mix of fishermen's families, early cull workers, and local business owners in the main dining room and a crowd of singles in the dogleg. A small boatload of younger people from the hotel on the southern side of the island—shift workers on their night off—mingling with a collection of rangers. Meg has spent the last hour wondering if she'd recognize any of the rangers—if they would recognize her.

"We feed and water them," Antonia says, eyebrows dancing. "Then the girls pick their prey and lead them up to the hot springs for canoodling."

Leira snorts, not turning from the stove. "What do you know about canoodling?"

Antonia rolls her eyes, smirking affectionately, but when her gaze falls on Meg, a worried frown creases her brow, and she nods toward the hall. Meg props the mop in its bucket and follows her into the narrow passage that leads upstairs to the private residence.

Antonia shuts the door to the kitchen and keeps her voice low. "What do you want me to do if Sargent comes tonight and your mother isn't back?"

Meg tucks her bare hands beneath her arms, and her throat dries a little. "I guess Cal told him we're here."

The heat from the kitchen dissipates, and the steam on Meg's arms grows chilly. "I'll have to see him sometime," she says, sounding more relaxed than she feels. "A heads-up would be good though."

Antonia nods, chewing her full lower lip. "And Cal—will you speak to him?"

Meg lifts her shoulders. They'd talked about the early-morning awkwardness when she came down from her room.

Her fears confirmed. Cal's a ranger. Antonia thought they knew. "I guess."

"He's a . . . good kid."

Meg shrugs like it's a given.

"Weren't you two thick as thieves?"

"We hung out," Meg mutters. "There weren't a lot of options."

"It hasn't been easy for him since . . ."

He got to stay. But Meg keeps it inside.

Antonia shakes her head. "He lost everything."

"I know."

Antonia watches her closely with narrowed eyes. Meg squirms inside, hating the thought that her mother's old friend, her old friend, must think she's a thankless brat who doesn't know how lucky she is, to be alive, to have any parents at all.

She wants to explain, justify herself, but there are no words, at least none that she can think of that won't make her sound petulant or worse. Finally, Antonia releases a soft, sad sigh. "It must be hard for you to see him wearing that ranger's coat. I remember you when you were eight years old. Little bow on your back, knife on your belt."

"Things change. People change."

"Sargent changed."

Meg can't meet her eyes.

"It's not your fault."

"Technically, it is."

"You were a child."

She presses her lips into the shape of a smile. How many

times has she heard those words from Cora? *It's not your fault.*
You were a child. Sargent made his choice. It's not about you. He's
the one with the problem. If only it made a difference. "I know.
I'm fine. It'll be fine."

Leira calls from the kitchen, and Meg follows, rubbing her
thumb across the lattice of scars on her palm. Her hands feel
naked and raw. She returns to the sink and pulls the rubber
gloves back on, safe and secure.

SETTINGS REWIRED

Cal trails Sargent down the dark track to Nero's Palace, off-kilter with the summons to follow and keep his mouth shut. He'd expected to spend an uneasy evening alone in the junior barracks "under the shun," and he knows better than to think Sargent is letting him off the hook. It'll be part of his punishment. More public humiliation. His body still aches from the strain of carrying the buck. His head still aches from the aftermath of Sargent's invasive interrogation. Every ranger in camp saw Cal's failure, Sargent utilizing the Voice of the Herd like a goddamn intercom.

He didn't have to. He could have kept it between the two of them, but Sargent's strategic like that. Why waste an efficient means of reinforcing the expectations of the community and the consequences of failing to meet those expectations? Added bonus, Sargent gets to show Cal's detractors that he hasn't forgotten the boy's an outsider.

Cal supposes he should be grateful he didn't get another broken rib, with Sargent's moods growing darker as they draw closer to the cull. The whole camp is on edge. Even the master rangers watch their mouths around Sargent, no joking or slacking off. Drills have grown tense, Bren and Nellie barking orders, impatient with apprentices' mistakes or the hint of slowness. Maybe it's the prospect of Nutris coming to the island that has Sargent in such a foul mood—the treaty so fraught with bad blood. Maybe it's the thought of facing Meg and Cora that has him wound like a barbed-wire coil.

Cal feels coiled too. Knotted tight. The fact Sargent's marching down the mountain tonight makes him nervous; he knows it won't be for the sake of food.

As he trudges along the track, his fingers drift to the scar on his jaw, but he catches himself and drops his hand. He's learned not to draw attention to the mark; it only stirs resentment among the apprentices. Rangers are generational, parent to child from long lines of families who formed the original guard when the Rift first split the mountain, millennia ago, disgorging horrors from another time and place. The scar reminds everyone that Cal entered the legend the wrong way.

Yes, it makes him useful to the community—Rift Sight is rare. He is the only current member who possesses the gift, thanks to his bite wound. Invariably, head rangers become head rangers *because* of their Rift Sight, and Sargent is the first to lead without the gift in generations. The apprentices believe it's what makes him so cranky.

Sargent's only extrasensory gift is his power over the Voice of the Herd, imparted during the endowment rite, a sacred ceremony held at the Rift Stone. Only master rangers are permitted to witness the endowment rite, and there are no written documents explaining what takes place. All Cal has gleaned from inferences is that it has something to do with the mythology around the very first head ranger.

Sometimes Cal wishes he didn't have Rift Sight, but he doesn't let himself wallow in ungrateful thoughts for long; it's the reason he got to stay on Black Water. While it disgusts the less tolerant lineage rangers to have the secrets of the island handed to an outsider, it *appalls* them that Cal might secretly entertain delusions of grandeur about his future. He doesn't.

To add insult to injury, Cal enjoys other benefits from surviving the bite. Improved night vision and an amplified sense of smell. If Cal were honest, *sniffing* wouldn't be his top pick for a superpower, but he can't deny it's been handy. One: it makes him awesome at tracking. Two: it's almost impossible for anyone to sneak up on him. Three: he can tell when people are lying. Lies smell sour.

He remembers the terrifying early days of his recovery after the attack. Like his body had been hijacked and all the settings rewired. The master rangers warned him he might notice changes, that bites from Rift Hounds come with *gifts*. They had books of handwritten accounts, handed down through generations. Turns out the ones who could smell things and see in the dark were the least interesting. Cal wonders if part of Sargent's change in personality is primarily bitter disappointment to wake up after the attack and find himself with nothing more than fairly unexceptional night vision.

After all, some of the old head rangers, like Devros Arken, could see the future, read minds—like civilian minds—and had nothing to do with the Voice of the Herd. Cal's favorites were the ones who could heal themselves or heal the sick with a touch: Nathaniel Loam, Temple Sacht, Cadon Gemmel. One had the gift of silence, Salma Keen. God, Cal wishes he had that—that he could stare at the apprentices who talk behind his back and take the voice from their throats. There was a woman who could make plants grow and another with the gift of sleep. Cal wishes he could put Sargent into a deep slumber. Would he fill his dreams with peace or terror?

The first time Cal sensed the presence of death, he was nine years old, checking rabbit snares with Joss. Joss found a young rabbit tangled in the snare. Cal froze to the spot, his breath turning white and patches of ice forming around his feet. To put the little thing out of its misery, Joss clubbed it on the head. Cal knew the instant it died. Goose bumps flashed up his arms and neck, with an eerie feathering sensation behind his ears. Death was there, brooding and aware. Cal passed out.

After that, it got gradually worse. He couldn't hunt. He couldn't be present while others hunted. He couldn't bear to eat meat. And it became harder and harder to deal with human touch. It wasn't just death he could feel. It was life too, and it was almost just as unbearable. Shaking hands, hugging, brushing shoulders, sparring in the training rings—unbearable. The slightest connection would send a jolt through his system, the wallop of life.

When they reach the foot of the cliff, Cal hears the muted noise coming from the restaurant, and his nerves jangle. He was ravenous in the junior barracks, but now he's not sure he can stomach a mouthful of anything, certain he doesn't want to be caught between Sargent and his daughter in a public showdown.

Cal wonders if she will acknowledge him at all and runs his hand through his hair, tucking it back behind his right ear. At least he's clean. He smells like soap and the mint leaves in his shirt pocket. His clothes are freshly washed, holes mended, boots polished. He breathes into his palm and smells toothpaste. Sargent gives him a narrow look over his shoulder, and Cal jams his fists into his pockets.

Sargent mutters, "You listen with your ears and your nose. You keep your mouth shut."

Cal nods, but warning chimes in his head. Sargent wants him to read her scent.

SOUTHERN GABLES

Meg dodges the swinging arm of a woman in her early twenties gesturing extravagantly as she tells a loud story to an audience of eager-looking ranger men. A brief glance confirms none of them are Cal or Sargent, but it doesn't keep the flutter from her throat as she makes her way through the crowd to clear the table.

Antonia wasn't joking about the Southern Gables girls and the few eager young men who came with them. Some of the boys have paired up to drink and talk intently in the corner, oblivious to the girls center stage. Meg counts seven young women. Ponytails and glistening loose curls. Impressive lashes and glossy parted lips. Their hunting ground: the short leg of the restaurant where a long table dominates the end of the room before a blazing fire. This is where the single rangers take their evening meals.

The girls seem to be making most of the noise while the

more confident rangers lounge at the table or lean on the bar, murmuring their replies, watching, waiting, enjoying the attention. Some of the older rangers observe from the periphery, sipping drinks, alternating amused or warning looks with their younger counterparts.

She can't deny the rangers make a heady impression packed together. Short, tall, curvy, or slender, everything about them speaks of the strength and physicality of an outdoorsy mountain life. More than one set of broad shoulders and muscled forearms catches her eye, but she doesn't look long. She knew most of the ranger kids when she lived here, and after failing to recognize Cal, she doesn't feel confident identifying the others. Instead, she keeps her head down.

It makes her heart sting to think she could have been one of them. This could have been *her* regular Friday night, but she promised herself she would never be angry with her mother again if the chemo worked, and it did, so she pushes the bitter thoughts aside.

When she makes it to the table, she becomes aware of eyes tracking her movements. Her hands start to sweat in the latex gloves she snatched from the kitchen. Conversations still, and awareness makes her cheeks warm. She stacks plates and used cutlery onto her tray, refusing to rush despite the up-tempo thump of her pulse. Letting her gaze sweep casually around the table, she stiffens when she finds multiple pairs of ranger eyes watching her.

Some of the visiting girls exchange confused looks.

A cleared throat. "You need a hand with that?" a young man

asks from across the table. His gaze is intense, smoky-blue, and unwavering. He looks young, her age maybe, a handsome face full of freckles and a wild thatch of red-blond hair. *Joss Fenchurch?* "Looks heavy," he says.

Next to him a dark, voluptuous girl wilts when he pulls his arm from her shoulders.

"I've got it," Meg says, an involuntary snap in her voice. She looks down at her work, but she catches the sweep of his gaze across the room and the subtle jutting of his jaw. A signal? Conversation restarts.

He leans on an elbow, lowering his voice. "Meg Archer?"

She cringes inwardly. Why pretend? "Ah . . . Joss, right?"

His face lights up with a grin. "You remember me?"

"I remember you used to cheat off me in math."

This only makes his grin wider. "Your mother gave me gold stars."

"She gave everyone gold stars."

"That's what kept us coming back."

She snorts softly and reaches for a heavy jug, her face burning. Why can't she be cool about this? Three rangers slip to their feet. Joss takes the jug. A hulking older boy with coffee-colored skin takes her tray. The name *Abbot* leaps into her head. Antonia's nephew. He smiles tentatively. He knows who she is. She does an automatic scan of the room, looking for his serious younger sister, but Rilke's not there. Next to Abbot a pale, slender boy with white-blond hair steps forward, his name out of reach in the back of her mind—something nature-related? She can't remember. He directs the crowd to part and smiles warmly. "Miss."

The volume dips with the rush of gallantry. One of the Southern Gables girls gives her a wink and thumbs-up.

"Really, I can manage. You don't need—"

The side door to the restaurant opens, and the chill night air sweeps in. Meg shivers, and two large shadows unfold on the threshold. Sargent steps into the firelight, Cal at his shoulder appearing to wince behind his mop of hair. Meg freezes. The whole room freezes.

Sargent's gaze is steady and stern as he takes her in. The one eye of Cal's she can see, not covered by his hair, looks anywhere but at her. Their size and presence seem to shrink the room. She hadn't counted on dealing with them together and certainly not before an entire room full of rangers who all seem to know who she is and probably what this moment means.

Sargent nods at her. "Meg," he says, his deep voice triggering a flood of sense memory.

Dad.

She doesn't say it. Instead she echoes his nod. *"Sargent."*

It gets so quiet she can hear the fire crackling in the hearth. Joss with the smoky-blue eyes puts the jug back on the table and clears his throat. "Hot pools?"

A mass exit occurs; bench seats scrape and bar stools vacate. Abbot and the boy with the white-blond hair take the tray of dirty plates and the jug of water to the kitchen before she can protest. The Southern Gables visitors move eagerly after the rangers. Cal presses himself against the wall to let them depart, until he, Meg, and Sargent are the only ones left.

Meg's pulse is a calamity, but she steels herself and lifts her chin. "Have you eaten?"

"That's why we came."

"You better take a seat then."

FIRE-BREATHING HYDRA

Cal sits at the table with Sargent, a good foot of space between them on the bench. Faces leer from the polished knots of wood grain, and he blinks to clear his eyes. Meg says something about something, then disappears into the kitchen with a toss of her dark ponytail.

"What does that nose of yours tell you, boy?"

"Nothing."

"Liar."

The air is full of traps.

Cal clears his throat. "I can't read you."

A twitch at Sargent's lips might be a smile.

Meg returns with heaped plates of roast meat and vegetables. Her arms are toned, and her body is athletic, hard and soft together. He wants to hold his breath, but he knows Sargent will drill him for information and call him a liar again if he messes this up. So he lowers his head toward his pocket for a quick breath of cleansing mint and waits for her scent to hit him.

She deposits the food before them, plastic gloves hiding her hands. He waits for the first waft of hot food to pass. Then he breathes and lets her scent fill his lungs, fill his head. His whole body wakes up and pays attention as she joins them at the table. Meg Archer isn't an eight-year-old girl anymore. Her anger and resentment, bitterness and guilt . . . the subtle thread of longing in the undercurrent of her scent rattle him. She smells like Cal's own skin. He can't look up. He can't eat.

"You look different," Sargent says, stabbing his fork into his food and taking a bite.

"I'm eighteen."

"In two days." He chews and swallows. "I liked your hair short and off your face."

"I remember." She brushes her little finger down the long tendrils framing her face, then crosses her arms on the table.

"And your glasses?"

"I didn't need them after the attack."

He cocks his head at this and forks more food into his mouth. Cal stares at the roast beef, bleeding on his plate. His stomach curdles. Meg says nothing, and when Sargent says nothing, she shifts in her seat.

"Something wrong with your food, Cal?"

He lifts his head and forces himself to settle into her hawklike stare. "I'm not hungry, Meg."

"He doesn't eat meat," Sargent says.

Cal ignores the smirk on the head ranger's face.

Frowning, Meg begins to rise from her seat. "Let me get you something else."

He shakes his head. "It's fine. I'm fine."

Studying him, she says, "I see you avoided Social Services."

Before he couldn't look up. Now he can't look away. He shrugs.

"We had an opening," Sargent says.

She catches her bottom lip in her teeth. "I'm glad."

She's not. Cal scents the sourness in the lie, but there's shame in it too, and he guesses she feels bad about not meaning what she says . . . or not meaning it without the tangle of dark feeling that goes with it. She tips her head down, running her finger along the wood grain. He imagines her thinking something along the line of *fisherman's son*.

Sargent's scent, however, remains unchanged. He's giving nothing away. Whatever resentment Meg might feel about Cal's position in the rangers, he can't help but wish for her sake that Sargent wasn't such a hard-ass. Can't the man let his guard drop for a moment to express some emotion? This is his daughter, his only child, he's seeing for the first time in nine years. Cal clenches his jaw.

"Cora's at the post office, inspecting the apartment," Meg says.

"She really wants to sell?"

"*I* want to sell."

"Seems a waste." Sargent shrugs. "I offered to cover her medical bills."

Meg's lips slowly part. She blinks a couple of times but keeps her expression impassive.

"She didn't tell you?"

Cal wishes he had Nayland Moor's gift of invisibility. Almost eight hundred years ago, Head Ranger Nayland Moor survived a bite from a Rift Hound and discovered he could obscure the vision of those in close proximity to him, making himself undetectable.

"We don't need your money."

Sargent keeps his eyes on his plate, chewing steadily. "Your mother's a strong woman."

Meg's mouth twists, and Cal doesn't need to read her scent to know she's struggling against a flare of temper. Cal bets she'd like to reach across the table and slap Sargent's face.

"She had to be," Meg says.

Sargent lowers his fork to his plate and rests his elbows on the table, loosely linking his fingers before him. "What do you want, Meg?"

"Nothing from you."

A lie. A seething, many-headed, fire-breathing-hydra kind of lie that makes Cal hold his breath. He doesn't want to read her anymore — it taps at his own dark feelings. He presses his knuckles to his nostrils to block her scent.

Sargent runs his tongue around his teeth with a brief sucking sound. "You need my signature."

Cal stops breathing altogether.

"Did you bring the deed?" Meg's voice gets choppy. "Antonia's in the kitchen. She can witness the handover."

Sargent narrows his eyes. "I think we have to wait till you turn eighteen. Come to the camp tomorrow night. We're having a cookout. Plenty of familiar faces."

"We're not here for a cookout."

"Can't hurt. Talk to your mother."

"You think either of us wants to come to your rangers-only party?"

"If I remember correctly," Sargent says, "it's all you ever wanted when you were a child."

Meg's jaw inches forward, and her eyes harden to flint. "I grew up."

DELIBERATE OMISSION

Squinting against the glow of the gas lantern, Meg leans over the bathroom sink and covers her face with a warm, wet washcloth. Her hands won't stop shaking. It's only 8:00 p.m., but Antonia took one look at Meg's face after her encounter with Sargent and sent her to bed. She must have looked like she needed a good cry, but she can't produce tears and she can't settle. She hopes Cora returns from the post office soon before Meg's brain explodes.

Maybe washing her face and brushing her teeth, the rituals of presleep, will calm the tremor in her body. In the mirror, shadows plow the skin beneath her eyes.

"What did you expect?" she mutters.

For the hundredth time, she replays the moment Sargent stepped into the restaurant. She tries to imagine him making his way around the table, stopping before her, searching her face, opening his arms, and murmuring her name. It's like forcing stop-motion animation in her head: jerky, disjointed, and impossible to render. Would she have let him hug her if he had tried?

What is she supposed to do with the fact he offered to pay Cora's medical bills? Why would her mother say nothing? Her shaking intensifies, and she buries her face in a towel. A few rough swipes and she tosses it on the sink. Pressure builds in her chest. Jerking the lantern from the floor, she shoos shadows back into the pretty guest bedroom, past the big white bed and its soft cream pillows. Yanking the balcony door, she dumps the lantern on the fire escape and wraps her gloveless hands on the rail. She leans out into the cold night air and stretches her mouth wide in a long silent scream.

The stars are hidden behind low clouds, and there's no sign of the moon. The forest cuts most of the view of the bay. She could reach out and swipe the rustling leaves. The steep track to the rangers' camp winds up past her window, and that tingling in her chest comes back with the yearning to climb it. She pictures Cal trailing Sargent up the slope, shoulders hunched. He barely said a word, and she wonders why Sargent made him come. Clearly, he'd made him. Cal looked so uncomfortable she thought he'd drill a hole through the table with the focus of his stare. Facing Sargent had required all her nerve. She hadn't left much in reserve for Cal.

He seemed . . . guarded, watchful, tightly wound, though she supposes the same could be said about her. She certainly noticed the improvements wrought by a shower and clean clothes. So he's turned out good-looking—in a roundabout way—an odd mix of hard lines, mouth, jaw, nose, and brow, counterbalanced by the kind of eyes that might make a girl jealous. But who he has become since she last knew him is all question marks.

She rubs her rough hand along her jaw, thinking of the scar Cal hides behind his tousled hair. She supposes her efforts to hide her scars are just as obvious. She doesn't like the idea of him thinking about her hands and feels guilty for the hypocrisy of thinking about his jaw.

Does Sargent look the same?

She wishes she could make herself cry. Bawl her eyes out and smother it all in a pillow. She's spent half her life rehearsing speeches for Sargent, and tonight was like she had been scraped hollow and stuffed with . . . an altered version of herself. Something silent and venomous. Maybe he's been scraped out too.

She shivers, turns on her heel, grabs her coat and gloves, and heads for the hall.

* * *

The main road of Black Water village is completely deserted. The lights of Nero's Palace reveal a small crowd of fishermen still lingering at the bar. The lights at the boardinghouse glow at the entrance. The rest of the buildings hemming the street are dark below with yellow light seeping through the cracks of curtains in the private residences above. Though fog hangs over the bay, there's enough streetlight to make her way to the post office without a lantern.

As she mounts the rise to the long, flat road, a sharp laugh catches her ear above the sound of water lapping mournfully at the beach. She stops in her tracks. Sargent? The sign swinging from the arm of the building reads "Bertrum's Butchery." She remembers it from childhood. The alley that runs along the left-hand side of the building leads to the kill yard. Perhaps Sargent is checking the details of the buck Cal delivered to Nero's Palace this morning. Processing unsanctioned kill is illegal. Carcasses seized from poachers are often burned, antlers and all, to discourage copycat attempts.

". . . difficult to judge . . ." The voice is definitely Sargent's. ". . . nights till full moon . . . best conditions. The bait will draw them to the summit. A strong distress signal will rattle the gate, but if that doesn't work, you need to have your men on the mountain. The map shows the three main lodestones."

"We have no interest in wasting time."

The upward lilting voice. The Fortune Hunter? Suspicion and curiosity war with Meg's instinct to run back to Nero's. She holds herself still, afraid to even rustle her jacket.

"Is he ready?"

Sargent grunts. "That's irrelevant. He's the most gifted member of the community."

"But is it worth the risk?"

"The endowment rite . . . controlled transition. And the more senior rangers with . . . the better."

"A lot of variables at play."

"Isn't that what we pay you for, Spear?"

Spear? His name is Spear?

"Franklin Abel pays me to ensure the future of his investment."

"No greater insurance for the Old Herd. Nine years without Rift Sight has been a pain in the ass. Besides, fresh blood ensures a . . . there's potential for a bonded lineage mate, guaranteeing compatible offspring for future vessels."

"Nutris will be glad to hear this."

"Nutris can kiss my ass; this is for Fallon."

Spear chuckles. "Give me your arm."

A moment of silence, then a grunt of pain and a muttered curse.

Meg's brain spins and trips, trying to piece the details together. Sargent is working with this man. What on earth is he doing to his arm? *Nine years without Rift Sight* catches her like a pinched muscle. *Nine years.* He said Fallon, but Fallon is a myth. A story about the origins of the Old Herd, the pregnant wife of Actaeon, caught in her husband's curse, delivered as a doe to the island by the hand of the goddess. Meg loved the story, a deviation from the old Greek myth. The goddess, filled with remorse, rips a hole in time and space to save the innocent woman. The cursed stag, pursued by hunting hounds, slips through the hole just as it closes, forever searching for his mate. That's how the feral dogs get their backstory. What does Sargent mean, *this is for Fallon?*

"And how long will *this* take?" Sargent says.

"Hard to say," Spear murmurs. "In the lab, we saw results less than . . . hours after application . . . carcass more than twelve hours dead, I'd guess . . ."

"... Lower Slopes only. Once the gate is open ... will spread ... all the way down to the Lower Slopes, ready for the cull."

"Here. Clamp this. And the tape. You are a man of vision, Sargent Archer."

The click of a gate and footsteps in the alley. Meg darts away from the building and walks briskly across the road to follow the seawall back toward the restaurant, hair prickling at the nape of her neck.

"Meg?"

Cringing, she stops, her pulse leaping. She turns slowly, feigning cool surprise.

Her father approaches, rolling his sleeve down over his bandaged forearm, his eyes narrowed. Jackson Spear strides beside him, hands inside the pockets of his coat, a knowing gleam in his eye. Meg considers bolting back to the restaurant and hiding under the bed.

"What are you doing out here?" her father demands.

"Walking."

"Walking?"

"Minding my own business."

Jackson Spear smirks, his eyes devouring her face, her body, her feet. She waits for him to acknowledge her, to tell Sargent how he *met* her and Cora on the dock. He says nothing. She says nothing. In the space of three seconds, she feels complicit. In what? *Say something. Call him out. Tell Sargent about the desperate father and the wallet and the money.*

"It's cold," Sargent says.

She holds up her hands. "I have my gloves."

He blinks at her fingers and meets her eye, but Meg can't read any emotion in his gaze. He clips a nod. "Yak fur."

"Meg, is it?" The Fortune Hunter holds out his hand. "Jackson Spear."

She considers not taking it, her body flashing hot and cold, but she thinks of her mother who's been cleaning for the last few hours and the full day of cleaning before them tomorrow. Now is not the time to antagonize the person who has the power to determine the sale price. She takes his hand and endures his power shake, the compression of her bones.

"And how are you two acquainted?"

"Her mother owns the old Black Water Post Office," Sargent says, perfectly bland. "They're hoping to sell it to Nutris Pharmaceuticals. I informed them you'd be here for the audit and recommended they present their offer in person."

Spear raises his eyebrows, looking back over his shoulder in the direction of the post office. She's too winded by Sargent's deliberate omission of her identity as his daughter to think of a coherent response.

"Shall I inspect the premises?"

"We're cleaning tomorrow," she says. "Maybe late afternoon?"

"I'll stop by."

Sargent stares past her shoulder, his expression grim. She wants to shake him. Punch him. Scream in his face. "Good night, then." She turns and walks away, slipping into a jog, goose bumps prickling her skin, as though predators mark her steps.

RIFT HOUNDS

Rough hands rip Cal from the womb of sleep. He lashes out, his elbow colliding with unforgiving muscle and bone, eliciting pained curses that snap him conscious. Nellie and Joss crowd his cot, pale freckled faces of mother and son blanched whiter still in the murky light. Across the room someone lights a lantern. Joss rubs his shoulder, mouth screwed up, hair mussed, sleep-swollen eyes. Everyone in the junior boys' apprentice barracks is sitting up in their beds, heads cocked, eyes fixed on the ceiling, windows, door. Howls echo outside. Close. Loud.

Cal freezes, picturing the source of the cry, prowling right beneath the shutters. Another howl undulates through the darkness. The sound makes Cal cold, his scar aches, and he knots his fists in his blankets to stop from touching the mark on his jaw. He did this. Knowing sickens him.

Nellie's already moving to the door, fisting her arms into the sleeves of a wool sweater, emerging disheveled. "Sargent wants you. Now."

The other apprentices turn wide eyes on Cal as another howl rises, more distant than the last, a long, shrill knife gutting the dark.

"The rest of you guard the camp," Nellie snaps, boot up on a bed frame, yanking her laces into brutal knots.

Cal fights his sleep-heavy muscles back into the clothes left limp on the end of his cot, hating the breathless stares of the others as they fumble for pants and socks. Sargent needs him. He hasn't seen the head ranger since they went to the restaurant. Instead of interrogating Cal about what he read in Meg's scent, he'd abandoned him on the veranda, said he had business in the village.

"Cal," Joss hisses. "Be safe. Ma, you too."

Cal doesn't reply, doesn't look at the boy, unwilling to catch the fear in his eyes as he shoots out into the cold mouth of the saddle. Nellie doesn't speak, ruffling her son's hair as she goes, cupping his cheek. Out in the cold air, Cal wets his lips, but his whistle is boneless, and he has to try twice more before it's clear enough to summon Reeva. The link flickers then settles, alert in his mind. He listens for the flap of her wings. Rushing to the tack room, Nellie grabs a rifle from the rack. Bullets are no use against Rift Hounds, but there are boars on the Upper Slopes, and they can be a problem. Nellie jimmies the lid on a rusty paint can, scooping out a fistful of dried rue. She selects a clean machete and rubs it on the blade, muttering the Latin. A hummingbird flits into the shed, circles Nellie, and lands in her hair.

"Yes, Flint, I know it's very late," Nellie murmurs. "Yes, you were sleeping, but I need you now."

With a terse peep, the little bird darts up, his wings blurring, and flies back out the door.

"Don't be grumpy," she calls.

Cal feels her turn and look at him. When he doesn't look up, she rests pale fingers on the blade of his machete. He pauses yet still can't bear to lift his gaze.

"You're not the first to lose one of the Old Herd," she says softly. "Yes, the Rift has opened. The Hounds have come. Now we do our job. This is what we trained for. Defend the Herd."

Cal swallows, unable to voice the terror cinching his throat. What if someone dies tonight? What if Nellie dies? How would he face Joss? He'd have to leave the community, leave the island. His head swims, but he gives a small nod. She pats the blade as though she were patting his hand and turns away. His fingers tremble as he completes the ritual with the rue, nostrils pinching against the acrid scent. He slings the strap of the rifle across his chest, clips the tether of the machete to his left hip, and sheaths a knife into his belt. He slings a quiver of ash-wood arrows on his back, their tips coated in rue, and selects his favorite bow.

They take no light. Cal's eyes have already adjusted, and Nellie cracks open a tin of Yarra leaves, sticking a wad beneath her tongue, chewing and blinking. They are about to run for the forest when Rilke comes skidding into their path. She has her oilskin over her pajamas, and her boots are laced tight.

Nellie sighs. "We don't have time for this."

"I'm ready," Rilke begs, fighting her thick curls into a ponytail, not even acknowledging Cal's presence.

"You've lost your scout, sweetheart."

Rilke flinches, and Cal's stomach twists for her. Rilke's finch died two weeks ago. Black and tan with a bright red bill, Queenie was fifteen, and her heart gave out. Rilke's too. Cal smells the grief on her like rain.

She juts her jaw. "I'm at the top of the leaderboard for defense drills."

"This isn't a drill," Nellie says, licking her fingers and wiping the Yarra juice over her eyelids.

"I have the best time for the six hardest etudes."

"Rilke . . ."

"*I'm ready*, Aunt Nellie. Please."

Cal is taken aback. It's easy for him to forget Joss and Rilke and her brother Abbot are cousins. Rilke's father, Bren, the rangers' chief physician and second-in-command to Sargent, was married to Nellie's twin sister, Anne. Anne died when Rilke was twelve years old.

The girl faces her aunt with steely determination. There's something about the set of her jaw, an echo of her aunt's, that makes the physical differences seem less pronounced. Nellie softens and brushes her knuckles across the spray of freckles on Rilke's cheek. "You know your mother would be so proud of you . . ."

Cal hears the *but* in her voice. Rilke does too, and she jerks away, eyes glittering.

Nellie gives another weary sigh. "The junior apprentices have been instructed to secure the camp. I expect you to follow orders." She leaves no room for argument, jogging away with a gesture for Cal to follow.

He gives Rilke an apologetic grimace and takes off after the master ranger, catching the sound of Rilke's muttering behind his back.

"It's not bloody fair. I'm older than him. He's just a . . ."

Fisherman's son. Cal ignores the sting.

The surrounding forest gains definition. He can tell when the Yarra takes effect because Nellie picks up the pace, more surefooted in the darkness. They clear the camp buildings and slip through the thick wall of trees.

Nellie makes room for Cal to take the lead. Cal struggles to shake the oppressive fear clouding his mind, to let his awareness rise, when another howl reverberates across the mountain. It's so loud and close he expects the reek to fill his nostrils with every breath. The track snakes in sudden upward lunges to each new plateau. He wills Reeva to come, but the next howl slits the darkness, and sense memory thrusts him back into his eight-year-old body. His scar stings. His chest compresses—he can't get air. Stars ignite in his peripheral vision. He stumbles against the trunk of a tree and gasps for breath.

Nellie stops beside him, hardly panting from the run. "Cal," she murmurs—a hesitation, knowing Cal hates to be touched—then her hand settles on Cal's back, bracing him between his shoulders. "We're out of time."

Cal grunts, gritting his teeth at the bolt of life—Nellie's signature—firing through his system. She's only trying to help, but the distraction doesn't stop the memories forming behind Cal's eyelids. He turns his head so Nellie won't see his face. He wants to throw up.

A rustle of leaves and the flap of wings. Reeva lands on the branch above him. Relief floods his limbs, and his chest unclenches. The bird doesn't cry out, doesn't squawk at all. She peers down at him, and something passes between their link that loosens Cal's breath. The stars fade in the corners of his vision. He pulls air into his lungs, the breath of loam and rot and ice. His eight-year-old self folds tight in his diaphragm, and he presses it down to his stomach.

"Go," he croaks, and with the silky rustle of her wings, Reeva launches upward. His awareness amplifies immediately, his certainty with it. "There's two." And he grips his bow and starts running again.

"Two?" Nellie mutters behind him.

Cal gnaws at the same question as he slips up the mountain, full stride, long limbs pulling him up and up, and his muscles begin to heat, quads, glutes, calves. He feels the twinge in his still healing ribs and the omen in that injury. He thinks of the strangled buck on the Northwest Loop. The arrival of Meg. Now Rift Hounds? Like some kind of twisted déjà vu.

In minutes, Cal leads them to the ridge of Little Peak and toward the towering redwoods that mark the border to the Old Herd territory.

The air ripples around him as Cal crosses the ley line—a

stinging snap against his skin, a deep centering electric surge calling him to the mountain. He braces for the Voice of the Herd to roar into his mind, but there's nothing. The Voice of the Herd is accessible all over the island, and in their warded territory, it should be like open broadband. The absence of that ancient presence frightens Cal more than the howls, more than the prospect of facing a Rift Hound, and he skids to a halt. Nellie stops by his shoulder and says nothing. She's listening too, her face taut with confusion and worry.

"What's going on?" Cal whispers.

Nellie scans the darkness as though looking for some sign of the Herd. She frowns. "Flint is searching for Sargent and Bren. Is Reeva picking up anything?"

Cal concentrates, finding his connection with Reeva, and his vision skews with an image of the forest from above as she skims the trees, moving south, deeper into Old Herd territory. She sends Sargent's face, sensing the head ranger deep in the forest. He must be with the Herd. But how can it be silent? Being untethered from the Herd makes Cal shaky. "She can't find them either. She's going higher."

A howl rips the silence, and the stench comes with it. A feral reek of dead meat and sulfur, eclipsing the scent of rue. Nellie unclips her machete, turning it in her hand, a dull glimmer on the blade. Cal switches his bow into his left hand and brushes his fingers over the handle of his machete. Nellie moves so they stand back-to-back. "Where?" the master ranger whispers.

He opens his mind, blinks to clear his eyes, and the forest

is superimposed with a second skin. His scar's most coveted gift: Rift Sight. Otherworld shadows revealed. The scar on his jaw tingles and throbs. He ignores the aura of natural things, trees breathing, a stoat curled midburrow in the underbrush, an owl unmoving in the branches above. Deep in the trees the glimmer of unearthly blue eyes.

He shifts his heel to nudge Nellie. Difficult as it is for Cal to bear the brief bursts of Nellie's life force sparking through his system, at least each brush of her shoulder blade, elbow, or hip says *Alive. Alive.* Alive is what they might not be any second now. He tells himself Nellie has nine kills under her belt. Nine. He adds it to his tally of three. He amplifies the odds, grows them like a hothouse, twelve between them. That's magic. They're heroes. They should be dead twelve times over.

Cal doesn't take his eyes off the shimmering blue, hovering higher than a grown man's eyes. He shudders to imagine the size of the Hound—the bulk of its chest, the power in its invisible haunches. Cal shivers and doesn't stop shivering.

The blue eyes narrow, and a growl like the slow tumbling of massive boulders shakes the ground and Cal's bones.

Nellie pants, nudging around in two shuffling steps so they both face the sound side on. The woman's scent is rife with terror, but she doesn't shake. "Where, Cal?"

Cal points at the blue lights and drops to one knee. "It's coming."

Nellie grunts, adjusting her stance. Still, Cal wonders at the woman's resolve. How can she stand it? Not knowing where death stalks toward her. How does she hold herself in place?

How does she not run? Panic spools ice through Cal's veins.

He lets his body slide into a familiar etude, the seamless shift of weight, the stretch of his triceps, reaching back for his quiver, the returning arc of his arm. He nocks the arrow, sights the target, draws the bow, and holds.

"Cal?" she says tightly.

"It's not solid yet." He won't waste an arrow firing at smoke. The split second it takes to reload is all it would need to assume full corporeal form and rip their heads off.

The stench makes his eyes water, shadows move like windblown mist, then ten feet away the creature finally begins to form around the blue pricks of light. Cal's mouth dries. The Hound is bigger than him. Its chest and shoulders are muscled and taut, flesh like a mottled bruise gaining definition. The body is sleek, black shadow rising like smoke from its back, the haunches compact but quivering with power, and the tail tapers from thick bone to a knifepoint tip. He knows one whip of that tail could cave his lungs.

Cal exhales and releases the arrow.

The shaft sinks into the Hound's shoulder, flesh rippling like water, unable to close over the shaft of sacred wood. The beast howls, a cannon blast of rage. Nellie roars too, leaping forward, machete swinging with only the arrow to guide her.

Instinct unlocks his muscles, and he unhooks his machete, lunging beside Nellie to slash at the beast. It leaps away, trying to shift back into its ephemeral form, but the arrow holds it in flesh and bone. Its frustrated snarl curdles the air, and Cal chokes as he rights himself. Nellie swings, powerfully yet too short, in the space the Hound used to be, following the etudes—cycling three times through three moves covering 360 degrees. Dizzying. Lethal. The Hound crouches away from the blade.

"Ten o'clock," Cal warns as the Hound circles left and Nellie thrusts her machete like a sword. Cal charges, and the beast ducks and weaves past him. The defensive move confuses him. Rift Hounds don't dodge. They attack. They kill. "He's waiting for his pack mate," Cal mutters through rough breaths. "Six o'clock. Watch your left!"

A flash of steel. Nellie's knife, slipped from her belt and thrown just inches left of the buried arrow. The Hound swings away from the blade—too slow—and the knife rips open its chest. The shriek of fury turns Cal's bowels to water, and his joints stiffen, marrow siphoning from his bones. He can't move fast enough. The Hound swipes its massive paw, claws unsheathed and flashing down Nellie's body. The sound of ripping. Jacket, wool, cloth, and flesh. A slash from shoulder to hip like a word crossed out with red pen.

Cal abandons his bow and throws himself between the Hound and Nellie, falling to one knee, both hands wrapped around the handle of his machete. The Hound charges, but he drives the blade up beneath its jaw. The crunch of skull bone vibrates through his arms, followed by a warm flood of reeking blood over his hands. Thick black smoke pours from the wound before billowing inward, obscuring Cal's vision. The Hound implodes, solid flesh dissolving to putrid smoke.

He takes no comfort when the air clears; he knows the

second Hound is coming, and he won't leave Nellie's body unguarded to collect his bow. She makes a gurgling sound behind him, as though she's read his panic. Then Reeva connects with his thoughts, blasting him with her fear, her warning—the second Hound approaches.

A new roar breaks through Cal's mind. The Voice of the Herd at full volume. A blast of pain and loss that almost buckles him over. His vision blurs, and he ducks his head against the internal noise. Nellie cries out, and Cal can't tell if it's a response to her injuries or the blast of terror from the Voice of the Herd.

The sound of a heavy body moving at top speed toward them is the only warning as the second Rift Hound appears in full corporeal form, skidding to a halt, jaws slavering. It's smaller than the first, snout more pointed and eyes closer together on its lowered head. Its hackles ripple, and the stench leaves Cal momentarily senseless.

"Stay back!" he shouts, his voice catching and tearing in his dry throat, eyes streaming from the Hound's fuming breath. His fingers slip on the sticky handle of the machete, but he holds fast as the creature sniffs the air in front of him. Pawing the leaf mold, the Hound rends the night with barking.

Nothing about the Rift Hound's hesitation makes sense. The Old Herd's panic reaches a crescendo. The Hound turns its head, sensing the distress, and darts back through the trees, returning to mist.

The volume drops in Cal's head as he pulls his focus away from the Voice of the Herd and the roar dulls. Nellie groans, and he turns to her. His neck prickles with his back to the forest where the Hound disappeared, but Reeva sends affirmation of the all-clear. She tracks the beast up the mountain as it heads back to the Rift.

"Please," Nellie croaks as her tiny hummingbird flits down through the trees. Flint trills and darts back and forth in frenetic bursts. "Tell me."

Though it goes against every instinct in his recoiling skin, Cal wipes the blood from his fingers and brings his hand to Nellie's chest, finding the wet skin beneath her collar. The connection is instant. *Alive-alive-alive.* The song that all bodies sing, insistent and fiercely clinging to the fragile cord of life. Around Nellie a pale flickering aura. Cal blinks, realizing he's still seeing with Rift Sight. He doesn't need it and blinks it away.

Trembling, he bows his head and listens closely for the whisper of death. Knowing creeps up over Cal's shoulders, feathers just behind his ears, needles into his head. The air grows cold in his mouth, throat, lungs. He can feel the tingling frost gathering around his knees and feet. Death is near . . . near . . . considering. He waits, and then the knowing fills him. He releases a shaky breath, trembling uncontrollably. "Fight, Nellie. You're staying."

A soft cry and Nellie shakes too, like she's been holding herself close, her muscles winched. "I don't know if I should thank you," she says, lips trembling. "Not dying hurts like hell."

JARRING RECALIBRATION

Wrung out from a restless night, Meg pauses before the post office, hunched in her coat against the morning chill. Mist shrouds the forest above slate cliffs, and the sky pearls gray on heavy gray. It's another moment of jarring recalibration. Staring at the narrow, two-storied building, she waits as the bones of memory clunk back into joint. Fading white paint peels on the windowsills, and there are no flowers in the beaten yellow planter boxes, no welcome mat on the step. Nostalgia hovers above her like a fist about to swing.

Flung from sleep in the small hours, Meg had lain awake shaking in the aftermath of a nightmare. Fangs and blue eyes and god-awful howling. She's not surprised. Coming home was sure to trigger the old nightmares, stir up bad memories. At least Cora was beside her, having slipped into bed at some stage. She considered waking her, just to distract herself from panic, but didn't want to start a fight before dawn.

She must have fallen asleep because the next time she found consciousness, it was seven thirty and the bed was empty again beside her. When she made it down to the restaurant kitchen, Antonia informed her Cora had already set out to start Team Big Clean and hadn't wanted to wake her. She suspects Cora is avoiding her; Antonia will have told her Sargent came to Nero's last night.

Now, she steps back from the post office and stares up at their old kitchen window. When she was little, it didn't strike her as odd that her father lived at the rangers' camp. He joined them for evening meals three or four nights a week, breakfast on the weekend. Most other people's dads were fishermen, and they were away at night too. It wasn't until she moved to the mainland and made friends at school that she realized *most* families, where the parents were still together, live together *most* of the time.

Down the side of the house, the back gate swings open, and Cora appears in her denim overalls, bright red bandana tied in her hair. Her cheeks are pink, and there's a streak of dust on her nose. She holds her wallet and keys in one hand and a sheet of crumpled notepaper in the other. Nostalgia punches Meg right in the guts. This could be a scene torn straight from her Black Water childhood. The only differences are the color of Cora's hair and the slight limp as she walks.

"Oh, there you are," Cora says, not fully meeting her eyes. "Sleep all right?"

"Why didn't you tell me?"

Cora licks her lips. "About?"

"About?" Meg raises her eyebrows. "About Sargent's offer to pay your medical bills? What else are you keeping from me?"

Cora slumps her shoulders. "He offered. I said no."

"When?"

"January, I wrote to confirm we were coming on your birthday to collect the deed to the house and negotiate a sale with Nutris. *February*, he bothered to reply only to demand why. March, I replied that it was none of his goddamn business. April, I get a check in the mail with the exact amount to cover my debts."

"Why didn't you cash it?"

"Why?"

Temperature rising, Meg unzips her coat with a sharp yank. *"Yes. Why not?"*

Her mother swells like she's being pumped full of air. "Because the man who abandoned us doesn't get to swoop in and be the hero that saves the day. Because investigating my financial problems without my permission is a gross invasion of privacy. Because I will not owe that negligent, mercenary narcissist a single dollar."

Meg stares across the road to the pebble beach, breathing hard through her nose. "What did you do with the check?"

"I burned it."

"Shit."

Her mother doesn't respond, but Meg feels her regret, her shame. She should say something reassuring. She can't. "So we have to be all noble, and he gets to punish us for nine years with no consequences."

"Punish?"

"For leaving." Meg is careful to keep the judgment from her voice, remembering her promise not to blame Cora for keeping her from returning to Black Water.

Cora flips her keys in her hand and clenches them in her fist. "As much as I'd love to blame Sargent for my cancer . . ."

It happens quickly—a landslide from sullen frustration to hot anguish, tears pricking Meg's eyes. "Why can't he just forgive us? Why can't he forgive *me*?"

Cora steps directly in front of Meg, grasping her firmly by the arms. "Where is this coming from? What did he say to you?"

"Nothing," Meg says, her throat screwed tight. "He could barely look at me in the restaurant. Then I was going to come see you last night, but he was out here with that Fortune Hunter. He wouldn't even acknowledge me as his kid."

"That's on him, Meg. Not you."

"Fergus Welsh died because of me. Sargent almost died because of me. I ruined everything."

"Fergus Welsh died because he was a ranger," Cora snaps. "Sargent almost died because he is a ranger, because of what's on that bloody mountain. That's what rangers do, Meg. They live short, pointless lives, sacrificing everything for a herd of bloody deer. That is why we left—because I want you to have a long life. I want you to see the world and find out who you can be beyond Black Water Island."

It takes all Meg's strength not to scream that Black Water is all she has ever wanted. That oilskin coat, those soft leather tracking boots, a bow in her hand, the ancient forest on all sides, and the bones of the mountain beneath her feet. She has to cross her arms tight around her waist to keep her hands from shaking.

Cora blows through her lips and rubs her face. "I begged Sargent to come with us. He *chose* not to."

"You know why."

"Don't give me that 'call of the mountain' bullshit. Your father is a grown-ass man."

Meg almost blurts, *I feel it too*—but she's sleep deprived, upset, and not thinking straight. Too many memories. A warped imagination thanks to a childhood soaked in ranger worship. She may not have had access to the secrets and lore they held close to their chests, but she'd overheard things, glimpsed things she may not have understood yet filled her with yearning. She spent half her life cultivating a fantasy that one day she'd return and they'd let her join the ranks. Reality is nine years of silence. More than a closed door. Judgment. Blame. For Fergus Welsh. For leaving Sargent. For tearing their family apart.

She tells her mother about Jackson Spear's intent to inspect the property this afternoon. Cora's mouth tightens, and she nods. "We can be polite. Professional."

"I heard them talking," Meg says. "About the Old Herd and stuff about Fallon. It was like Sargent was talking about a person."

"That's because Sargent drank the Kool-Aid; he *makes* the Kool-Aid."

"He said something about being nine years without sight."

Cora frowns.

"What do you think he means?"

Her mother shakes her head slowly, knotting her brow. "I have no idea, love."

"Nine years. It's about us. Blaming us." Meg looks to the horizon. Out past the mouth of the bay, a ferry chugs toward the island, sitting low in the water. "There was all this stuff about bloodlines and opening a gate."

"What gate?"

Meg screws her face up, struggling to access the details. She wishes she could have recorded the conversation and printed out a transcript. It was important. Secret alleyway meeting important. "Remember when we moved to the mainland?" she says. "I'd rush home from school every day to check the mailbox?"

Cora sighs. "It broke my heart."

"There was always this split second before I opened the box, this . . ." She scoops air with her hands. "Rush of hope, thinking . . . this time."

Cora swallows thickly.

"That was last night, being with Sargent. An empty box."

Her mother closes her eyes and exhales. When she opens them, her lashes glisten. "Two more days, kid. Three tops and we're out of here."

Meg glances at the post office and releases a shuddering breath. She can't articulate the contradictory tug on her heart—the longing for Black Water. Instead she nods. "He wants us to come to some cookout tonight up at the ranger camp. Says the Nutris reps will be there, and we can look at the paperwork."

Cora nods.

"You want to go?"

"If the Nutris guy will be there. Sargent. Antonia would come with us. Tick some boxes."

Meg hesitates before asking. "And . . . how do you feel about seeing him?"

Cora fidgets with the zipper on her wallet. "I've got a stomach full of bees."

"Reckon you could fire them from your throat like a machine gun?"

Her mother snorts. "Part of me was hoping he'd come look for me at the post office last night. Just to have that first contact without a crowd. I suppose he's still hot G.I. Joe, and here I come with my wrinkles and gray hair."

Meg recoils. "First of all, hot G.I. Joe? Ew. Stop that. Second of all, you are forty-three, not eighty-three, and your hair is silver, not gray, and you look completely badass. And why do you care what the *negligent, mercenary narcissist* thinks about the way you look?"

"I haven't had sex in a very long time."

"Right, well, now I have to go bleach my brain." Meg marches toward the post office, and Cora hooks her through the elbow, swinging her back toward the road.

"We have to buy some from Leaman's first." She waves her notepaper, which appears to be a list of cleaning supplies.

Meg shudders. "Extra-strength, please."

BRIEF CLARITY

Cal stalks across the yard toward the summer barracks, fine rain dazzling his sweater. He turns his bleary eyes to the mountain, but the Voice of the Herd is quiet. He'll need to find a ley line today, recharge, refocus. His bones ache for connection.

A few of the junior apprentices are working through defense drills in the yard. He pauses to watch, leaning against one of the corner pillars of the practice ring. Rilke steps in, stocky and stripped to the waist, like the others, just a sports bra and workout shorts to avoid creating extra laundry. The other apprentices shuffle back, giving her space. She flourishes a wooden machete.

Abbot, Rilke's burly older brother, watches his sister with worried eyes, arms crossed, biceps bulging. Beside him, Leif, sleek and tightly muscled, leans his chin on Abbot's shoulder. Leif spots Cal, and his face brightens; he lifts his machete in a silent salute. Abbot joins him, raising his wooden blade and giving Cal an approving nod, his expression open and sincere.

Rilke turns. When she sees Cal, her jaw hardens. She pivots, launching back into the etude, a similar 360-degree set to one Nellie used last night.

Sargent steps out of the master rangers' cabin, bloodstained bandages in his hands. Nellie lies in one of the back rooms that serve as infirmary, where Bren treats the sick and injured. The apprentices straighten around the practice ring, and Rilke increases her speed. Cal ducks his head and walks away, unwilling to face another public dressing-down. If Sargent wants to yell at him or strike him, he can do it without an audience.

Before the head ranger can make eye contact, Cal slips into the summer barracks. The kitchen is still open — an extra hour's grace for rangers who've been working during the active Rift. He follows the smell to the servery and stops short. Joss gives him a sleepy nod from the cramped stove. Eggs and bacon and stacks of toast. Otho dozes on the windowsill, his beak tucked into his little tawny chest.

He wants to apologize. Instead he blurts, "You shouldn't be on kitchen duty."

"Ma's out of it; Bren has her sedated to the eyeballs."

"Then go sleep. I'll take care of this." Cal stalks toward the kitchen, pushing up his sleeves. "I can't believe those assholes would make you cook."

Joss sticks out his spatula like a stop sign. "Leave it. I'd rather be busy."

They stare at each other across the counter, and Cal detects a volatile mix of emotion in the boy's scent, but nothing that smells bitter like blame or hatred. "Is it bad?"

"Big slash." Joss indicates the path of Rift Hound claws from shoulder to stomach. "Deep but didn't touch any organs. Bren had some freshly powdered Bane."

Cal sucks air through his teeth; raw Bane is potent and brutal. "Rough night, then."

Joss nods and rubs his eyes with his finger and thumb. He produces a colossal yawn. "The wounds are knitting well. The scar will look a lot like Sargent's when it's healed. Ma'll like that."

"I'm sorry, man."

Joss's eyes are red-rimmed and glassy. "You saved her life."

"I did nothing. I was useless. The whole thing was my fault."

"You put yourself between two Rift Hounds and my mother."

Cal groans, unable to bear Joss's kindness. "The only thing that saved us was timing. You felt the Voice last night? As soon as that distress signal came, the second Hound bolted. One of the Old Herd was in trouble, and it knew."

"After an easy kill?"

"Something like that."

There's an excruciating pause, then Joss sighs. "Don't torture yourself, Cal. None of us are safe up here. We're all on borrowed time, and because of you, Ma has more."

Cal casts about for a change of subject. "How was your date at the thermal springs?"

Joss straightens up. "A gentleman doesn't tell."

"So I guess you'll dish the gory details then."

Joss smirks. "There's something to be said for the Black Water thermal springs, my friend. Magical qualities in the water."

Agonized by the casual use of *friend*, Cal forces an amused snort.

With a knowing look, Joss leans across the counter. "Speaking of . . ."

Cal narrows his eyes. "Speaking of?"

"Meg Archer?"

A rush of tingling blooms from Cal's chest, but he keeps his expression cool and shovels scrambled eggs into his mouth to indicate silence on the topic.

Joss grins. "Sooo, we're pretending she's not hot."

Footsteps at the door and Cal can't catch the scent. He knows immediately that it must be Sargent, and the way Joss stiffens and turns pink behind the stove confirms it. Cal nearly spits egg all over the counter. *Please don't let Sargent have heard us.* Then the scent of blood confuses him. It's not Nellie's blood wafting from Sargent. Blood without a defining signature. Was Sargent hurt last night, too?

Otho wakes on the windowsill and hoots irritably, fluffing his raggedy wings before turning his back.

The head ranger stops beside Cal and helps himself to a slice of bacon, tearing it between his teeth. "Nellie looks comfortable."

Joss ducks his head. "Bren knows his stuff."

"Still," Sargent says, "it's tough, seeing your mother like that. You don't have to worry about the duty roster. I'll switch a few names."

"No, sir," Joss says, his eyes growing misty. "I'd prefer to keep busy."

Sargent studies the boy, and Cal looks at his food, waiting for the head ranger to turn on him and tear him apart with words or fists. Neither occurs. In fact, the man stays entirely calm. Disoriented, Cal looks up, catching a rare glimpse of softness in his face, a glimpse of his previous incarnation—the Sargent from before. It fills him with a painful cocktail of guilt and longing, wrapped weirdly with his grief about his dad—or dads in general. He probably needs more sleep.

"In that case"—Sargent scratches his stubble, revealing a thick bandage on his forearm—"how would you like to join Cal, tracking an injured deer? He'll find it. You put it down."

Thrown off by the offer and the realization the scent with the missing definition is Sargent's blood, Cal stutters, "It—it didn't kill the deer? The Rift is still open?"

"The Rift *is* still open. I need you to track the deer, put it out of its misery, and kill the distress signal. That should close the Rift."

"Sir," Joss says, "what's the point? Two more nights till full moon."

Sargent hardens his jaw. "It's the difference between the threat of a few Hounds breaking through and the whole bloody pack."

Cal blurts, "But I'm on probation."

"You saved a master ranger's life," Sargent says. "The audit is about to begin, and we can't afford to have anyone on the bench—not with Nellie out of the game."

Cal gives a stiff nod. "It saved us last night, that injured deer. The Hound took off after it as soon as the disturbance came through."

Sargent looks at Cal long and hard, his brown eyes inscrutable and his scent closed. Though he's rattled, Cal doesn't drop his gaze, doesn't blink, like his mettle is being tested in yet another stare down. He's had more and more of these disorienting moments with the head ranger peering at him like he's taking the measure of his soul.

Finally, Sargent looks away. "As far as I can tell, the Hounds that got to you and Nellie surprised the Herd on their way down the mountain. Set off a minor stampede. We think they hit a ley line, and the ones too scared to cross scattered from the main group. A mob of twenty or so ended up in the cleft of the mountain."

"An ambush?" Joss asks.

"I doubt Rift Hounds can be accused of strategy," Sargent says. "Instinct and stubbornness. Whatever the case, a third Hound came straight from the mouth of the Rift and plowed right through them."

"Three?" Cal murmurs. Guilt turns his throat to ash.

"I got there as the last bastard came through."

Horror and macabre fascination unlock Cal's jaw before he realizes he's gaping like a fool. He's pictured it many times, but never witnessed it: hounds emerging from the Rift, wild with the scent of the Old One, the Great Stag—the scent of his offspring so maddeningly rich in the mountains.

"Was he there?" Joss's voice drops to a reverential whisper. "Did you see him? The Old One?"

Cal holds his breath, the same question burning in his chest.

Sargent tilts his head, impatient with the suggestion. The Great Stag can break through only when the Rift is at its most unstable—at the full moon. Even then, sightings are rare. The pack of Hounds that come slavering after him ranges anywhere between one or two to half a dozen. These rare lesser raids are anomalies, usually only a rogue Hound. Three is a worry.

"The Rift started to collapse before the Hound could do much damage." Sargent licks bacon grease from his fingers. "It fought hard to stay and complete the kill, but the pull was too much."

It boggles Cal's mind to picture the beast being sucked back through the tear in time and space. He and Joss exchange similar looks of incredulity.

"We'll go now," Cal says, returning his plate to the counter, quickly calculating the whereabouts of his gear. Most of it is being washed. Joss will lend him a spare shirt.

Sargent shakes his head. "Nutris starts the audit tonight, and I need everyone here for roll call. I'm not giving Jackson Spear an excuse to claim Nutris treaty rights."

Cal shivers at the implications. If the rangers can't prove their capacity to administer the cull, which includes providing enough guides to accompany the Fortune Hunters arriving the following week and keeping the mountain clear of Rift Hounds, Nutris can claim treaty rights, giving themselves access to the Upper Slopes and the Old Herd. Unthinkable.

Joss dumps his spatula on the grill. "As soon as we're clear, give the word."

A small, approving smile turns Sargent's lips. With a parting nod, he swivels on his heel, then pauses. "Cal. I have a job for you in the village."

Summoned, Cal follows the head ranger to the door, friction in his reluctant limbs. He casts a parting *help me* look at Joss. The boy shakes his head as though Cal is being led to the gallows and mouths *Meg*, drawing his thumb across his throat.

* * *

Cal follows Sargent along the steep path down the mountain. He figures if Sargent was going to berate him for last night's horrors he would have come right out with it. In the same vein, if he was going to call him out for speaking inappropriately about his daughter—which technically Cal hadn't—he would have gotten to the point. An economical backhander across the face. A knee in the gut. No. This will be the interrogation he was expecting last night when they left the restaurant. At the time, Sargent had confused him completely by muttering about a meeting in the village. Cal had hiked back to Little Peak alone, dazed and anxious.

A muffled caw overhead. A black mass moving quickly

through his peripheral vision. Reeva lands heavily on his shoulder, mint leaves in her beak. Her life force is a soft, warm surge of energy through his bones. She makes her creaking door noise, rapid-fire from the back of her throat, punctuated by the depth-charge blip sound that reminds him of his father's fishing boat radar. He got to hear it only when they were well offshore, out of range of the island's electromagnetic interference. Reeva's depth-charge blip of indignation always makes his heart squeeze.

She sends images of Sargent into his thoughts, images of the rifle bouncing on the man's back directly before them, images laced with suspicion and dislike. Cal nudges her with his jaw and clicks his tongue. He takes the mint leaves, tucks them in his pocket, and gently thanks her by stroking the downy feathers at the top of her beak. She leans into his touch, making a contented hum, like a purr.

"Your bird doesn't like me," Sargent says without turning.

"Uh . . ." Cal can't see the man's face. He's right. Reeva doesn't like him. Never has. The only person the bird shows any enthusiasm for is Antonia. "She's not much for making friends."

Sargent snorts. "You're a good match."

Cal is struck by the comparison. Is that really how others see him? Prickly? Unfriendly? He just keeps to himself.

"You know it pisses them off," Sargent says, "the *fisherman's son* with a scout."

Cal found Reeva on his tenth birthday. Fallen from the nest, she was hopping and hissing on the forest floor with a broken wing by Burntwood Lodge. She tore Cal's fingers when he tried to pick her up and crashed away through the undergrowth, bawling. He followed at a distance, and when she had calmed down, he scattered stale cookie crumbs fished from his pocket. Longing squeezing his throat, he lay a trail to the ley line close by. Hunger drew her on. When the pulse of electromagnetism hummed into his bones, he lunged and caught her.

Reeva's little life force was a revelation, a sensation like electric butterflies in his chest. Holding her before his face—just short of pecking distance—he stared, unblinking till his eyes grew painfully dry. She stopped savaging his fingers and returned his stare, cocking her head. Cal drew a deep lungful of air and breathed over her face, whispering the words Nellie had taught him, and that was that.

"I had a scout when I was your age. Centuries ago," Sargent says with a rough chuckle. "Barn owl. Huge, handsome bastard. Filthy temper. Hated everyone and everything. Sometimes hated me. But he was loyal and sharp as a tack. Saved my life countless times."

"Can I ask . . . what happened?"

"Broken wing," Sargent says, his voice a little hollow. "Wouldn't heal. Couldn't hunt. Wouldn't take anything I killed for him. Too proud and furious. Had to snap his neck in the end."

A jolt goes through Cal. He thinks of Reeva's silky black head nudging his jaw, the way she tips her beak up inviting him to scratch her feathers. The thought of her tiny bones gripped in his hands, the pressure it would take to wrench and snap her spine. He swears, leaning the side of his face against her, needing the softness of her feathers.

"Hell of a thing," Sargent says. "Never formed another animal bond after him. Couldn't bring myself to it, to be honest. Like it would be unfaithful to even try."

Cal finds himself nodding, and Sargent's cloaked scent gains a brief clarity. A clean smell—like fresh air. It strikes him that it might be the most unguarded thing he's ever heard Sargent say.

The roof of Nero's Palace comes into view, and Sargent stops in his tracks and turns to face him. Reeva makes an unhappy sound and launches off Cal's shoulder and flaps up into the trees.

Sargent gives him one of those long, uncomfortable looks before casting his gaze toward the restaurant. "I want Meg to come to the cookout tonight."

Cal's brain blanks.

"I didn't handle things well at the restaurant." He shrugs. "I want you to invite her."

"Me?"

"She doesn't trust me, but she trusts you. She likes you."

Tingling erupts somewhere behind Cal's sternum, and he wills the heat to stay beneath the tide line of his collar. "I don't know if I'd go that far. We barely exchanged words."

"Will you do it?"

Heat reaches his ears, scalding the tips, and he's grateful for a mop of hair to hide behind. "I . . . guess I can ask."

"Invite her. Tell her you *want* her to come. That you want to talk to her. To reminisce or whatever . . . about old times."

Cal's mouth grows dry, and he struggles to compose his face. "Sir, I'll ask, but I'm not sure she'll be interested. She's pretty angry."

"You read that in her scent?"

He hesitates. *This* is what he's been waiting for. He swallows. Though it makes him feel awful to confirm it, like he's betraying Meg's confidence, Cal nods.

Sargent plants a hand on his hip. "I don't need a gift to know Meg hates my guts."

Cal almost blurts, *That's not true,* that *the opposite is true, otherwise she wouldn't be so upset,* but it seems a step too far. "She's angry with me too. Look at me." He opens his arms and gestures between them and at the island around them. "I got everything she wanted."

"She's about to turn eighteen," Sargent says gruffly. "Her mother can't keep her from returning to the community if she wants to."

"You—you'd let her become an apprentice?"

"You know what she's been doing for the last nine years?" Sargent smirks, and it doesn't strike Cal as the affection of a proud father as he lists Meg's achievements in her outdoor pursuits, archery and rock climbing and survival encounters. "She's never lived here since she was bitten. If she has Rift Sight, she would be an asset to the community. I'd like her to stay long enough at least to see if being on the mountain stirs up any latent gifts."

125

Cal can't think of a single reply. While he's often wondered if Meg's scars had resulted in Rift Sight, he can't entertain the thought of her being thrust into a nightmarish experience like the one he faced the night before. Sargent's not exactly coming across like he's after a father-daughter reunion so much as sizing up a potential commodity.

It reminds Cal that this is how Sargent sees him, and it pokes at an old wound. Have the last nine years really hardened the man so much?

"She needs a reason to stay, Cal," Sargent says carefully. "And you two share a special . . . connection."

"Sir . . ." he croaks, but he's at a loss for words.

Sargent levels another one of those long throat-closing stares and drops his voice. "Do you think I'm hard on you, Cal?"

Instinct warns Cal it might be better to toss himself off the side of the cliff than get this wrong. He drops his gaze to his boots and lies. "You're tough but fair, sir."

Sargent snorts. "Last night was a good lesson for you—the lives of the community in *your* hands because of *your* choices. That's why I ride your ass, because I see your potential. You're fresh blood, Cal. Something the community has lacked for a long time. More than ever we need strong, gifted leadership and powerful alliances to ensure the ranger legacy."

"Sir," Cal says, blinking at the head ranger, ringing in his ears. "What are you saying?"

With a sigh of impatience, Sargent takes a step closer. "I want my daughter to stay, and I want you to help me convince her."

BERTRUM'S BUTCHERY

"What are you going to wear tonight then?" Meg asks, sinking her teeth into a candy bar. They're both a little smudged and sweaty after spending the first half of the morning cleaning. Taking a breather on the steps of Leaman's General Store, Meg struggles to imagine making nice at the cookout. She's still smarting after her encounter with Sargent and hates the idea that he probably thinks she's a sulky brat. The thought of having to suck it up to prove otherwise makes her want to knock his teeth out.

Cora gives her a sidelong look. "Why not take your gloves off? There's no one out here watching you."

Meg harrumphs and peels off the gloves. The cool air is bliss on her palms. "You didn't answer my question."

"I didn't pack a lot of options, to be honest." Cora cracks open a can of soda and tips her face to the sky as she drinks.

"You packed the *flirt shirt*."

Cora almost spits her mouthful and coughs and wipes her chin. "Excuse me?"

Meg wags her finger. "The *red* one you like to wear with your push-up bra."

Lifting her chin, Cora says primly, "Just because you have boobs that stay up by themselves."

"Smells like desperation."

Cora pelts her with a Milk Dud, and Meg yelps and laughs.

"How do you think you were conceived?"

"*Ugh.*"

"The first time I took the ferry from Southern Gables, I was a goner."

Meg shakes her head. She recounted the details of last night to Cora while scrubbing out the kitchen cupboards of the post office apartment. When her mother confessed she too was once a Southern Gables girl, Meg almost knocked herself out on the edge of the sink. Her mother had said, *Why on earth would I have applied for the position at the post office otherwise?*

"I took one look at him, leaning against the bar, and that was it."

"*Gah.*"

"I couldn't wait to get him up to the thermal springs," she says with a wistful sigh.

"You're talking about the enemy."

"He wasn't always the way he is now," Cora says. "He was kind and funny and . . ."

"I remember."

"Now he's . . . what he is . . . and that is not your fault." Cora reaches and captures Meg's free hand in her own. Meg fights the instinct to pull away, never entirely comfortable even with her mother feeling her rough scars. Cora reads it in her eyes and tightens her hold, her expression tender and fierce. "There's not an inch of you that isn't perfect, Meg Archer."

Meg's throat gets tight, and she rolls her eyes. "Take it easy, Hallmark."

Her mother chuckles and lets her go. "Fergus Welsh was the hard man before your father. I guess Sargent felt like he had to live up to that and fill his shoes."

Meg glares at the upturned dinghy in the bay. Trawlers dot the horizon. Gulls swoop and loop-the-loop above the jetty where three old-timers cast their fishing lines. The air smells of forest and mountains and sea salt. The ache in her chest grows tingly, and she wonders if Cal will be at the gathering tonight. She clears her throat. "Did Fergus Welsh abandon his family?"

Cora sighs. "He wasn't always kind to Hank."

Hank Hess, former head chef at Nero's Palace. Poor man. Meg can't bear to think of him. She ruined his life too. She wonders for the millionth time how things would be different if she'd stayed off the mountain that night. No feral dogs. No bites or burns to tear them all apart. She recalls her mother's abortive attempts to reunite with Sargent over the early years of their separation. Long weekends where Meg was forced to stay at their elderly neighbors while Cora took the Midnight Ferry and debased herself, begging Sargent to give up the oilskin coat and join them on the mainland. She'd return silent and teary. Once, she returned with a black eye. Around the same time, Meg stopped checking the mailbox every day and begged her mother not to try again.

A sudden roar flips Meg's thoughts, a rough, furious blast of noise. A woman's shriek follows, then a loud clatter and a hair-raising scream. Meg shoots to her feet, but her stomach threatens to drop out her ass. Cora rises beside her, and they take off up the street, gloves and chocolates dropped in a heap. They reach the downward slope of the road, passing the corner of Bertrum's Butchery. Another scream echoes from the alley between buildings. Meg skids right, down the narrow path. A corrugated iron fence forms a yard against the cliff base at the back of the building. A terrific crash and clatter interrupts the screams.

"Is someone hurt?" Meg calls, shouldering her way through the side gate.

"What on earth—" Cora mutters as she comes in behind her.

A middle-aged woman in faded blue coveralls waves a dripping hatchet toward the corner of the yard where a stag paws the ground, antlers cutting lethal arcs. The animal heaves to and fro, eyes milk-white. Something about the beast's movement is jerky and labored, like it's the product of poor animatronics. Nostrils flaring at their arrival, it produces another bloodcurdling blast of noise and rears like an angry drunk. Meg shouts and knocks into Cora. Almost doubled in height, it slashes the air with its hooves before landing heavily. The stag's front knees buckle before righting itself with a lurch.

Cora grabs a broom from the back step, brandishing it brush-up to deflect the antlers.

"It's dead!" the woman in coveralls cries, her dark skin waxy with fear, muscles straining in her neck, eyes showing white all the way around. "It's dead!"

"Move," Meg barks, unable to make sense of the woman's words. "Just run before it tramples all of us."

"But it's dead!" She waves her hatchet, a tarlike substance coating the tip.

The same black fluid coats the stag's teeth, dribbles from its mouth, and oozes from a raw wound in its neck. The stench is horrific and weirdly chemical. Meg notes the markings around its ears and is sharply reminded of the beast deposited by Cal at the door of Nero's Palace.

"Go!" she yells, pressing the back of her hand to her nose. "Give it space to get out. We'll leave the gate open."

When the woman fails to move, Meg grabs her by the elbow and hauls her toward the gate, pushing her out into the alley. Cora is about to follow when the stag charges, head down, antlers seeming to multiply. She leaps backward, her spine collides with the rail of the back steps, and she stumbles and falls. The stag catches the brush of the broom in its antlers and tosses its head. Unthinking, Meg jumps forward, grabbing the handle of the broom.

"Are you okay?" she shouts. "Can you get up?"

"Meg!" Cora cries, pain in her voice. "Let it go. Get out."

"You first!"

Raging, the stag drives the broom handle through Meg's

fingers, burning her bare palms. The force of impact drives Meg back against the side of the building and the handle through the wall, where it lodges and snaps in two. Meg jolts at a hot, sharp sting in her side, and Cora screams her name. A dizzying close-up inspection of the velvet tips of the stag's antlers makes her cross-eyed. The animal reeks like it's been dead for weeks.

Gripping the remaining piece of the broom handle, Meg smashes the brush end on the animal's skull, and it stomps backward, shivering and shaking its head.

Cries for help echo from the alley, heavy boots come pounding toward the yard, and then two large men barrel through the gate.

"Cora!"

"Sargent?"

"You have to move." Cal skids to a stop in front of Meg, waving his arms. "Now!"

Meg blinks, but her vision blurs at the edges. Cal's lips are turning . . . blue?

Sargent shouts words Meg can't comprehend. Another language? He cocks his rifle and shoots. Sound booms through Meg's skull, and she bangs her head on the wall of the building in fright. The stag doesn't fall, though a small black hole appears above its left eye. It roars and rears.

Cal shields her, forming a cage with his arms, hands on either side of her head and an inch between their bodies. A sudden chill makes her shiver. Bright hazel eyes. Cold sweet breath. She knows for sure she's banged her head too hard when frost forms on the high arc of his cheek.

Sargent fires again. Hooves slash the air, clipping the rifle. A violent toss of the stag's head and its antlers collect Sargent. His head whips back, gored from jaw to scalp, exposing a flash of white bone at his temple. He collapses at Cora's feet, and the rifle clatters to the ground. A tremor moves through Cal's body, his eyes widen, and he dives for the weapon.

Frozen, Meg watches her mother struggling to haul Sargent back from the stag's trampling hooves. He's so big, and Cora is small and injured and crying and shaking. She manages to tug him against her, his head lolling on her stomach. She doesn't know where to put her hands. "Oh, God," she says. "Oh, God."

Dropping to one knee, Cal lifts the rifle, making quick, deft movements as he positions the butt against his shoulder, aims, and pulls the trigger. A dull click and his jaw drops. The chamber is empty.

Another body storms the yard. The Fortune Hunter, Jackson Spear. He carries a machete in his hand. He charges toward the stag and swings. Meg flinches, closing her eyes tight. Feels the thud through the bottom of her feet as something heavy hits the ground. She turns her head before she opens her eyes, unwilling to see the stag. There she finds her parents, tumbled together like they've fallen in a drunken embrace, covered in her father's blood.

OUR LAW

Cal remains upright. The shock of it — not passing out — causes a brief delay while he stares at the severed head of the buck. He scrambles for the Voice of the Herd, something to tether him to the moment, guide his response, but his brain has been replaced with a sucking hole. Everything is wrong. Blood pools thick and black. Something chemical laces the scent, making his eyes water. The presence of death hasn't lifted, cooling his lungs, making his skin crawl, feathering behind his ears.

How is he still conscious?

Jackson Spear crouches by the carcass and scoops black goop into a little glass vial. He caps it and slides it into his coat pocket. "Well, that was something." He grins at Cal, eyes lit. Then his expression grows curious, and he straightens up. Cal ducks his head to swipe the thin veil of frost from the side of his face. He runs his teeth over his lips, willing heat into his skin.

Cora whimpers.

With a slight wobble, he turns on his knees. Sargent lies splayed on Cora's lap. Meg slumps against the wall of the building, gray-faced and panting.

"Don't move," he says to Cora. "Just . . . just stay there and I'll—I'll . . ." He looks around for something to staunch Sargent's blood.

"Help him!" Cora cries. "He's hurt. It's bad. Oh, God. Sargent!"

Cal feels as though *his* head has been detached from his body. Where is the Voice of the Herd? Sargent isn't moving. Cal hesitates. If he touches Sargent—tries to lift him—he'll pass out. If that's so, it means Sargent *is* dead, and Sargent *cannot* be dead. He can't be. His daughter is here. The cull is coming. Nutris will claim treaty rights. There is an injured deer on the mountain, and the Rift is unstable. If he touches Sargent, he'll know for sure, and Cal doesn't want to know.

"Towel," Meg croaks, lifting a shaking hand in the direction of a clothesline by the fence.

Jackson Spear steps past Cal, rips a yellowing tea towel from its clothespins, and hands it to him. Cal wads thick folds against the wound on Sargent's face. He presses his fingers to Sargent's neck, as though searching for a pulse. No surge of life punches through his system, and his chest hollows out. Death is as close as if it were standing beside him. Frost forms by his boot, and he shifts his foot to hide it. *Please . . . please . . .*

There.

Thin as a gossamer thread.

Alive . . . alive . . . alive.

Cora gasps. "He's okay?"

"There's . . . a faint pulse."

"But he's alive?" Cora demands.

"He is . . ." Cal stares briefly into the middle distance, searching for Reeva's presence in his mind. It takes only a couple of heartbeats before he's aware of her. The sound of her wings follows. Cal rises to his feet using the rifle as a prop and searches the trees.

"Whoa!" Spear ducks as Reeva swoops in and lands on Cal's raised arm.

Before Cal can give her any instructions, the bird puffs her feathers, thrusts her beak at the Fortune Hunter, and shrieks. Spear jerks back. Everyone in the yard cringes. She shrieks again and with a baleful look turns her back to the man.

"Hey." Cal clicks his tongue. "That's enough." He takes a mint leaf from his pocket and thinks of Sargent, his wounds, and Bren. Reeva cuts him off with a grumble, stabbing his fingers as she takes the leaf, as though to say, *Obviously.* He lets his fear fill the connection with urgency. Reeva's acknowledgment is a simple flicker of affirmation followed by a parting remark—an image of Meg propped against the wall, clasping her side. "I know," he murmurs.

Reeva launches at Spear's head, making the man yelp and duck, as she takes off into the trees.

"Is that normal?" Spear asks.

Cal pinches the bridge of his nose; he's so cold he can't feel his lips. "She'll bring help. Thank you for stepping in when you did."

"I'm sorry about your boss," Spear says, sizing Cal up. He drops his voice. "You recognize your buck?"

"We can talk about that later."

"The zombie deer?" Meg rasps.

"Cal," Cora says. "We need to hurry."

"Bren will come."

"Sargent *needs* hospital care," Cora says, struggling to control her voice. "An MRI at the very least. He could have swelling in his brain or something. We need to get him on the ferry."

"You know our law," he says quietly. "The head ranger stays on the island."

"*Our law?*" Meg lurches upright. "Don't give me *our law*. You're a *fisherman's son*. I'm Sargent's *actual* child."

Spear looks at her with sudden interest. "You're Sargent's daughter?"

"*Yes,* and Cora is still his wife," Meg says. "Next of kin. We decide."

Cal doesn't flinch, but it hurts to meet those yellow-green eyes. "No. You don't."

"He's had his skull cracked open!" she cries, wobbling dangerously.

He takes an involuntary step toward her, but what can he do? Prop her up? Help her sit? She looks like she might actually punch him if he tries. He doubts he could take the bolt of her life force, anyway, not in his oversensitized condition. He stalls before her. "You're hurt."

Cora groans. "Honey, you're bleeding."

There's blood on Meg's fingers where she presses her side. A hot surge of anger bubbles inside him, irrational rage at the thought of her pain. On the upside, the sudden heat thaws his stomach and lungs. *Go,* he thinks at death. *We don't want you.*

"Can you sit?" He gestures at the step, but she doesn't move, frozen in shock.

Jackson Spear grunts with impatience, stepping in to take her by the arm. Cal almost growls through his teeth.

"I can do it myself," she snaps, wrenching free of the man's hold.

"I've saved your ass twice."

Cal moves between them, meeting the Fortune Hunter eye to eye. "Twice?"

Raised voices rumble in the alley. Three men crowd through the gate, Spear's team of Fortune Hunters, the men from yesterday morning. They wince at the smell, covering their noses.

"Judas Priest . . . I wouldn't have believed it."

"It worked."

"Less than twelve hours."

"Unfrozen specimen."

"Old Herd."

"You collected the pretest sample, Spear?"

Spear clips a nod.

Cal tightens his knuckles to fists. "*What* are you talking about?"

Puffing, Antonia appears through the gate. "Abigail Bertrum is raving in the street. What is going on . . ." She pushes through the huddle of men, brow furrowing sharply as she takes in the scene. She pauses by Meg, her hand stretched out, a question and offer in one.

Meg shakes her head. "I'm fine."

"Antonia," Cora sobs. "It's . . . it's bad."

Antonia drops to her knees beside Cora, clasping her around the shoulders. She presses her palm to Sargent's chest, right over his heart, head cocked as though listening. "Cal," she calls. "What are we doing?"

"I—ah . . . Bren is coming. We need to keep him stable."

"Can we move him?"

"No." Cal blinks rapidly. "At least not far. Not till Bren arrives."

"The restaurant?" Antonia says. "Has to be more sanitary than a butcher's yard."

"I . . . yeah, I guess." He rubs his face, feeling all eyes on him, his breathing loud and labored in his head. "Okay, we'll move him."

"Well, don't just stand there!" Antonia snaps her fingers at the Hunters. "Two on either side. I'll support his head. Cora, can you walk?"

"I think so," she says, voice breaking.

The men shuffle forward, reluctant as schoolboys, Spear cool and unruffled. None of them meet Cal's eye.

"Careful," Cora cries as they gather and begin to lift Sargent.

Cal watches on, useless. *Worse than useless.*

"Oh, no," Meg murmurs.

Cal swings toward her.

She looks ready to puke or pass out. Having peeled back the hem of her shirt, Meg gapes at a bubbling hole in her flesh. The shard glistens in her hands, and Cal connects the broken broom handle to the picture. She balls her fists, eyes growing glassy and wide before rolling all the way up. She tips forward. Every cell in his body snaps to attention.

Bam!

Her life force punches right through his core. *Alive! Alive! Alive!* A bolt so fierce in contrast to Sargent's it makes him want to shout or sob with relief. His arms scoop and lift like it's all been hardwired, like he has nothing to do with it. She's tall and heavy and soft and bony and . . . the most intense thing that has happened to his body in nine years. Life, breath, scent, skin. *Alive! Alive! Alive!*

"Meg," Cora gasps.

At least Cal thinks it's Cora; all his sensory awareness is profoundly preoccupied. "I have her," he says. "She's okay."

He lets the men carrying Sargent go first out the gate, Antonia and Cora close behind them. When the way is clear, he follows, using the strength in his legs to hoist Meg a little higher. Her face rocks against his neck, a sensation so foreign and intimate it almost takes his breath. The pulse of life sings through his bones, and by the time he strides out into the street, the chill of death is gone.

For a moment, he feels taller than his six feet three inches, stronger and more aware of the power in his biceps and shoulders, more centered than when he touches a ley line or connects with the Voice of the Herd. He forgets his scar and his awkwardness and his aversion to human contact. He forgets his internal walls and his instinct for withdrawal and avoidance. Right now, he could carry her all the way to the top of Little Peak Saddle and . . . what?

He shakes his head, heat in his face at the foolishness of his thoughts. Then he sees the gathering crowd of villagers and Fortune Hunters. Clarity—like a slap—reminds him of his scar and his awkwardness and his aversion to human contact. The furious joy of connection skews, amplifying the volume on Meg's life force to an obliterating wall of noise that burns through brain and bone. "Stand back!" he shouts at the press of people. "Move! Now!"

Abigail Bertrum's cry rings out. "It was dead! It was dead!"

SUBOPTIMAL TIME LINE

Meg wakes with a hiss, fire blazing white-hot in her side. She reaches to cover the wound and finds thick bandages. When she draws her knees up, as though to curl around the pain, it only makes it worse. She rolls the other way and nearly topples off the edge of the table — a dining table in Nero's Palace. Cora catches her shoulder and hip and holds her still. "It's okay, love. I'm here."

So is everyone else. Rangers crowd the restaurant, eyes fixed on the long table in the short leg of the dining room where they usually take their evening meals. From what she can see, Sargent is laid out, stripped to the waist. From collarbone to navel the hard-packed muscle has been embossed with dense crosshatching. Meg's pulse pounds in her ears and behind her eyes. She grips the edge of the table so tightly her fingers ache, waiting for the shock wave to recede. It is the first time she has seen her father's scars.

How many times has she traced the rough skin on her palms and thought of her father's torn chest?

She imagines these scars mark the moment life stopped and a fold in the space-time continuum shoved them into a divergent, suboptimal time line. It's a fair explanation for nine years of displacement and separation. The original Meg, back in the first time line, is congratulating herself on not dragging Cal up a mountain to hide in a cave. No one dies. Fergus Welsh lives a long, happy life. Sargent remains Sargent. Okay, there's no logic in the idea that Cora remains cancer-free in the original time line, but the fantasy persists. Her parents stay madly in love. They all live happily ever after. Together. On Black Water.

No feral dogs.

No zombie deer.

None of what's happening right now.

A tall man rises from a stool by Sargent's head. Meg recognizes him as Bren, Antonia's brother. She's there too, waiting with a silver bowl. He rinses the blood from his hands and dries them on the white towel. They exchange an unhappy look before Antonia turns away. She finds Meg and Cora watching, and her frown tightens in sympathy. She takes the bowl to Leira, waiting behind the bar, and places it in her hands, briefly touching her cheek before coming to Meg.

"Is he . . . ?" Meg's throat catches.

"Lie still." Antonia pats her arm. "I'll get you some water."

"They can't stop us from taking him," Cora says. "They can't keep him here."

Antonia offers no comforting reply and returns to the kitchen.

"Cal?" Bren murmurs.

Cal stands well back from the table, arms folded, jaw set. It's the buffer of space around him in the crowded room that sets him apart. Just looking at him ruins Meg's whole alternative time line theory. Not going up the mountain doesn't save Cal's father from Nutris Fortune Hunters. There's no happily ever after for Cal in that time line or this one. Either way, he is alone.

Every set of eyes swivels to find him, but he stares at Sargent and gives one small shake of his head. "No change."

"Anyone can see that," an apprentice calls.

Cal masters his face, but Meg can tell he's biting his tongue.

"That will do," Bren says with a weary familiarity, folding the towel and placing it neatly on the table.

"What's the point in keeping him if we don't use him?" someone else mutters. "Isn't that the whole point of the fisherman's son? He's supposed to be useful."

"Shut your mouth," Abbot says, uncrossing his arms where he stands by his father. Bren presses a hand lightly to his son's chest. The master ranger obviously wants to keep things calm, but the atmosphere is static-charged.

"It's not going to hurt him to try again," a girl says softly. While she keeps hostility from her tone, impatience and frustration are in the choice of words. Her expression is grim, and her arms are folded tightly across her chest. She's short and stocky, and Meg can see her arms are muscular. She's strong. It's the freckles and wild curly hair that finally place her in Meg's brain. Rilke. Abbot's younger sister.

Bren narrows his eyes at his daughter in warning before addressing Cal with an apologetic look. "Do you have a sense about"—he casts a cautious glance toward Meg and her mother—"the outcome?"

Cal meets Meg's eye for the first time since she came to and looks away before replying. "It's . . . uncertain."

"What's uncertain?" Meg and her mother demand at the same time.

Heads turn, but Meg ignores the other rangers, waiting for Cal to explain.

He doesn't.

"And where's the Nutris guy?" Meg demands, struggling to sit up. Craning her neck, she sees no sign of the blond Fortune Hunter or the other three men from the kill yard. "Jackson Spear had something to do with this. He was collecting samples of the black blood and acting like it was . . . I don't know, something he expected."

"Spear killed it," Cal says.

"It was already dead," Meg says. "It was the deer you brought down from the mountain yesterday morning. Spear and Sargent were in the kill yard last night. I heard them talking. They were planning something."

This sends the whole group into a frenzy of muttering. Several apprentices cast dubious looks at Cal. Bren struggles to call the room to order, his hands raised, patting the air. "Sargent liaises with Nutris; there's nothing suspicious about that."

"We're down two master rangers in less than twenty-four

hours," Rilke says in that same quiet but implacable voice. The room shuts up, and Meg is impressed at how someone so young and small, by ranger standards, commands attention.

"Nellie is healing," Bren says, jaw tight.

"Who was alone with Nellie on the mountain?" Rilke asks.

Abbot shifts his weight, giving his sister a hard look. "What are you saying?"

"Who found the deer?" Rilke purses her lips. "Who was with Sargent when the buck charged?"

"You think *I'm* responsible for all this?" Cal matches the girl's quiet intensity, but Meg can see his fight to stay calm.

"You're the common denominator," Rilke says tightly.

Murmurs of agreement rise around the room.

"Real nice." A pale, blond boy, standing close to Abbot, shoots Rilke a look of disgust.

Rilke shrugs. "We have to consider the facts, Leif."

Leif gives Abbot a look that says *She's* your *sister*. Abbot scowls. Leif isn't satisfied, leaning around the large boy to address Rilke directly. "Cal puts his ass on the line for this *whole* community every time a—" He hesitates, glancing at Meg and her mother. "Every time things go down. He saved your aunt's life."

"Enough," Bren says.

"Something happened to Nellie Fenchurch?" Cora asks, apparently landing on the one thing she can wrap her head around in all the confusion.

Bren folds his arms. "These are private matters."

Cora jolts like Bren has prodded her with a sharp stick,

and she takes a step toward the table, gesturing at Sargent's unconscious body. "Well, *this* is *our* private matter. Don't start with the secrets, Bren. Not this time."

"Cora." Bren hefts her name like it's a lead weight. "I will do everything in my power to help Sargent."

"Which is what?" she snaps. "Pack the hole in his head with your magic deer powder?"

The man's chest swells. "There is no more potent healing compound in the world than Actaeon's Bane."

"It didn't heal me."

He frowns, opening and closing his mouth, clearly struggling to find the right words and manage his tone. "I am . . . *aware* some conditions have proven resistant to—"

Cora folds her arms in a mirror of the tall man's posture, her jaw thrust forward. "I'm sure you're very good at what you do, Bren, but you live on an island with *no fucking electricity*."

"Cora." He lifts his hands.

"You better have someone bring my husband's belongings because the next ferry that comes in, I am taking my family and we are returning to the mainland where they will be treated in a hospital, with medical equipment, like monitors and scanners and actual antibiotics." She turns her back to him and settles a shaking hand on Meg's shoulder.

"You and your daughter are free to go," he says.

Meg stiffens, and Cora snaps upright. "You can't hold my husband hostage."

"He is not our hostage," Bren says softly. "He is our brother. Our leader."

"They can't deny him medical care," Meg croaks, gripping her mother's arm.

"He *has* medical care," Bren says. "And you both know well enough that Sargent would not leave Black Water even if he had a choice."

Only a flicker in Cora's eye hints at the wound she's just taken. Meg doesn't move or speak, but her heart is a cave-in. They hold each other, shoulder and arm, while the Rangers begin to move. Someone produces a sturdy-looking stretcher. Men surround Sargent and begin to lift him onto it. Cora rushes over and yanks on the nearest elbow. "No. You can't just take him. He needs help."

Across the room, Cal presses back against the wall, wincing as the other rangers cross before him. "Are you going to let this happen?" Meg demands.

He finds her with that laser-beam hazel eye, and the agony reflected in it stokes Meg's panic. She slips off the table, hissing at the stabbing pain in her side. Staggering toward her mother, still struggling with the young ranger, she bats at arms and shoulders, but the pain makes her efforts weak, and she resorts to shouting. "Back off!"

Tiny galaxies spin in her peripheral vision, sweat beading her upper lip. Meg stumbles, and Antonia catches her, tugging her away. Cora is openly sobbing, slapping, and pounding hunched backs. "You can't do this! I'll—I'll go to the mainland and bring back the police. Bren! If he dies, it's on you! Do you hear me?"

"Come on." Antonia clasps her hand, and finally Cora wilts

and collapses against her old friend. They all bump together, Antonia not letting Meg go. Cora weeps, and Meg shakes, staring at the door. The men file out, bearing Sargent between them, quiet and solemn. Cal pauses on the threshold looking back at her, his face divided by shadow, the sharp angle of his jaw, the strong line of his nose, the high arc of his cheekbone. He looks brittle enough to shatter.

"We'll do everything we can." He turns his back and ducks beneath the lintel, stepping out into the milky afternoon light.

LOW BAR

Cal waits by the common room door of the master rangers' cabin, a sturdy clapboard shared by the single senior members of the camp. Bren directs the settling of Sargent onto the infirmary cot. The master rangers are careful, almost reverential, laying out their leader. It only intensifies Cal's sense of doom—the behavior is too funerary. He wants to snap "Sargent's not dead," despite the chill in Cal's lungs from standing at this proximity. Of course, he knows what he thinks or says will have no impact on Sargent's survival. Experience has taught him that death keeps its own counsel, an arbitrary predator with an endlessly hungry mouth.

Knowing this doesn't counteract the instinct to *do* something. In fact, Cal is the hoarder of endless tissue-thin superstitions about death. Don't look directly at it. Don't talk to it. Don't act like it's won. Don't mention it by name. Don't bluster or beg. Don't show fear. Don't make promises.

Don't cry. The rules generally form after he breaks them.

Bren inspects the bandage and turns to look for Cal.

He doesn't wait to be asked. He steps into the room, his bones so heavy he could sink to the floor and fall asleep against the wall.

"I'm sorry," Bren murmurs, running a hand over his face. None of them have had enough sleep.

Cal dismisses the apology with a small shake of his head and extends the tips of his fingers to Sargent's forearm. No jolt but a faint pulse. He tries to remember if this is what feeling a pulse was like before he was bitten. The quiet, steady flap of valves. But death is there too—another body in the room—watching, waiting. Though the air cools in his lungs, Cal can't see his breath, and there's no sign of frost; the Bane must be doing something. "He's stable, but it's still undecided."

Bren gestures toward the door, and Cal follows the remaining master rangers out into the common room. Joss watches from the doorway of his mother's room across the cabin. Behind him, Nellie lies propped on pillows in the bed beneath the window. "What's happening?" she calls. "Is he going to make it?"

"Ma." Joss pats the air. "Relax."

Bren repeats Cal's update.

"Get him up to the Rift Stone," Nellie says, panting with the effort to lift her head. "It's his best chance."

"It's not that simple," Bren says. "It's not safe with an injured deer on the mountain, so soon after last night."

"We can't afford to lose Sargent," Nellie says. She collapses back on her pillow, her chest straining against the pull of her bandages. "Cal isn't ready."

Cal's guts drop to his boots. "For . . . what?"

Bren and the master rangers exchange uncomfortable looks. The four men who carried the stretcher take it as their cue to exit. The others fall silent until the men are gone while Cal's inner contest of fight or flight fixes him to the spot.

The door clicks closed, and Nellie pipes up. "You're the only Rift Hound bite survivor in the camp."

Cal opens and closes his mouth, blinking like he's just been poked in the eye.

"Let's not jump the gun," Bren says, warning and weariness making him gruff.

"Come on." Joss opens his arms, hands spread. "He's the only existing ranger with actual Rift Sight."

"*So?*" Cal drops his voice to a harsh whisper, as though death might hear this from the infirmary. "That doesn't mean anything. Sargent was appointed head ranger without any sensory gifts. It's not a prerequisite. The old lists include plenty of head rangers like Sargent."

"They don't last long," Nellie grumbles, slinging a thumb in the direction of the infirmary.

Cal stalks across the common room and closes Sargent's door softly before swinging back to face them. "Fergus Welsh was younger than Sargent when he died, and he had gifts."

"He was an exception," Nellie calls.

"There is no pattern," Cal hisses. "It's whoever's willing and you all agreeing. I am *not* willing, and there is no way in hell anyone would agree, even if I was."

"*I* agree," Nellie says with a harrumph. "I'd just prefer another ten years on your shoulders. Settle you down a little and round off the rough edges."

Cal makes choking sounds and looks for moral support.

Joss offers none that Cal wants. "I agree, too," his friend says. "You saved Ma. You're not an asshole. People listen to you."

A bitter and half-strangled laugh bursts from Cal's throat. "No one listens to me."

"That's only because you never say anything," Bren says with a sigh. "When you talk, people listen."

"People hate me!" His voice winds high in an embarrassing corkscrew. "Your own daughter thinks I'm the *common denominator* in all this; she can't even look at me."

"She's jealous," Bren says.

"Jealous?" Cal shakes his head. "She's right. Sargent's in there because of me."

Bren waves the idea away. "Sargent's in there because of Nutris. And nobody hates you. There might be a little resentment about your lineage, but you're not the first person to experience prejudice, Cal."

Cal shuts his mouth, and Bren gives a single nod to punctuate his point.

"There are more pressing issues than our succession plan," Bren points out.

Joss straightens up, gesturing at Cal. "Sargent asked us to track the injured deer."

"What about Jackson Spear?" Cal asks, trying to shake off the disorientation of the previous topic. "He had something to do with the buck."

"Sargent's dealt with Spear before," Nellie says. "He's shady."

"Let me go find him," Cal says. "Bring him back to camp. You can question him yourself."

"Spear is already coming. We were supposed to have a cookout," Bren says. "Whatever the case, we must appear to have everything in order. We'll take Sargent up the mountain at first light. In the meantime, get some rest."

* * *

Rolling the chalk between his thumb and forefinger, Cal eyes the sparring roster with a scowl. Willful engagement in physical contact. Despite the backlog of fatigue, he's just too wired to relax. The distress signal from the injured deer is still there, a discordant note deep in the Voice of the Herd. If Hounds broke through because of the first deer on the Lower Slopes, what hope is there that the Rift will hold with a distress signal in the Western Reaches of the mountain, a day closer to full moon? No hope at all. He wishes Sargent had let him go first thing; he'd be more than halfway to the Rift Stone by now, and the wasted time fills him with bitter, twisting desperation. Part of him is tempted to slip away, but he doesn't want to jeopardize the delicate situation with Nutris on top of everything else. They must present a full force at the meeting, and there's no getting around the fact he'll have to get at least a few hours' sleep.

In the meantime he needs to purge the energy in his body or he'll burst a blood vessel. The junior apprentices try to bait him into the ring every now and then. *Come on, fisherman's son. Get your hands dirty for a change.* This is meant to be a jibe about his privileges in general. He doesn't spar. He doesn't hunt. Sargent doesn't require him to. Not even small game like rabbits, possums, or stoats. Cal considers this the small benefit of Rift Sight—a hall pass from killing things or touching people.

Cal scratches his name in the third column. One of the apprentices will leap at the chance to kick his ass. He hopes it's someone big and mean. Someone he won't feel bad about thumping. He drops the chalk in the tray and ducks out of the summer barracks to head for the barn. Joss's words still ring in his ears. *You saved Ma. You're not an asshole. People listen to you.* A pretty bloody low bar for leadership. The way the master rangers had exchanged looks—like they'd talked about this before—it wasn't a new idea. Bren's *let's not jump the gun* had offered no comfort. The gun was way jumped, and Cal couldn't begin to process the ramifications. Truth is, he has no desire to be in charge. He simply wants what he's always wanted: to belong. To not have people muttering behind his back and calling him *fisherman's son* like it's a contagious disease.

Cal scowls and rubs his arms to make some heat. The

afternoon is frigid, the air heavy with moisture. Rain will follow in the hour. His stomach growls, but it feels like more than just hunger for food; his whole self feels hungry, restless.

There are a few apprentice rangers in the training yard running drills with wooden machetes before sparring practice at four. Expressions are grim, the atmosphere is tense, and he can't tell if the looks he's getting are laced with suspicion and mistrust or worry for Sargent.

Bren emerges from the master rangers' cabin. He carries a plastic tub with bloodied bandages. He gives Cal one of those pressed-lip smiles where the corners of the mouth don't turn up. Cal trusts Bren. The man is reserved and serious, unlike Nellie, whose style is more "rambunctious aunt," but fair and kind without fuss or sentiment. Bren nursed him through his own recovery nine years ago. Cal was unconscious for three days reacting to the Rift Hound bite, writhing on the same bed where Sargent lies now. Three days. Probably absorbing curse toxins or losing his soul. Something useful like that.

When he regained consciousness, he didn't think much about the rustic cabin's "luxury" separate bedrooms, common room, and bathroom; he was a kid who'd run from his home in a frenzy of grief. He'd naively expected to return to his father's house and his comfortable bedroom—after Social Services gave up the chase. Of course, he didn't understand that the house belonged to the Seafarers' Union, and no one would let a boy live there by himself, or rent-free, until he was old enough to skipper his father's trawler. But when you're a kid you don't think about things like that.

Sargent recovered from his own injuries, at the time, and saw Cal's Rift Hound bite as an opportunity. He had the master rangers petition Social Services for guardianship. With no known relatives to hamper Cal's desperate wish to remain on the island, Social Services sent an agent to inspect the camp and satisfy their bureaucratic checklist. Papers signed, Cal was shifted into the junior apprentice barracks with the other kids and tried not to mourn too much for the privacy of his old bedroom down in the village.

He stalks through the camp, making his way past the outbuildings, and pauses before the doors of the huge wooden barn. He knocks first and listens for the rustling of hay or telltale heavy breathing—there aren't many options for privacy in the camp unless couples want to take to the bushes. Nothing. He pulls the rope handle and slips inside, giving himself a moment to let his eyes adjust. It's a degree or two warmer. A loft divides the roofline, gaps in the wall paneling permit smoky shafts of light. The air is thick with the pungent smell of hay and grain and damp wood.

He heads for the huge woodpile in the corner, peels off his sweater and shirt, and hangs them on a nail jutting from one of the support beams. Goose bumps flash across his chest. Restless energy snakes through his bones. He grips the smooth handle of the ax and swings the weight of the iron head onto his shoulder. He hefts a jagged chunk of elm onto the block and positions himself. Stretching his arms back over his head, he relishes the tightening through his shoulders, triceps, and biceps. He ignores the twinge in his ribs and swings hard.

THWACK!

The whiplash of Sargent's head. The flash of red on the side of his face.

THWACK!

The buck's severed head. Stinking black blood. A glass vial.

THWACK!

Meg's yellow-green eyes wide with dismay. Blood on her hands. The slow tip of her body toward him.

CRACK-crunch!

He shakes out his hand and sucks the bruised inside of his thumb. He can still smell her on his skin. He's not sure the electricity has fully left his body—as though his bones still vibrate with the echo of holding her.

He *held* her.

He can barely hold a conversation, but he held her.

By the time he made it to Nero's Palace, he imagined his bones might disintegrate or his brain might turn to ash . . . but before it got bad, before he felt like he was going to die, it was . . .

He drags a chunk of maple onto the block. *THWACK!*

BLACK WATER

Meg slips into the liquid heat of the thermal pool with a sound like a whistling kettle escaping between her teeth, followed by a few choice curses. Finding a secure boulder for her feet, she crouches low and bobs neck-deep, huffing and cringing, one hand gripping the smooth volcanic rock that forms the rim.

"Let the water get at it." Antonia gestures at the wound. "I promise it won't be as bad as the first dose."

Her wound had received a second application of Actaeon's Bane, a paste made of raw ground horn mixed with aloe and Yarra root. The first dose made her scream. It took a few hours, but the tissue sealed. Antonia has brought her to the pools for the soothing, antiseptic qualities in the black water.

Gritting her teeth, Meg uncovers the wound, and the paste begins to emulsify in the wash. She holds her breath as the sting ramps up and up and . . . levels out, cutting off the peaks of pain that almost made her pass out at Nero's Palace.

"Told you it wouldn't be as bad." Antonia screws the lid on the jar and nods at the terrace to the four main pools fed by trickling falls from the mountain and the bubbling springs beneath. "Bren says there's a ley line that runs through here. The electromagnetic juju's supposed to help. I never felt any different, but some people say they can feel it, like a tingling sensation through the rocks."

"I remember," Meg says with a grunt. She never felt anything when she was a kid, though not for lack of trying. On every boulder in every pool, she laid hands with a hungry reverence, breath held for . . . what? Proof? Evidence to lay before Sargent and Fergus Welsh and the men and women who smiled and patted her head when she ran through the rangers camp with her little bow and arrow. It makes her face hot remembering her desperation. Though right now she'd be willing to swallow her pride and hug every boulder on the terrace if it would take the pain away. "How long will it take to fully heal?"

"There's healed, and there's *healed*," Antonia says, warning in the press of her lips. "Cora won't be thrilled about you going up to the camp without her."

"Please don't wake her," Meg says. Cora had sobbed herself into a migraine, and Leira had put her to bed with a cold wet cloth and medication.

Antonia sighs. "Forty minutes. Maybe an hour. But hoofing it up Little Peak Saddle won't do you any favors."

"Neither will sitting at Nero's waiting for news," Meg says

with a grimace. "They've got another thing coming if they think we're just going to roll over."

Antonia shakes her head and rises to her feet. "You've got an hour and a half of light left. Either way, you need to be up there or down at Nero's before dark. No point healing the hole in your side to wind up breaking your neck in a crevasse or plummeting off a cliff."

"I'll be at the camp," Meg says.

Antonia places Meg's towel and discarded clothes on a log beside the pool. "They care about your dad, Meg. They're not the bad guys."

Dad.

Meg offers a noncommittal nod.

Antonia sighs. "I don't understand all the secret ways of the ranger community. I never felt the ley lines or any of that stuff. I went to the mainland and became a lawyer yet still ended up back here. This place is special, Meg. Sargent wouldn't want to leave. You know it. Your mother knows it."

Part of Meg wants to shout and bawl, but her heart knows Antonia's right. "I'm sorry we drove all your customers away this afternoon."

Antonia waves, brushing the apology aside. "You take care and watch the light." Cautious on the slippery terrace steps, she makes her way back up to the track.

Meg bobs across the pool, gingerly navigating the uneven footing, unwilling to stub her toe or bark her shin on hidden rocks. She finds a shelf seat beneath a smooth boulder and settles back, groaning at the blissful heat in the stone. She breathes in the steam, determined to calm her churning thoughts; she hasn't stopped churning since she came to in the restaurant. She probably needs to have a good cry; the pressure is all there, but again she can't quite crack the dam wall.

She closes her eyes, and Sargent falls. The red wound carving the side of his face and the wink of bone, that's what pinned her to the wall of the butcher's yard. Not the zombie deer. Not the shard of broken broom handle in her side. It makes her nauseous to think that yet again Meg being in the wrong place at the wrong time results in ruin for her father. It's like she's cursed. Or she's *his* curse. But how could she have stopped it? What brought him down the mountain that morning, if not her and her mother being in the village? She should never have come home.

Shaking her head, she scoops black water into her palms. It's the tiny fibrous mineral deposits that give the clear water a black effect. She lets the fibers slide across her hands and catch in the valleys created by her scars. She rubs the deposits with her thumb, and they dissolve, leaving a silky residue. She scoops water up her arms, careful not to jar her injured side, and marvels at the satiny sheen left on her skin. Another scoop to smooth up the column of her neck, across her shoulders and collarbone. She slips her bra straps aside, slow fingers triggering a delicious rush of tingling. Her thoughts drift and catch on the image of hazel eyes.

The tingling travels to her spine and spreads across her shoulders, where her body meets the boulder. *Tingling*. Her brain crash-lands, and her mouth pops open. She holds her breath as though listening for a subterranean hum. Immediately the tingling increases, as though paying attention amplifies the effect.

"No way," she whispers, and her pulse leaps. Swallowing, she leans away from the rock, and the tingling ceases. *"No way."*

She places only a hand on the rock. When nothing happens at first, her stomach drops, but then comes a gentle hum building slowly, creating a soothing vibration up her arm and into her chest. With a little gasp, she pulls her hand away, and the vibration stops. She tests the sides of the pool and feels nothing. Her heart pounds anyway. She works her way around the rim slowly until she reaches the tingling boulder, anticipating the hum even before she puts her hand on the rock. "Ha!"

She wraps herself around the boulder like a limpet. The hum is in her bones, a deep, centering hum. *Home.* An inexplicable sensation bubbles inside her—something like sorrow or joy or the two mixed together—producing a raw sob. The irony of it is too bittersweet, to feel it now, when she can't even go running to her father to break the news. Would it mean anything to him? Would he be glad or indifferent?

Scritch-scratching near the top of her head interrupts her moment of grief and wonder, and she opens her eyes. A raven perches on the boulder less than two feet from her nose, shifting its weight from claw to claw.

The bird is big—small-dog big.

It cocks its head, blinks a beady black eye, and then thrusts its beak toward her.

Meg produces a strangled yelp and a violent shudder, but somehow remains pressed to the rock.

Gur-gur-gur, the bird croaks. Again it cocks its head, and Meg notices the edge of something in its beak, a crushed leaf.

"Reeva?" she murmurs.

It pulls back and hops from foot to foot, then extends its neck toward her again and drops the leaf on the boulder. The whiff of mint.

"Reeva." The vibration of the rock against her belly and chest increases. The bird bobs its head, that wicked beak glinting in the low light.

"Is this from Cal?" she asks, feeling instantly foolish. Does she expect a reply? Does she really think it understands her? Why would Cal be sending her mint leaves? She jerks upright. "Is it Sargent? Has something happened?"

The bird caws, turns its back, and puffs its feathers.

Meg blinks, trying to calm herself. "Not Sargent?"

Reeva smooths her feathers and turns to face her.

"I'm losing it. I am officially losing it."

Extending her neck, slowly this time, Reeva taps her beak on the mint leaf.

Meg reaches slowly for the leaf, not taking her eyes off Reeva. She gets thumb and forefinger on the half-chewed offering when the bird hops and lands on the back of her wrist. Meg gasps. The bird is heavy, and the talons pinch a little, but there's no pressure or tearing. Openmouthed, Meg stays frozen, caught in the raven's unblinking gaze. Reeva walks up her arm, *pinch, pinch, pinch,* until she's inches from her face, untroubled by Meg's panicked breaths ruffling her feathers. The vibration through the rock is deep, pulsing, hypnotic. The bird lowers her beak until they are nose to nose, and Meg whispers, "How is this real?"

Her vision blurs with a disorienting image. She sees two men, heads bent in conversation. The angle is confusing, distorted, like she's spying through a fish-eye lens. Her shock is eclipsed by recognition. Sargent and the Fortune Hunter Jackson Spear. She can't hear what they're saying, but the emotion overlaying the scene is wary and urgent. Sargent passes the man a folded piece of paper. The blond man tucks it in his pocket and shrugs in that same lazy manner from the butcher's kill yard.

"What is this?" Meg's throat has gone dry, and her heart pounds in her chest. She blinks hard, and the image dissolves. Reeva still pins her arm to the rock, her beak so close to Meg's face, Meg goes cross-eyed.

Her vision blurs again. Colors flash, and she sees herself through that fish-eye lens, standing waist-deep in the pool, dark hair slicked back. Her pale skin glows, arms and chest glistening, the fabric of her bra made translucent in the wet.

"Whoa!" Meg jerks upright. Reeva lifts from her arm, and Meg falls backward into the pool. Finding her feet, she splashes to the other side, the effort sending pain through her wound. She grasps the log at the edge while she splutters and spits and wipes water from her eyes. "What is happening?"

Reeva lands on the boulder and flaps her wings, cawing and hopping from foot to foot.

Without the reassuring vibration of the rock, Meg's anxiety ramps up. She wraps her arms over her chest and darts nervous glances at the thick forest hemming the terrace. "Cal?" she calls, then louder, "Cal? Are you here?"

No reply.

Licking her lips, Meg speaks slowly. "Reeva. Are you . . . are you *making* me see things?"

The raven *gur-gurs,* and Meg's vision blurs, and she sees herself in Cal's arms, from high above, as he carries her down the main street of the village, her head lolling against his neck. The image is filled with warmth and fascination.

"Okay," she says, panting and dizzy. "Okay, so you saw me with Cal and—and you saw Sargent with Spear, and you saw me in the pool. *Where* is Cal? Is he near?"

A flash of color and she looks down on a shirtless man from the rafters of a large wooden building. His muscled back gleams with sweat as he swings a heavy ax, splitting a chunk of wood in a single stroke. Dust motes float in the air. Light and shadow move over the man's torso. He straightens up, drawing lungfuls of air. His head tips back, and damp brown hair falls back from his face. Cal.

Meg stops breathing as he runs his hand up into his hair, pushing it right back off his face. His scar is like a half-moon imprint on the side of his jaw. Light and shadow accentuate the strong planes of his face. He purses his lips, narrowing his hazel eyes right at her. Meg gasps and ducks low in the water.

Not her. The bird. He's looking at the bird . . . or is he?

"Reeva!" She splashes upright. Her vision swirls, and she's back in the hot springs, and the bird is sitting on the boulder, watching her. "He can't see me, can he?"

The bird flaps her wings and lifts off, stirring steam in a white whirl.

RESENTMENTS FLARE

Cal swings, bringing the wooden blade in a swift upward arc just hard enough to block Rilke's overhead thrust. The blades connect in a bone-rattling smack, and he can tell that Rilke isn't holding back in the slightest. They separate and circle each other. Gritting his teeth, Cal digs his toes into the pine needles, keeping his center of gravity low. He darts a pleading look at Abbot, who drew Cal's and Rilke's names for this bout; it's a ridiculous match, and everyone knows it.

At six foot three, Cal towers over Rilke's five foot five inches. While Rilke's muscular and undoubtedly in excellent condition, Cal is a bloody ox by comparison. He shook his head when Abbot read their names, gesturing for the older boy to draw again. Rilke had bristled, muttering about cowardice. He pretended not to hear, but Abbot had given his sister a dark look and pointed them both into the ring to the hoots and catcalls of the rest of the apprentices. Now he faces the option of looking like a jerk for using his height and weight against her or looking like a jerk for letting her win.

Backing around the ring, he lets Rilke take the middle, lets her think she has him on the retreat. A faintly smug twist to the girl's mouth signals her expectation to win the next point. She strikes with quick fierce jabs, and Cal deflects. She twists away to try again, changing her stance and the balance of her weight. Panting hard, she thrusts up beneath his chin, and he blocks her to keep his head in place, gasping a little at the ferocity of her strike. And so it goes for another five, ten minutes, both of them working up a sweat.

Lanterns light the training yard. Everyone is present. The Nutris reps will be here in the hour, and the atmosphere of tension has been building all afternoon. The news of Sargent's condition sits heavily on every pair of shoulders. The weight of worry makes tempers short, and the last few sparring pairs have fallen into outright brawls. They use blunt wooden blades for a reason. Resentments flare. Mistakes are made. The stink of sweat and aggression sets Cal's teeth on edge. He's heard nothing but muttering and speculation behind his back since he came from the barn, and he still has plenty of pent-up frustration to burn.

"Stop being a bloody gentleman," Joss yells. "Get in there."

Leif chuckles next to him, sheened in sweat and bloody-lipped from the previous bout with *a boy his size*. "She's your cousin."

"She spent most of our childhood knocking me on my ass."

Abbot snorts, but Rilke doesn't smile. She's breathing hard, and frustration etches her face. She knows Cal's just waiting her out. With a shout, she lunges. Cal ducks low to the side and swings his elbow beneath the girl's overreached arm. Rilke's momentum does the damage, her ribs ramming into the point of Cal's elbow with a solid *thwack* that makes everyone around the circle groan in sympathy.

Cal immediately feels bad. "Sorry."

She coughs, gasps, and stumbles to her knees. Cal needs those seconds to recover from the uncomfortable bolt of Rilke's life force. Goose bumps shiver over his shoulders. He casts Abbot another pleading look; they've been sparring for at least ten minutes. The older boy's stern expression softens with worry, and Leif looks at his partner with a sympathetic frown.

Something in Cal's peripheral vision catches his eye. Reeva landing on the rim of the head ranger's veranda. The bird caws her disapproval. She's not happy to see him sparring. She caws again, and Cal shakes his head, flicking his wrist to signal for her to go away and not watch.

Rilke picks herself up as Cal's vision blurs with Reeva's sending. The image skewers Cal in place. Meg waist-deep in black water. Steam billowing around her. Hair slicked back. Pale skin gleaming in the low light. The raw wound on her ribs. Her wet bra. Blood rushes from his head, and he doesn't see Rilke coming. Something like a sledgehammer connects with his jaw. Lights explode behind his eyes, and he's falling through space and never hitting the ground.

It's a couple of seconds before sight and sound return to him. When he blinks his eyes open, there's a circle of faces above him, hands hovering and uncertain about touching him. "Don't," Joss says, his arms out to hold the crowd back. "Give him some space."

Abbot pushes through the press of bodies, his brow bunched into a hard knot.

Cal's eyes blur in and out of focus. He heaves himself up onto his elbows, and the others back up, leaving a margin of space around him. His head feels like it's full of porridge. Rilke stands just beyond the group, her dark skin shining with a sickly pallor. Her expression flickering between guilt and rage. "You just stood there."

Joss shakes his head, squatting beside him. "What happened? You kind of blanked out."

"What are you trying to prove?" Panting hard, Rilke spits. "That you can take a hit?"

"I was distracted."

She curls her lip. "You're an asshole."

"You need a hand?" Abbot asks him, hesitating with the offer.

Cal shakes his head. His jaw aches. He can feel Reeva firing sendings at him—her worry and fear. He doesn't open his mind to her. One glimpse of a mostly naked Meg got him into this mess. He groans. "I need an aspirin and a cold shower."

LIMITED REANIMATION

Antonia was right. Meg grits her teeth and leans heavily against the back wall of the summer barracks. It's cold this far up Little Peak, but the back of Meg's neck is slick with perspiration from the hike and the pain in her side. Careful not to rustle her jacket too loudly, she peels a glove from one hand, lifts the hem of her sweater, and tests the wound for wetness. The scar is raised and tender, and her skin is damp, but when she holds her fingers up before her eyes, squinting through the gloom, there's no blood.

Blowing through her lips, she closes her eyes and tries to settle her breathing. There's no way she's stumbling into camp, puffing and gasping for breath. It's bad enough her determination to throw down with Bren and the master rangers eroded with every step up the mountain. The problem is, she kind of gets it now. What she felt, pressed to that boulder in the hot pools, the sense of living energy thrumming through the island itself—no wonder they don't want Sargent to leave. If that's what they all feel when they connect with the ley lines, if it's more than a warm buzzy feeling, why would she want to separate him from something that potentially gives him life?

She's jumping the gun. What she needs is answers—about what it means and whether it means anything. Likely, she's conflating her encounter with the vibration with all her childhood desperation to be counted worthy of joining the rangers themselves. She has to keep a clear head. Besides, she's not ready to abandon faith in science or the benefits of modern medicine.

Voices rise in the training yard, and Meg pushes up from the wall, forcing her wobbly legs to move. Slipping around the end of the kitchen, she sees a crowd of rangers assembled around the fire pit. She freezes when she recognizes the Fortune Hunter, Jackson Spear, standing on Sargent's porch with Bren and three older women Meg recognizes as master rangers.

"Limited what?" someone demands.

"Limited Reanimation." Spear displays a small round canister. "Test results range from a 13 to a 28 percent increase in the potency of ground Bane. And we're talking about frozen samples harvested in the previous cull. Imagine what we can accomplish with fresh kill."

A brittle silence solidifies in the air as rangers exchange looks varying from incomprehension to outright hostility and disgust.

"You're . . . raising the dead?" the pale blond ranger asks. Leif, Meg finds the name. His handsome face contorts, and he shakes his head at the huge young man beside him, Bren's son, Abbot.

Abbot crosses his arms, presenting the full threat of his biceps. "That some kind of sick joke?"

"Raising the dead is a fairly hysterical interpretation," Spear says. "You apply the paste to the gums. The permeable membrane absorbs the product, and within a couple of hours, the nanotech travels to the brain, inducing varying degrees of Limited Reanimation depending on the state of decomposition."

Someone swears. Others shift in their seats. Meg stands stunned.

"It simply reignites electric impulses," Spear says, his tone matter-of-fact. "A brief charge, firing muscle memory. It's especially useful in animals that have died traumatically. It reverses the taint of chemical panic, dramatically improving the potency of Actaeon's Bane even beyond nontainted levels."

"Improving your profit margin," Leif mutters.

"That's why we're here."

"It's not why *we're* here," Bren says, his voice flat.

"Dimensional Rift aside . . ." Spear says, cold and droll, but Meg doesn't hear what comes next because her brain lodges on *Dimensional Rift*, drawing a blank. ". . . dealing with practicalities. *Your* job is to protect the Old Herd and manage those bloody Hounds. My job is to complete the audit and to advance the work of Nutris Pharmaceuticals. Research and development is a part of that advancement, and Limited Reanimation is . . ."

"Your *research* has endangered the life of our head ranger," Bren says, grinding the words in his teeth. "How do you imagine civilians would cope with your research? Limited Reanimation is too unpredictable to introduce to a cull environment."

Spear gestures to the document Bren has been waving. "Sargent believed otherwise. He provided clear sanction for testing."

Bren rips the document in half.

Spear produces his lazy shrug. "It's already on record, and my men have already deployed to audit the Lower Slopes. They will be looking for testing opportunities along the way."

"That is unacceptable," Bren says, his voice rising sharply with the murmurs of disapproval rumbling around the fire pit.

"You have enough to worry about with getting Sargent up to the Rift Stone; I believe that's your best bet for saving his life. Meanwhile you have an injured animal to track. Sargent assured me that your most talented tracker would take care of that problem. I have thirty-five Hunters arriving for the cull in less than a week. You owe me a minimum of seventeen guides and a mountain free of Rift Hounds. Failure to meet any of these requirements, and I will assert treaty rights—"

"That won't be necessary."

"You're down two key players from what I understand, and you're running out of time. I suggest you get on with your job while I get on with mine."

Without waiting for a reply, Spear adjusts his rifle on his

back and steps off the porch. Several rangers rise too and block his path, Rilke at the forefront. The Fortune Hunter pauses and cocks his head, narrowing his eyes, fanning those deep crow's feet.

"Let him go," Bren says.

Rilke scowls at her father before she and the other rangers clear the path. She spits at Spear's feet, but the man merely smirks and stalks away. The assembled group fall immediately into grumbling and loud debate. Bren and the master rangers huddle together.

Is this why Cal sent Reeva to fetch her, so she'd hear all this? She frowns, eyes boring into the abandoned blaze in the fire pit. Her brain grinds with the efficiency of rusted gears. She needs sleep and food and painkillers. So much of what was said went straight over her head. Dimensional Rift? The only salient detail was the mention of taking Sargent up the mountain. A Rift Stone? She shivers, imagining something like the boulder in the hot pools, a rock thrumming with power, and her hope surges. She can't ignore Spear's more ominous mention of Rift Hounds and shivers again, sweat turning cold on her skin. Does he mean the feral dogs that trouble the Upper Slopes?

Instinct warns her that her original intent to walk boldly up to Bren and start making demands is the wrong move. She needs to stay hidden until she has more information. She needs to talk to Cal. She searches the milling crowd, where discussion has grown tense. A scuffle breaks out. Bren and the master rangers drop down from the porch to intervene, calling for order. Long shadows lunge in the firelight, and Meg ducks back. Where is Cal?

"We move at first light," Bren shouts above the noise, and the volume drops. "Apprentice rangers *must* remain on the Lower Slopes." Gasps of outrage rise, Rilke's foremost. Bren ignores her. "If you encounter Nutris Fortune Hunters, do not engage; you may confiscate anything that looks like Nutris R and D, but do not interfere with the audit."

"Was it really Sargent's signature?" Abbot asks.

"Until we can confirm that, we confiscate."

"What's this about an injured deer?" Rilke demands. "No one's mentioned anything to us about an injured deer. If the Rift is unstable, you need all of us on the Upper Slopes."

Bren sighs with a heave of his shoulders. "Sargent earmarked Cal and Joss for tracking this morning."

"Joss?" Rilke chokes. "But not me?"

"Sargent—" Bren begins wearily.

"And what do you mean this morning?" Rilke demands. "Why haven't they already left? They wasted the whole day! We could be crawling in Rift Hounds by tomorrow night!"

"Fine," Bren says, gritting his teeth. "You can join them at first light. Perhaps your efficiency will speed up the process."

Rilke's mouth snaps closed, presumably shocked to get her way.

"You are, after all, coming to the end of your apprenticeship, and Cal is the most talented tracker we have. Consider it a learning opportunity."

Rilke's face drops.

Bren turns to the remaining group. "At first light, senior and master rangers will escort Sargent to the Rift Stone. Now get some sleep."

Meg edges back along the building, her mind whirring.

A wet crunch echoes behind her, and Meg spins. A young man leans against the side of the building, chewing an apple. He peers past her shoulder at the gathering in the training yard and shakes his head. His hair sticks up, and even in the shadows, she can make out freckles on his pale skin. It's Joss Fenchurch. Bouncing his eyebrows at her, he regards her with amused curiosity and digs in his pocket, producing another apple. "Hungry?"

SECRET THINGS

Stepping out of the summer barracks, Cal squints at the dawn sky, heavy gray with a pink tinge. No howling in the night. He doesn't know what power to give thanks to. Drizzle patters his face. But drizzle down here may well mean heavy showers on the Western Reaches, up past Fallon's Landing, or torrential rain in the Rift.

He trudges across the training yard, poncho flapping, pack on his shoulder. His body aches from the last few days of abuse. His jaw is stiff, and the skin on his cheekbone smarts. With each step, his lower back pinches, and he rubs his temple to ease the persistent throb behind his left eye. Sparring with Rilke—what was he thinking?

His gaze slides to the master rangers' quarters, a brick in his chest. He shivers, imagining the chill that might be waiting for him in Sargent's room. What if he's dead already? He looks away, hitching his pack higher on his shoulder.

No. They would have woken him to confirm it.

He pictures Meg's blanched face in Bertrum's kill yard, Cora's cries ringing in his head. He remembers being eight years old in Sargent's arms, carried away from the crowd at the dock, throat raw from screaming, the warmth of Sargent's breath on the top of his head. *Easy, little man. I've got you.*

This Sargent might be cold and humorless, but he wasn't always so. Cal shakes his head, searching for other words . . . capable? Decisive? Uncompromising? Everything a head ranger should be. Part of him wonders if Sargent would have kept his warmth and kindness if leadership hadn't been thrust upon him. Would Cal? He scrapes his hand over his face. Truth is, everybody already thinks he's cold and humorless. Halfway there.

He ducks into the tack room and refills his stocks of rue and Yarra leaf. He cleans and coats his machete, dips his arrow tips in lard and rue, oils the hinges of his crossbow, and tries not to hear Bren in his head: *When you talk, people listen.* It makes his gut churn. Nellie nodding in her sick bed, Joss grinning at him across the master rangers' common room. No. He's not angling for the top job. Cal doesn't need any more reasons for people to resent him. Besides, it's not just Rilke who blames him for what happened to Sargent.

After the tense roll call last night, he'd retreated to the master rangers' cabin. He listened by the window, frost on his cheek as he kept watch beside Sargent. Jackson Spear's threats. Rilke's outrage. Bren's frustration. He draws a wary breath through his nose, filling his lungs and—

Meg.

His spine stiffens.

He sniffs his shirt.

No.

He showered and changed his clothes last night. He breathes again, softly this time, cataloging the layers. Damp pine needles, wet wood, rust, mud, herbs, grease, tar, tin, lantern oil ... lily and chamomile soap.

He leans on the tack bench, locking his elbows and closing his eyes, body charged by the lick of adrenaline. By reflex, he reaches for the Voice of the Herd. It rumbles through him, deep, reassuring, aware. What's he looking for? Gravity. Recalibration.

Meg is here.

Is it really a surprise? She's probably come to check on her dad. It wouldn't have been easy with a wound in her side. How will he face her? He cringes at the thought of her pain and the argument to come. How will Bren explain their plans to take Sargent up the mountain? What if she expects to come? There's no way Bren would let her anywhere near the Rift. He'll say no, and Meg will be furious, and then what? Some poor apprentice will have to drag her back down Little Peak to Nero's Palace. He does not envy that person.

He leaves his gear in the tack room and steps out into the rain. There's movement in the training yard, apprentices beginning to collect supplies for the hike into the mountains. He wonders if Rilke is up and prepped, and Cal grits his teeth at the prospect of the forty-eight hours ahead. The moment he steps away from the tack room, Meg's scent fades. He frowns, backtracks, and follows the trace of lily and chamomile around the side of the building to the back of the kitchen. His stomach rumbles at the waft of breakfast, and his mouth begins to water.

He concentrates past the demands of his stomach to find Meg again and follows the scent to the back wall of the summer barracks. Suspicion halts him. The track from the village to Little Peak leads directly into the training yard. She would have had to edge around the camp to come this way. Hiding? He breathes again. It's not the rain that's dampened her scent; the scent is hours old. She was here last night. He blinks and widens his eyes, trying to recall what was said around the fire pit.

Shit.

So many things.

Secret things.

He clicks his teeth and whistles for Reeva. He listens for the sound of her wings. Nothing. He starts walking again, following his nose straight to the outbuildings. His skin feels tight and his insides twitchy. Meg? Out here? Did she sleep in the barn? It would have been freezing. A whiff of bacon and toast confuses him.

Where is Reeva?

The barn door sits slightly ajar.

Someone chuckles.

Someone else makes a shushing sound.

Cal slips through the door and stops in the shadows, disbelieving.

Joss and Rilke sit with their backs to the door. Rilke pours coffee from a large thermos into three tin mugs arranged on an upturned bucket. Joss lounges with his back on a support post, legs stretched before him, ankles crossed, chuckling at Meg. Meg sits opposite them, swathed in a thick blanket, clicking her tongue, eyes on the rafters. An oil lantern, perched on a barrel, washes her face in buttery light. She murmurs soft words and tears a corner from her toast, wiggling it at the roof between her gloved fingers. Placing the toast on top of a sack of grain, she leans away, biting her bottom lip. Reeva drops from the crossbeam above like a black arrow, making them all yelp as she dive-bombs, nabbing it in her beak. Shooting back to the crossbeam, she tears it to shreds, showering the group below with crumbs, causing more hushed laughter.

Rilke covers her mug, shaking her head. "That's straight witchcraft."

Joss waves a strip of bacon at her. "Cal's going to spit when he finds out you've broken his scout."

"Serves him right," Rilke mutters.

"Don't start." Joss waves the bacon at her.

"I'm just saying, it's an upgrade for the bird."

Meg frowns, chewing her toast. "I did nothing. She turned up."

Cal considers stalking out of the barn, marching up the mountain, and throwing himself through the Rift. Why are his biceps cramping? He's balled his fists so tight he could snap a tendon in his knuckles. He glares at the back of Joss's and Rilke's heads; he needs his knuckles. Relaxing his stance, he steps into the light, making his voice as bland as he can manage—murderous. "What is going on?"

Meg bounces on her bottom, eyes popping wide. Rilke sloshes coffee over her wrist, cursing. Joss goes rigid, then leans around the post, his smile overly-bright. "Breakfast?"

Squinting into the rafters, Cal doesn't whistle for Reeva, but he almost shouts her name in his mind. She drops and swoops to Cal's arm. Her cawing sounds off, and she dips her head in an odd bowing gesture, waddling to his shoulder, flicking her wings. *Is she showing off?*

Reeva sends a slew of images, one after the other. Meg on the veranda of Nero's Palace. Meg in Bertrum's kill yard. Meg in Cal's arms. Heat floods his face, and he clears his throat with a tight shake of his head. It doesn't stop Reeva. Meg climbing the mountain track. *Meg in the hot pools.*

"Oh—um . . ." Meg bolts to her feet, clutching the blanket around her, her face bright pink beneath a wool beanie. She almost trips in her thick oversize socks as she scrambles toward them. "I—I came as soon as I got your message, but I couldn't find you, and Joss turned up, and we had a talk, and Rilke agreed, so I'm coming with you. You—as in all of you. The three of you . . ."

Cal stares at her feet, his brow knotting tight. "Are those my socks?" The blanket . . . the beanie . . . from his supply chest? He glares at Joss.

Joss hikes his shoulders to his ears, turning his palms up. "You weren't using them."

"Oh, sorry." Meg grimaces and starts peeling herself free of the blanket and beanie and socks. She almost shoves them into his chest, her warm sleep scent billowing from the fabric, mixed with his scent. "Joss said you wouldn't mind."

Momentarily punch-drunk, Cal swallows hard. He bites back the urge to apologize, but it only makes him sound terse. "What message? Coming with us where?"

She digs inside her shirt, blushing hotter. Retrieving a crushed mint leaf, she rolls it on the palm of her glove. "To the Rift Stone."

GOD'S GIFT

Meg's face burns. Her ears burn. Cal glowers at the leaf, then glowers at her, that hazel eye scorching a path right through her. She's so hot she wishes she could strip to her skin and lie on the half-frozen ground. After everything she overheard last night, and her subsequent interrogation of Joss—and Rilke grudgingly filling the blanks—the idea of Reeva delivering a mint leaf shouldn't be the impossible detail.

It's hardly *less* likely than a dimensional portal, Rift Hounds, or magic deer. Certainly more believable than a telepathic hotline to said magic deer or animal bond-scouts that give their rangers second sight. If anyone gets to be outraged and disbelieving, it's her. Finding out that the stories she grew up with were historical facts and not myth and legend is a pretty big ask; she had to put her head between her knees for a solid twenty minutes. By comparison, Meg's suggestion that Cal had summoned her to Little Peak is perfectly reasonable.

Her humiliation is only heightened by the flood of Reeva's telepathic snapshots confirming her suspicions. Cal can see what she sees. Has seen? Will see? The tiny secret part of her tempted to find this exciting is swiftly extinguished by his prolonged glower. Clearly, he didn't send the leaf. He doesn't want her here. He's horrified by the suggestion, offended by her use of his belongings, and appalled at the idea that she is any wiser about the secrets of Black Water Island. Meg would like to punch him in his perfect jaw, though, judging by his bruises, someone already has.

"How . . ." Cal runs his hand over his face, pinching the bridge of his nose. "What exactly do you think is . . . I mean, how is this even . . . ? *Joss, can I speak to you outside?*" He dumps the blanket on a barrel and turns sharply, forcing Reeva to unfurl her wings with a snap to keep her balance. She produces a loud grumble.

Meg gapes at Cal's departing back, the stiffness of his posture, and his bunched fists. "Who exactly does he think he is?" she says, not troubling to lower her voice.

"God's gift to Black Water," Rilke mutters.

Joss points his finger at his cousin's chest. "What did I say?"

Rilke rolls her eyes. "I'm not starting anything."

With an apologetic grimace, Joss jogs after Cal, who strides toward the forest like he has a murder to commit.

"I have a right to be here," Meg calls after him.

Joss half turns, patting the air in a shushing gesture. At the same time, Rilke places a silencing hand on her shoulder.

Meg drops her voice, hissing, "If anyone gets to be furious, it's me."

"No argument here."

"Rangers and their *secrets*." She marches across the barn, shakes out her jersey, and rams it over her head. Sitting heavily on an upturned grain sack, she jams her feet into her hiking boots and yanks her laces into knots. Rising, she whips her coat from the hook by the woodpile. The image of ax-wielding, shirtless Cal invades her thoughts, but she shakes her head briskly and makes for the door.

"Whoa." Rilke blocks her path. "Where are you going?"

"I'm not sitting here while *Cal West* decides if *I'm* worthy to go up the mountain. I'm going to talk to your father."

"Bad idea. We talked about this."

"Rilke," Meg says, hating the sound of pleading in her voice. "I don't care what Cal says. I won't abandon Sargent again."

Rilke frowns at her boots. "No one thinks you abandoned your father. You were a kid. Your mother took you."

"He never forgave me."

"There's nothing to forgive."

"You don't understand."

"We'll get you up the mountain, Meg, but it has to be a secret. Otherwise, the master rangers will flip."

Meg draws a shuddering breath. "What about him?" She nods in the direction of the forest, straining to hear raised voices. Nothing but early morning birdsong and the creak and shuffle of trees.

"Cal's annoying, but he's no fool; he knows he can't stop you. Besides, you actually deserve to be here. You've got ranger blood, Meg. You're one of us."

Meg tries to calm down, heartened by the girl's generosity. "What do you mean, annoying?"

"I don't know." Rilke folds her arms, then frustration gets the better of her, and she flings them open again. "The master rangers think he's the golden boy, and he's done *nothing* to earn it. He wouldn't even *feel* the ley lines if it wasn't for his bite. It's not in his blood, like us. Never mind me working my butt off, and I'm *still* stuck on junior duties. I'm three months older than him." She cuts off, screwing her lips up, then bursts out muttering again, "And the whole tortured orphan routine is getting tired. Look around, Cal. How many ranger kids have got two parents to rub together?" She stops suddenly, an expression of horror dawning on her face. "I'm so sorry, Meg. I can't believe I said that. I'm sure Sargent will—"

Despite the sting, Meg waves the apology away; she doesn't want the girl to feel bad, and it's not like she hasn't harbored her own resentment toward Cal for his place in the community. Just then a shadow passes the door, and Rilke steps back, mouth hardening to a thin line. Cal steps in like the end of days, Joss grimacing at his shoulder. Meg takes a few backward steps as Cal walks right into her personal space and fixes her to the spot with that fierce hazel eye.

"The *only* reason I'm going along with this is because I know if I don't say yes, you'll follow us anyway."

"That's—" She coughs to clear her throat. "That's right."

"I could tie you to this post and send a message with Reeva to your mother in a day or two."

Rilke expels air with a *pfft*.

A nerve pinches in Meg's cheek. Cal's a big guy. She's seen enough of him to know he has the goods to follow through. Her heart kicks, and her breath comes short. "You're being a dick."

"*Cal,*" Joss says, shaking his head.

Cal presses his fist beneath his nose, drawing a deep *help-me-God* breath. "Promise me you'll do what I say—what *we* say."

She scowls.

"How do you think I'll face your mother if I don't bring you back in one piece?"

"That's not your responsibility."

"We're *all* responsible," Joss says.

Rilke sighs. "This is overkill."

"We're not leaving until she promises."

"*She* knows how to follow instructions," Meg snaps.

"Meg," he says, his voice suddenly soft and low and pleading. It makes her toes curl and the fine hairs rise at the nape of her neck. That fierce hazel eye softens too, and what she sees is worse than anger and frustration: it's genuine fear.

She wants to touch him, reassure him, but she keeps her hands to herself. "Cal." She lifts her chin. "Have a little faith." Then she digs in her pocket, retrieving the photo of the little boy with the tumor on his heart. "You need to let Bren know what he's dealing with. Spear can't be trusted, and I'm not sure my father can be, either."

WESTERN TRACK

Cal eyes the milling crowd of rangers like it's a tank of electric eels. He keeps as far to the side of the track as he can, positioning his gear on his arm as a buffer against accidental zaps. Even at half their number, the rangers accompanying Sargent's stretcher pack the crossroads. They'll follow the northeast path; it's wider, the slope more gradual, making the most of the deer trail and wide switchbacks, better for a large party with a heavy load.

Cal will track directly west to Burntwood Lodge and Fallon's Landing. The climb is steeper and narrower, but it also leads directly into the heart of Old Herd territory. It's the most likely place the injured deer will have taken refuge, hemmed by ley lines and a deep gorge. Even though it's almost twice the distance, with only four of them they'll make the Rift Stone before Bren and the master rangers by almost half a day—if they keep good time and the Rift holds.

He lifts his face to the sky: only a few spots of rain. If he could catch a break—if it cleared altogether—it would make all the difference. He wonders if Reeva has delivered Meg's message to Cora. He's not sure what details she gave in the rolled-up piece of paper, but he highly doubts it will allay her mother's fears for her daughter's safety. He cringes picturing her face, replaying her desperate cries the day before, begging for them to let her take Sargent to the mainland.

Bren signals, and the men part, making way for Cal. He grits his teeth; he knows he looks ridiculous passing through the crowd like the oracle of doom. He can't bring himself to meet anyone's gaze for fear of the blame he imagines must be burning in so many rangers' eyes. The sudden hush only makes it worse, the anticipation. Cal's gift isn't generally put on display. Anyone who's seen Cal's lips turn blue or frost appear on his face is generally seeing the last thing they'll ever see or watching someone they love die. Still, people talk. He's grateful at least that Meg is hiding farther along the western track, well out of sight.

He makes no comment and gives the moment no ceremony, dropping his hand lightly onto Sargent's shoulder. He doesn't close his eyes or lower his head. Staring briefly into the middle distance, he feels what he felt less than an hour ago when he last checked. Sargent's pulse is stronger than the previous night, steady and stable yet no jolt of life. Cal's breath grows cold, his lips too. The watchful presence lingers. Whispers rustle out through the ranks.

He comes back to himself, feeling watched and contagious,

and quickly rubs away traces of frost from his fingers.

Bren waits, his expression grim with fatigue and worry.

"No change," Cal murmurs.

"You heard," Bren says, his voice like a bark. "We break at Flint's Gully."

As the Rangers move out, Cal stays still. Bren stands with him, providing an extra buffer without comment. Abbot passes with a nod and a sympathetic smile.

Leif lifts his hand in a parting gesture. "Good hunting. Stay safe."

"You too," Cal says, noticing how Bren lingers, bracing for what might be said.

The older man drops his voice. "I appreciate this isn't easy."

Cal isn't sure whether he means being the camp death detector, carrying the burden of responsibility for locating the injured deer, or being saddled with Rilke as a hunting partner.

"But we're grateful," Bren says, and though he bolsters his voice, his scent is laced with grief and fear. "The community is grateful."

Cal doesn't believe him; Bren is just being kind. He clears his throat. "Sir, if what Meg overheard was true and Sargent and Spear are working together, should we be going to the Rift at all?" He said all this when he first took the photo Meg gave him to Bren this morning, but he can't shake the bad feeling. He wishes he could extract the snippets of Sargent and Spear's conversation straight from Meg's memory and dissect the details. All she could make of it was talk about the Old Herd and a gate and Fallon. What else could the gate be but the Rift? "Maybe it *would* be better if Cora took Sargent to the mainland. To a hospital."

Bren's expression closes. "You know Sargent would *never* agree to that, and you know that liaising with Nutris is the head ranger's job. I don't think we should read too much into an overheard conversation."

"Spear's proven he's ruthless," Cal says. "He beat up that kid's dad and took his money."

"None of that changes what you need to do now. Find the injured deer, end the distress signal, and meet us at the Rift Stone." Bren tilts his head, forcing Cal to meet his eyes. The man looks exhausted and desperate. "We need you, Cal. Prove your detractors wrong."

It's like being handed a boulder. Cal swallows and gives a single nod. "We'll see you up there."

* * *

Two hours up the western track, Cal's muscles are beginning to loosen and warm up. Though he feels no better about Sargent and Spear, he tells himself to focus on what lies before him; he can't control anything else. The mountain is cloaked in mist, and the air is sweet. It must be heading on midmorning, and the sun hasn't burned through the cloud cover. It makes the forest quiet—as quiet as it can be with Joss and Rilke and Meg, who don't seem in any hurry to shut up. Though their conversation has grown more breathy and Meg's replies are shorter. He supposes he should be grateful there's no chance of stumbling into an irate boar with their voices clearing the path.

Joss has established that Meg is enrolled to begin a bachelor's degree in biology and environmental science, works part-time as a climbing instructor, has a collection of hand-made bows and arrows, and loves Mexican food. Mexican food takes up a good twenty minutes of conversation. Cal loves Mexican food. He says nothing. Rilke follows with a grilling about football, teams Meg supports, and games she's been to.

They may as well be talking about life on Mars.

The conversation turns to Little Peak, the rangers' routines and traditions. Meg keeps her voice even, betraying no outward signs of bitterness or resentment, showing polite interest in every detail. She asks about the bonded scouts, amazed she never knew about them when she was a child. Rilke falls silent, the death of Queenie too fresh and painful to dwell on. Joss bridges the awkwardness with a brief lighthearted joke about Otho, his grumpy little owl, too blind to travel far these days. Then, smooth as anything, he changes the subject.

A couple of times Meg's laugh rings out, a sudden, uninhibited burst of amusement. He doesn't know whether he'd like to wring Joss's and Rilke's necks or thank them for easing her burden, distracting her from the fear and grief draining the light from her eyes. She's funny—like Joss, a quick, sharp wit. All the snappy comebacks. Even Rilke—when she's not complaining—is funny. It makes Cal lengthen his stride.

A nudge in the back of his thoughts makes him look up. There's a small black smudge moving high in the overhanging trees above the ridge. He reaches for Reeva in his mind, like flexing a muscle. She's too well camouflaged to make out clearly, but he can feel her, watching, assessing. The bird fires images into his mind: Cora opening the note, her face contorted in fury and fear. His chest tightens. Should he say something? He can't bring himself to.

Sighing, he acknowledges Reeva's good work and sends her a warm thought. However, he hasn't gotten over what he saw this morning: Reeva *playing* with Meg. Dive-bombing for treats. *In front of an audience.* When Meg pulled the mint leaf from her bra, he was floored.

He fires the image at Reeva, the mint leaf in Meg's hand.

There's a second or two, then Reeva sends rapid-fire images of Meg, like it explains everything, the same ones she sent him in the barn, including Meg in the hot pools and the translucent bra. He almost trips.

Meg yelps.

Cal spins.

"Gotcha." Joss clamps her upper arm. Meg has sunk to one knee, her other foot having slipped off the edge of the muddy bank. The pack she borrowed from Rilke has slid up behind her head. The bow and quiver Joss stole from the tack room hitches awkwardly around her neck, and arrows are scattered in the mud. Rilke lifts the pack off her shoulder while Joss hauls her back to her feet. Meg hisses a little, squeezing her elbow to her side. From knee to foot, her tights are coated in mud, and pink splotches stain the apples of her cheeks.

Stop staring.

"You have to watch your footing in the wet," he says.

Rilke rolls her eyes.

"I *was*," Meg insists.

Joss gives Rilke a warning look while he wipes arrows on his sleeve. "Sorry, did I pull too hard?"

Meg shakes her head, brushing the palms of her gloves together, but they're muddy and damp, and she closes her fists to hide them.

"We can dry them out," Rilke says. "Hang them off your pack."

"It's fine." Meg offers a tight smile, not meeting Rilke's eyes. "They're built for the conditions—Tibetan yak fur."

Rilke raises her eyebrows.

"Fancy," Joss says.

"Sargent sent them for my birthday."

"When was that?"

"Ah . . . today, actually." A wobble in her lip suggests this is a detail she hadn't intended to let slip. The boys find other things to look at.

Rilke pats her shoulder. "Happy birthday, Meg."

"Thanks," she mumbles.

Joss murmurs, "Um, what do you think, Cal? An hour and a half till we hit the Western Step?"

"At least," Cal says, leaning his arm in the strap of his crossbow. "We can stop here though, if—you know—anyone needs a break."

Meg looks at Rilke. "Do *you* need a break?"

Rilke shakes her head.

Meg cocks her head at Joss. "*You?*"

"Ah . . . I'm good."

"What about you, Cal? Do *you* need a break?"

He clicks his teeth. "Nope."

Meg lifts her chin. "Then I guess we're all good."

"*Fine.*" He turns his back and stalks on.

IN AGONY

By the time they reach the steep narrow track to the Western Step, Meg is hot and puffing. She tries to disguise the sound by breathing through her mouth. Conversation dried up after her slip off the track, and they've been walking uphill for almost a solid hour. Her guides don't look *close* to breaking a sweat, no hint of panting from Cal up front, Rilke before her, or Joss behind. Meanwhile, her side burns like there's a blowtorch searing the wound. She wishes she had spent longer in the hot pools with Actaeon's Bane.

Shoving her hood back, she wipes the slick nape of her neck, brushing wet tendrils off her skin. She fumbles for the water bottle in her pack.

"Hold up," Joss calls, and the apprentice rangers stop in their tracks and look back. "Thirsty." Joss grabs his own water bottle. Meg gives him a small grateful smile, and he winks.

She leans against the mossy bank, not minding the cold

dampness soaking the seat of her pants. Everybody takes a water break. It's been a while since she could take her eyes off her feet, navigating the track; the grim beauty of Black Water is something else. Jagged peaks looming above primeval forest. Sudden vicious gullies and blade-sharp cliffs. Raw cuts of green. Ancient formations of rough-hewn stone thrust up by tectonic shifts long centuries before, thick pelts of emerald moss coating the undersides, too high for hungry deer to reach.

Ahead, the track narrows to a steep bottleneck. She watches Cal's back as he assesses the path, the broad stretch of his shoulders as he digs one hand up into his hair. Meg has an itch to see what that gesture looks like from the front, his tousled hair pushed right back, the full, honest picture of his face. He drops his hand, and his hair falls back over the edge of his jaw before he swings around.

"Joss, you take the lead here."

He offers no reason. Joss asks for no explanation, simply nodding and moving to take the lead. Cal leans out over the drop, bracing his arm around the trunk of a tree, and Meg frowns at the effort he makes to keep clear. No smart comment from Rilke about it. Meg slings her pack in place, gritting her teeth at the slice of pain in her side. Cal sees her grimace but doesn't mention it as she passes.

A few minutes into the climb and Meg is in agony. She has to reach above her head to secure holds for each step. As much as possible, she favors the arm on her good side, but she can't completely avoid using both. The track is slippery, a muddy channel in the rock. It's deep enough that she doesn't have to worry about plummeting over the drop but steep enough that she might crash on top of Cal if she loses her grip. She's embarrassingly slow for someone who claims to be a climbing instructor, and she can't stop thinking about Cal's view of her ass. His silence beneath her only makes her more aware of his presence and the contours of her activewear.

"Nearly there," Joss calls.

A silent prayer of thanks and Meg pushes up, all her weight on her right foot to save straining her side. The muscles in her thigh tremble with the effort, then *schlep!* Her foot slips, and she can't contain a cry of pain.

"Rilke!" Cal calls, close below her.

Scrabbling her fingers on the wet rock, Meg presses herself to the track to keep from falling. It takes Rilke a couple of seconds to clamber down and grab her wrist.

"Other arm!" Cal shouts, too late, as Rilke pulls.

Forks of lightning blaze through Meg's wound, and she cries out again.

Cal swears.

"Sorry!" Rilke repositions herself to take Meg's other hand.

She feels heat close to her thigh and glances down. Cal has both hands poised to catch her, yet he doesn't touch her. Rilke hauls her slowly upward.

"I got it," she says, breathless and weak.

The rest of the way, Rilke stays within reach, but Meg makes it up to the plateau without another slip. She walks as steadily as she can to a formation of rocks, well back from the edge, and sits with a suppressed groan. Carefully, she slides her pack from her back, then her bow and quiver, and considers removing her raincoat. Her side feels wet, but she can't tell if it's general sweatiness or if she's opened her wound. She doesn't want to inspect it with anyone watching her.

Rilke mutters about needing to pee, stalking into the forest with a face like a thunderclap. Cal and Joss stand at the cliff edge, conferring, Cal partly turned away, Joss facing him, fighting a teasing grin. She ducks her head to hide the heat in her cheeks.

PEOPLE STARE

Cal stands on the Western Step, breathing deeply, trying to clear his head. He pretends to survey the jagged horizon of cliff, sea, and sky, but his body is an electric light show. Firecrackers burst in his chest, corkscrew down his arms and legs. He needs to climb out of his skin or wrestle a boar. The way Joss is grinning at him, he may need to punch his friend in the face.

"Don't." Warning adds a growl to his voice; Meg will know they're talking about her.

Joss snickers. "I'm just saying, Rilke and I won't always be the first ones on hand."

"It was one slip. She's not a klutz. She's injured. She's a *climbing instructor.*"

"She's going to notice," Joss says. "You're not exactly subtle."

"Lower your voice."

"You carried her to Nero's." Joss searches his face. "Was it that bad?"

A muscle pinches in his cheek, and Cal forces himself to unclamp his teeth. What's he supposed to say? How can he describe the intensity of someone's life force punching through his body? It's more than life and death; it's . . . intimate. His cheeks get hot. "Yes."

"Really?"

Cal rubs his face, a rough swipe. "No . . . then yes."

Joss narrows his eyes.

"I don't know. I don't want to talk about it."

A new grin stretches Joss's lips, his face alight with knowing. "She's under your skin, Cal. All that shared history. She's gorgeous and angry and carrying a weapon. No wonder you're freaking out."

"You *let* her sleep with my blanket on purpose."

Shoulders bouncing with suppressed laughter, Joss backs away.

Cal turns to check on Meg, catching the unguarded expression of pain in her face and the swift way she hides it when she realizes she's being watched. He sighs and grits his teeth and makes his way across the patchy grass, Joss whistling as he follows.

Cal stops a few feet from where she sits, giving himself a moment to readjust to her scent. He's still half drunk from the climb, when the smell of her skin was so deep in his head, he could barely think straight. He nods at her side. "How is it?"

"Fine," Meg says. "Pulled it a bit with that slip, but I think it's okay. The Bane and hot pools pretty much worked a miracle."

He unslings the crossbow from his back and sets it nose-down against a boulder. "We should rest."

"I don't need to rest."

"I do," Cal says, stepping up to take a seat on a rock a safe distance from hers. Upwind. She purses her lips—she doesn't believe him—but he can hear the heavy pull of air into her lungs as she tries to catch her breath.

"You're not even winded," she says.

"Got to pace yourself."

Joss opens his pack and chucks them a loaf of bread and a couple of chunks of cheese. "Cal's got the apples. I better make sure Rilke's not pitching herself into a ravine."

"It wasn't her fault," Meg says. "I'm fine."

"Don't worry." Joss shoulders his pack. "Rest. Eat. Catch up."

Cal flares his eyes wide, the full don't-you-dare-leave-me-alone-with-her death stare.

Joss grins and swivels on his heel.

Neither Cal nor Meg moves, staring at Joss's retreating form. Finally, Meg lifts her head. "You really think Rilke's upset?"

Cal breaks the loaf in half. "She won't be thrilled that she hurt you while I was bellowing orders. She's annoyed that her dad put me in charge."

She regards him for a moment then shifts, turning her back. After peeling off her gloves, she tips water on them to scrub out the fabric.

"You could leave them off," he blurts, and cringes.

"You could tie back your hair."

He snaps his mouth closed and glares at her back. "Doesn't it get hot and irritating?"

"I was going to ask you the same thing."

Cal clicks his teeth, wishing he could think of a snappy comeback, and sighs. "You get used to it."

She stops scrubbing and leans on her elbows. "You do."

Tearing a hunk of bread between his teeth, he chews slowly, his brain hitting high revs. He can't believe they're having this conversation. "People look at faces. They don't look at hands."

"You'd be surprised."

"But wearing gloves all the time just draws attention."

"And wearing your hair like that doesn't?"

"People stare."

"They do. At least your scar makes you look badass."

Cal almost chokes on his bread. "Badass?"

"Like a pirate, or something."

"A *pirate*?" He snorts. "With a hook and a patch and a wooden leg?"

Her body rocks with a soft laugh.

Cal's stomach flips, a pike double twist. "People are nosy and rude. They always want to know, *What happened to your face?*"

"And mutant space dogs won't cut it?"

Caught off guard, Cal laughs. It shakes him from the belly up.

Meg swings to look at him, eyebrows winging high, mouth stretching in a grin.

Cal's stomach flips like an Olympic gymnast. *Gold!* He's glad he's upwind; if the full blast of her scent hit him now, he'd pass out drunk at her feet. "Can't say I've mentioned the space dogs."

She turns away again, wringing out her gloves. "Just tell them you saved a girl's life."

It hits him like a bucket of ice water. If Nellie and the other master rangers hadn't turned up, Meg, Sargent, *and* Cal would have died in that cave too, not just Fergus Welsh.

She tugs her gloves back on and turns and picks up the bread, giving it her full attention. Her bangs fall forward, and Cal's fingers itch to brush them back, tuck them behind her ear.

"Can I ask you a question?" she says, not looking up.

Cal swallows his bread, and it goes down like a hard plug. He doesn't want to stop this. He doesn't want to close the door, but the urge to duck and run makes his heart trip like he's being chased by a swarm of bees. "I thought Joss and Rilke covered everything? Joss said you grilled them for hours last night."

"They were a bit vague when I asked about you."

Meg *asking about him?* He frowns at the rocks. "I'm sure Rilke had plenty of charming things to say."

"She said nothing."

"I find that hard to believe."

"Why'd the rangers take you in?"

He cocks his head. "Like a stray dog?"

"That's not what I meant. Their rules are entrenched — the traditions. You're —"

A fisherman's son. Neither of them says it.

"Well, it wasn't pity," Cal mutters. "Or the goodness of Sargent's heart."

She looks up then, hair falling in her eyes.

If he could just bring himself to reach . . .

"Was he different . . . right away?" Her voice is steady enough, but even upwind, he catches the longing and heartache in her scent.

He can't lie, but he says it softly. "Day and night."

She presses her lips together, exhaling through her nose. "Will you tell me what it was like for you—afterward?"

"It's pretty blurry."

"Did you want to stay? Were you happy? Are you like them? You feel the ley lines and hear the voices?"

"Voice."

"Okay. What's it like?"

"That's five—six questions."

"I have more."

"Meg." He drops his head, digs his fingers into his hair. "Will it make anything better?"

"Did you *want* this?" She gestures at his poncho and gear, her wide mouth puckering with the strain of holding it together. "This . . . life?"

He swallows and forces himself to meet her gaze. "I didn't want to leave the island—that's all."

She stares at him a long time, her eyes glistening, a twitch in her lip. "Me neither."

Cal looks away. *Apologize. It's your fault. What happened*

nine years ago—what's happening now. Everything she's lost, everything she's losing, is because of you.

Reeva interrupts his thoughts. She sends an aerial snapshot of the two of them sitting on the rocks. Meg looks up like she's heard her name called, then looks away. Cal looks up, then back at Meg and frowns. "What have you done to my bird?"

Before she can reply, Reeva sends another image, and Cal jerks to his feet. Rilke and Joss and a zombie deer.

BADASS DOUBLE-BULL'S-EYE

Meg makes more noise than a rhino, charging through the forest after Cal, who is so silent she wonders if his feet touch the ground. How does he do it? What's more galling is the feeling that he's not even running at full tilt like Meg; he's holding himself back so she won't get lost.

A whistle brings Cal skidding to a halt, followed by a sphincter-clenching roar. Meg stops short of crashing right into his back. They stalk toward the stamping and bawling through a thick copse of trees, stripped of their lower branches and foliage thanks to overbrowsing. The whole ridge looks bald. She spots the deer, crashing drunkenly, a tether tied to its back leg. She covers her mouth to smother a gasp.

Another whistle. Somewhere overhead. Meg searches the higher, leafy branches until a large shadow moves, Rilke gesturing. She holds her hand up and signals, displaying three fingers, then a fist, cup, twist, flick. Cal nods. Rilke presents her middle finger—a signal even Meg recognizes.

They creep closer until they're only a few yards from the animal, and the stench hits her. This deer is no less alarming than the buck from Bertrum's kill yard. Missing one antler, it staggers, lopsided. Its eyes are milky white, and three black holes pepper its shoulder, each dripping tarlike ooze. She guesses Spear's men have been up this way—or Spear himself. They've marked the tree with bright pink spray paint all around the trunk.

The markings on this deer are different. It's smaller for one thing, and the fur around the hooves and ears is pale. The snout is shorter too. This must be a Lower Herd deer. The animal's joints jerk, its legs splayed for balance. Its head swings blindly to and fro, and the sound it makes sends shivers down Meg's spine. She notices the rough cutting around the antler stump. They must be intending to come back for the other. Perhaps to test the difference in results?

Bile rises in the back of her throat. "You think it's in pain?"

"It's dead," Cal murmurs, his breath puffing white. "I don't know if it feels anything."

"It's not right."

"It's Nutris."

A flicker in the back of Meg's thoughts has her checking the trees for Reeva. The bird has landed in the tree above them. Reeva cocks her head, and Meg can't help but smile. When she looks down, she finds Cal frowning at her, his lips puckered so tight they're almost turning blue. He looks pale. Without thinking, she reaches to touch his face. At the same time she remembers she's wearing gloves and that touching Cal's face would be super weirdly intimate, he flinches away. "I didn't mean—you look a little washed out," she says, rushing to beat the flood of heat to her cheeks. "Do you need to sit?"

"I'm fine," he snaps, turning his head so his curtain of hair blocks her out. "Why don't you wait back there?"

"I'm not *waiting back there*."

"You promised to follow instructions."

"*Ugh.*" Meg takes a spot behind a thick pine trunk that still allows her a good view. She rests her bow by her feet and gently probes her aching side. Joss drops from a tree on Cal's left, and she stifles a gasp; how did she not see him? He uses hand signals, and Cal nods, swinging his crossbow before him. She can't see Rilke from here, but she hears the cocking of her rifle. Joss slips his machete from his belt. Meg holds her breath.

Boom! Rilke fires. The animal rears, roars, and *boom!* She fires again. The animal doesn't fall, despite the black oozing holes in its forehead. A click and Cal fires a bolt; the arrow slices through the rope holding the deer in place. It staggers two steps clear from the tree, and Joss charges forward and swings his machete. Again, Meg closes her eyes tight and waits for the thud. A soft thump is followed by Rilke's voice. "That is messed up."

Joss kneels beside the carcass and mumbles. Cal and Rilke join him and wait. They're silent for a moment, and then Rilke and Joss both look at Cal. He nods. And Meg can't stand it anymore. What is going on? What are they looking to Cal for?

She steps out from hiding, ready to demand answers, when

a shadow looms fifty yards to the right; another white-eyed deer careens into the copse of trees, a broken tether trailing from its hoof. Her vision blurs as she drops to her knee and snatches up her bow. She sees the scene from above, hears Reeva's belated shrieking, feels the pinch in her side as she reaches back for an arrow. Her vision clears in time to see Cal and the others whirl and scramble for their weapons.

Meg draws and fires, nocking a second arrow as the first finds its home, the shaft buried deep in the weeping white eye. The deer screams and tosses its head, but it doesn't stop running, charging straight for the others. Her second arrow skewers the same spot as the first, the force of impact shoving the beast off balance. Its front leg buckles, and it crashes to one knee with a horrific snapping sound. She closes her eyes at the glimpse of white bone and black blood and Joss swinging his machete again.

* * *

Meg drops her pack and slumps on a boulder. Four hours north of the Western Step, leaning hands on thighs, she catches her breath. Even Joss, Rilke, and Cal are breathing audibly—some small relief: they *are* human. Burntwood sits before them, a rough longhouse buttressed against the mountain.

There are no signs of rangers or Fortune Hunters in the longhouse, no boots under the covered porch, no smoke from the chimney, no light in the windows. The sun is going down, and Meg's courage is fading fast. Fatigue doesn't help. She is starkly aware of being far from the fishing village—far from the rangers' camp and higher in the mountains than she has ever been before. Childhood tales about feral dogs were bad enough—now she knows the truth, and this far from civilization, every shifting shadow and snapping twig hauls her back to the night of the attack.

Cal wanders to the edge of the ravine, catching his breath. Joss shucks his poncho and the layers beneath down to his bare chest, flinging the garments over the rope strung between a post and the longhouse. Something about the makeshift clothesline strikes her as oddly domestic and brings a small smile to her lips. Rilke follows suit, wholly unselfconscious, stripping down to her bra. Meg tries not to stare, but she can't help admire the view. They take turns at a barrel dunking their heads, splashing their chests, the backs of their necks and armpits. Rilke is stocky, a muscled hourglass with a tapering waist and lovely wide hips. Joss is lanky and lean, yet every inch of his pale torso is sculpted.

Meg looks away and sheds her own layers. She wishes she was brave enough to strip down to her bra, but she leaves her tank top in place and frowns at her hot, irritating gloves. The cold air nips at her skin, offering a moment of blissful relief. Joss scrapes his boots on an iron peg protruding from the door post and clomps inside. Rilke picks up her rifle and flashes her teeth, winking. "Dinner," she says, before disappearing back into the trees.

Cal stands at the edge of the ravine staring west at a densely wooded plateau on the other side. Lit by a rare break in the clouds and the sinking sun, he looks tall and solid and made for the landscape and achingly lonely. She opens her mouth to close the gap between them—to see if she can get him to look at her—but hates to interrupt his moment of peace and closes her mouth again. The view is staggering. It deserves silence. Or lovers.

Cal begins to lay aside his gear; he keeps his back to her. She looks while there's no Joss to catch her looking. Crossbow, satchel, belt, and machete. When he hauls his poncho over his head, his shirt lifts. Meg nips her bottom lip between her teeth. The brief reveal of tapered lower back and hips. Meg's stomach performs a hungry little flip-flop. Movement in her peripheral vision—Joss stands at the longhouse window, watching her watching Cal. He turns away, and Meg's face blazes. Was he smirking? That was a smirk. She gets to her feet, grabs her pack, and heads into the longhouse.

* * *

Meg sits with her back to the fire, gloves off as she eats. She feels less nervous now that she's inside and can't deny that the presence of three capable apprentice rangers helps. However, the longhouse isn't huge, and even though Cal sits well back against the wall, there's only a few feet between them. Despite her exhaustion she is hyperaware.

The meal is silent except for the sound of Joss's reverential *mmm*ing. She can't tell if Rilke's pheasant is this delicious simply because of hunger or if it's the addition of the spices she produced with a flourish from the front pocket of her pack. Meanwhile, Cal tucks into a plastic container of some vegetarian dish he's brought with him from camp. They take their time eating, and Meg is too exhausted to think beyond her immediate fears and physical needs. *They are on the mountain. At night. She is spent. Food is good. Cal is here.*

Sargent. Her mother. Jackson Spear. Debts. Deeds. Overdue rent. It all floats out of reach, like slow-moving fish in a murky aquarium, glass four inches thick. Sargent is dying. Her mother must be sick with worry. Meg saw Reeva's sending of Cora's reaction to her note. Jackson Spear is a snake spreading poison. She can't even muster guilt for her lack of emotion; she understands her body is at its limit. She's participated in a couple of survival encounters as a part of an outdoor education unit. It's like her system shuts down to bare, immediate essentials. *She is spent. Food is good. Cal is here.*

"A toast is in order." Joss fills enamel cups with water from his pouch. Rilke retrieves a tin from her pack and unscrews the lid on a peach-colored powder. She sprinkles a pinch in each cup, and Joss hands them out.

Meg cocks a wary eyebrow. "You lacing my drink?"

Rilke snorts. "It's dried miller root with a few grams of Actaeon's Bane. It's like a turbo boost of electrolytes, replenishing nutrients for healing muscle tissue. Dad taught me how to make it. Nutris would love to get their sticky fingers on it."

Meg swirls her cup, watching the powder sink and dissolve. "What does it taste like?"

"It's kind of sweet," Cal murmurs, drawing every set of

eyes with the break of his silence. He drinks until he's drained his cup.

Meg stares at his wet lips and the muscles moving in his throat. *Food is good. Cal is here.*

"I haven't made my toast," Joss says.

Cal holds his cup out, and Joss refills it. Rilke adds another pinch of powder, and Meg notices the exchange of looks between the two adversaries. A thaw in tension?

"How much can you have?" Meg asks.

"One or two will be enough for you," Rilke says.

"What are we toasting? Not being dead?" She bites her lips together. "Sorry, I'm tired, and I have no filter."

"To Meg." Joss lifts his cup. "For a badass double-bull's-eye on her birthday."

"Badass." Rilke grins.

Cal nods, his gaze moving over her face, a small smile softening his lips. "Badass."

They all drink, and Meg shakes her head. "Yes, I'm sure you were all in great mortal peril."

"Rangers take care of each other," Joss says.

Rilke nods. "You were watching our backs."

It's Cal's smile that defuses her protest, his grin widening until a brief flash of teeth transforms his face. Meg is momentarily dazed, glimpsing the eight-year-old boy she remembers from childhood, but that impression is swallowed up by the much more pressing reality of Cal now. Intriguing and compelling and frustrating and . . . She realizes Joss and Rilke have drained their cups, and she and Cal are still staring at each other.

She almost splashes her chin bringing the cup to her lips.

Joss fills the silence, speculating about the whereabouts of Jackson Spear and his men. Rilke launches into a diatribe about Nutris. Meg tries to listen as they discuss the likelihood of keeping Nutris from claiming treaty rights, but her body keeps narrowing its focus. *Food is good. Cal is here.*

Cal is here.

Cal.

She is distantly aware that she should stop staring, that she might be making him uncomfortable. After all, he made it pretty clear when she nearly touched his cheek that he's not interested in her like that. Right now, her body doesn't care. Her system feels magnetized. If Joss and Rilke weren't here, she'd be crawling across the floor.

Cal's lips move, and he cocks his head.

"What?" She shakes herself.

"Are you tired?" he asks. "If you're up for a little exploring, it's worth crossing the ravine."

She looks helplessly at Rilke and Joss, but both of them have night-before-Christmas expressions.

"Bit of a shift away from wanting to tie me up in the barn." She crosses her arms, tucking her hands out of sight. "One badass double-bull's-eye and you're ready to throw me out on the mountain in the pitch dark?"

He strokes his jaw, regarding her with unsettling intensity. "If you really want me to tie you up, Meg, I could take care of that when we get back."

She looks at him sharply. Is he flirting? That sounded like flirting.

"Um, hello?" Joss says. "We're still in the room."

Cal takes interest in a loose thread on the cuff of his shirt.

Meg tries not to stare at the muscles shifting in his tanned forearms. "Exploring?" she says, half strangled. "Out there? *In the dark?*"

"We won't go far, and it won't take long," Joss says.

"It's best seen at night," Rilke adds, leaning toward her with a mysterious smile.

"Um ... Do we have a lantern?"

"You won't need one," Rilke says.

Joss nudges her with his elbow. "We've got your back."

They're up and moving and dampening the fire, hauling on warmer layers and lacing up boots before Meg can even get her gloves in place. Her heart fires scattershot in her chest. The thought of being out on the mountain in the dark is honestly terrifying. How can she say it aloud? Rilke and Joss step outside, the door banging behind them. Suddenly it's just Meg and Cal, and the valve breaks. "I'm not sure if I can do this," she whispers.

Cal's guarded expression drops, growing instantly open and concerned. She moves right into his personal space, pressing her hand to the door to keep it closed. He catches his breath and almost topples back against the wall in his effort to make room for her in the narrow entry. *Don't stare at his mouth. He'll think you're a pervert.* "How are you not afraid?" she whispers.

His hair has slipped back enough to reveal both of his eyes and the very edge of his scar. He doesn't try to hide it, and Meg is careful not to stare. There's only a foot between them, and that space feels fully charged.

"This doesn't scare me." He turns his head to the door, and Meg watches the muscles in his jaw bunch and shift, the hollow below his ear, and the long column of his throat. He turns his gaze on her again, his eyes dark and warm. "It's protected territory, but it will be easier to explain why when we get there."

She presses her hand to her chest. "God, I think I'm having a heart attack."

"I promise," Cal says, "Rift Hounds can't get where we're going."

FALLON'S LANDING

"Careful," Cal says, wishing he could just take her hand and guide her down the step.

Meg shivers, zipping her jacket to her chin and pulling her beanie low over her ears. A drum rolls in Cal's chest, giddy with the freedom of looking at her face. The night must seem black as pitch to her, the sky so thick and low with cloud, no stars or moonlight in the sky. She stretches her hands out and almost stumbles off the porch before finding the step.

"Whoa, hold on," Cal says, lifting his hands as though he might catch her.

"I have Yarra leaf." Rilke comes beside them.

"Yarra?" Meg says, looking right past Rilke's shoulder. "Antonia said it was an ingredient in the paste she used on my wound."

"Cal," Joss calls, nodding for him to come away for a private word.

"It has a few uses," Cal says. "Antiseptic qualities. You can make soap from the bulbs—mash them into a pulp. Dried leaf tips boost night vision. Don't move till it kicks in, okay?"

"I'll be able to see in the dark?" she asks, doubt and wonder warring on her face.

"You pop the leaf on your tongue." Rilke opens the tin and digs out a leaf. "Press it to the roof of your mouth. Let it soak for a couple of seconds. You might need to take your gloves off to feel it."

Meg frowns.

"Just give her the tin," Cal snaps.

"You've got to lick your fingers and wet your eyelids," Rilke says, like she's arguing with Cal.

"Oh," Meg murmurs, chewing her lip.

"Just give her the tin and a bit of privacy."

"Okay, whatever," Rilke snaps, taking Meg's hand and placing the tin in her palm.

"Cal," Joss calls again.

"Wait with her," Cal says.

Rilke gives him a sour look, and Cal jogs across the swath of balding grass to join Joss. Joss is in the middle of smudging his eyelids with Yarra juice and blinks owl-like at him in the dark. He doesn't need much. Most rangers have decent night vision. "What?" Cal mutters.

"Dude," he whispers. "She is so into you."

"Shhh." Cal darts a furtive glance over his shoulder. "Don't be ridiculous."

"*If you really want me to tie you up, Meg . . .*"

"*Joss.*"

"She wants you to tie her up and dip her in honey."

"Don't."

"She's been eyeing you like the last glass of water in the desert, my friend."

Cal groans and covers his face.

"What are you going to do?"

"What *can* I do? *Nothing.*"

"Man, this is killing me."

"*Is it, Joss? Is it killing you?*"

"You're into her, right?"

"God, does it even matter?"

"Cal."

"It's never going to happen."

"Not with *that* kind of attitude."

"Yes, because it's my bad attitude that's holding me back, not my *total inability to endure human contact.*"

Unfazed, Joss opens his hands. "Maybe you could develop a tolerance."

"Maybe. Let's start now with me pounding your face."

Joss sighs, peering past Cal's shoulder at Meg blinking on the porch. He screws his nose up. "You could work around it."

"What?"

"I'm just saying that there might be ways around it if you're willing to be *creative.*" He puts air quotes around *creative* and wiggles his eyebrows.

Cal shakes his head. "Stop. Talking. Now."

Joss lifts his hands. "I'm just trying to help."

"This is unreal," Meg says, with a small hiccupping laugh. She waves at Joss and Cal, an incredulous smile stretching her mouth. *"I can see you."*

"Dude," Joss whispers again, waving innocently back at her. "She can *see* you."

"We're about to cross a ravine," Cal hisses. "It's dark and accidents happen, so I suggest you shut your mouth."

"Just give me the signal if you want us to give you two some alone time."

Cal gives his friend a dirty look and stalks away to the sound of chuckling.

"You know that's a chasm you're walking toward?" Meg calls.

* * *

The ravine is a giddy plummet to an arm of the river, Black Water's Lament, gleaming like a forgotten ribbon dropped among the crags. The air is magnificent, the fragrance of Fallon's Landing, lush, green, cool, and sweet. Cal strides onto the swing bridge, making the planks groan against the rigging, and turns to face Meg. "It's safe."

"You'll be fine," Joss says, patting her shoulder.

"It's lasted five hundred years," Rilke calls from the opposite bank.

"That doesn't make me feel better," Meg mutters, but she squares her jaw and takes a step, knuckles paling around the rope rails.

Cal's grateful to be upwind. The scent of her fear on top of her general scent could make him do something rash. Joss's words tunnel through his head. *Dude. She is so into you.*

Is she?

There's been a bit of staring, but he could be reading it all wrong. She can't be interested after his reaction this afternoon, flinching away from her like she might be carrying the plague. It eats him up inside. Why doesn't she hate him?

Whatever the case, he has a *job* to do and plenty more important things to spend his attention and energy on. Monitoring the Voice of the Herd. Plotting their ascent. Finding the likely refuge of an injured deer. Reuniting Meg with her father at the Rift Stone. Dealing with the fury of the master rangers. *Not* wasting his time obsessing about the one thing he's spent the last nine years avoiding.

Touch.

Touching her.

Meg.

Over and over, he pictures touching her.

Not lust-addled sex-fantasy-type touching—though resistance to this idea isn't so much about virtue. It's simply the sheer implausibility of overcoming the monumental obstacles that would *ever* make lust-addled sex fantasies anywhere near the realms of possibility. No. What he imagines is the simple brush of skin. The hand-to-hand contact. Fingers lacing together. Holding on. Not letting go. Not pulling away at the bolt of life. He imagines touching her face. Cupping her cheek. Tucking her hair back behind her ear. Tracing a finger over one of those hawkish eyebrows.

Connection.

Everything about today reminds him that he will never overcome those obstacles. Her slip on the climb. His flinch in the woods. Besides, whatever happens with Sargent, she'll be returning to the mainland, and then what?

Just like that, the momentary lightness he felt watching her take the Yarra—her uncensored delight as the darkness lifted from her eyes, that giddy-making smile of hers blasting right at him—dissolves before he makes it halfway across the ravine. The internal walls slam back into place, hardening his resolve to keep his distance, keep her safe, keep himself safe, do his job, and get Meg back to Cora.

He hauls himself up the slope of the bridge to Fallon's Landing, where Rilke waits smirking at Meg's careful progress. A hush mutes the thickly forested plateau, that feeling of being watched by ancient yet benign eyes. Mother's Arms, the master rangers call it, on account of the curvature of Black Water Peak surrounding the plateau. Fallon, the matriarch of the Old Herd, sometimes grazes here, and the sense of something otherworldly hasn't lifted from the place.

"Wow," Meg whispers, stepping up onto the plateau. "This is . . . It feels . . ."

Joss nods slowly.

"Just being able to see this without a flashlight or lantern . . ." Meg says, gazing into the forest. "It's incredible. Like being under a full moon."

Joss and Rilke exchange uncomfortable looks; Cal looks away. Meg must realize what she said and shivers at the thought of Rift Hounds. "Okay, so that was a bad comparison."

"Fallon's Landing is surrounded by ley lines," Joss explains, with guilty glances at Cal. He wasn't there when Rilke and Joss explained the workings of the Rift and the energy pulsing through the island because of it. Meg nods slowly, listening with the intensity of someone expecting to take an exam.

"There's a small bottleneck opening near Flint's Gully—" Joss points south—"that leads to higher grazing pastures. Rift Hounds won't cross the ravine, and they can't stand the ley lines. This is as safe as it gets this far from the village." He gestures for Cal to go on.

Cal faces the forest, turning his back to Meg, and closes his eyes, focusing on the vibration in his mind. He finds the Voice of the Herd reaching for him.

"What's happening?" Meg whispers.

"Cal's a good radar," Joss says.

"For the voices?"

Joss chuckles softly. "Voice."

"Big deal," Rilke says. "We *all* hear the Voice."

"What exactly does it sound like?"

"Noise," Rilke says. "Endless bloody noise."

"A vibration," Joss says, a smile in his voice. Cal can picture the expression on his face. "A hum in your mind and your bones."

"Right," Meg says slowly. "And Cal is particularly sensitive?"

"Special," Rilke says.

Cal grits his teeth and considers implementing a ravine accident. "This way."

"He doesn't need Yarra leaf either," Rilke says. "And he has a powerful sense of smell."

"Smell?"

Cal cringes, a rash of heat creeping up his collar. He should have elbowed Rilke's ribs a lot harder when they were sparring last night.

"Which makes him our best tracker," Joss adds, earnest in defense.

"And he can heel and sit and roll over—that's why the master rangers love him."

Meg chuckles quietly.

"People who don't want to be abandoned in the woods or chucked off cliffs should shut their mouths," Cal says, teeth gritted, ducking beneath the stripped branches of an elm tree.

"Sorry," Meg says, stifling her amusement. "Are we going to see the Old Herd?"

He doesn't reply, finding a worn deer track through the trees.

"Won't they run away?"

"They will if you don't shut up," Cal mutters.

"Now, now, pup—" Rilke begins.

A *thud* suggests Joss's fist has connected with Rilke's bicep.

Almost twenty minutes pass in silence, the vibration growing stronger in Cal's mind. A flicker deep in the shadows tells him the Herd is near and has likely already seen them approaching. He signals for the group to stop, sit, and wait. Meg sits on a boulder next to Joss. Rilke sits on the ground, and Cal finds a fallen log. He signals again for the group to keep their eyes on the trees to the west. Meg watches so intently her neck is fully extended, eyes wide as though to let in more light.

It's several minutes before the first nodding deer head appears among the trees, and Cal stops scanning the forest and lets himself watch Meg's face. She leans forward, hands on knees, eyes glued ahead. Then her mouth pops open. Wonder.

BEING SEEN

Meg holds her breath as a doe picks her way across the dead leaves and tangled roots, another following, ears pricked and twitching, delicate nostrils scenting the air. Three more step out from deeper shadow closer to Cal; he sits still as stone. They are tall and elegant, and their fur shimmers with a faint otherworldly sheen. When they swivel their heads, the true wonder is revealed. Light catches in their brown eyes, reflecting back a deep glimmering blue.

Meg claps her hand over her mouth. She looks to Cal, and he nods in acknowledgment and mouths, "Happy birthday."

A giddy, fluttering feeling makes her catch her breath. He did this for *her*.

Digging in his pocket, he produces a small pouch and tugs the cord loose. He licks the back of his hand and sprinkles something over the wet skin and extends his arm, resting it on his raised knee.

"Salt," Joss whispers beside her, offering her a pouch.

The first deer pauses, scents the air, and picks up her pace, heading directly for Cal. She stops before him and blows through her nostrils, nodding before extending her neck to its limit, stretching a delicate tongue for the salt.

Cal keeps very still, not even moving his head, nothing to startle the doe. He forms a striking tableau, the powerful curve of his body, arm extended. All that poised strength. Meg tells herself *any* guy would look dreamy in soft-focus light, in an enchanted wood with tendrils of mist curling among the trunks of ancient trees. For goodness sake, it's like a scene from a movie. The tightening in her belly and the fluttering in her chest are simple chemical reactions amplified by fatigue—her defenses are down. Cal *is* pretty. It doesn't mean anything. He's too serious and introspective, too reserved and complicated and pleased with his own complication, that's obvious, but . . . he's kind and gentle and good. *Ugh.*

The deer inches closer with each lick, lashes sweeping low over her almond eyes.

Cal looks up, his gaze sharpening on something deeper in the trees, his lips part, and his chest swells with an inward breath. Another doe approaches, much taller, her hide a ripple of silvers, charcoals, smoke, and shadows.

"Fallon." Joss gulps and grips Meg's wrist so tight she nearly yelps. "Meg. The salt."

Fallon? Surely they can't mean the doe from the story. Her skin prickles recalling Sargent's conversation with Jackson Spear in the alley by Bertrum's kill yard. *This is for Fallon,* he'd said. She tells herself this must simply be a deer they've *named* after the one from the myth, but her pulse picks up speed, and she fumbles with her gloves, awareness prickling behind her ears. She peels her hand free, licks the back of her fist, and spills a lot of salt trying to sprinkle it over her skin before passing the pouch back to Joss.

The doe paces through the trees, elegant hooves high-stepping through the undergrowth. The other deer lift their heads and watch her approach, and it's their attention that sends an eerie chill down Meg's spine. Nodding like she agrees and agrees, the doe walks up to Cal and tosses her head at the smaller deer, who skitters and trots away. The older doe — at least Meg senses she is older, much older — blows through her nostrils, and Cal slowly lowers his head.

Meg's eyes nearly pop. *What is going on?* Goose bumps flash down her arms and legs. The doe comes close to Cal, extending her stately neck, bringing her nose to the top of his head. Nibbling and nuzzling his hair, she huffs down the back of his collar, and Cal's shoulders begin to shake with suppressed laughter. She rests her forehead against Cal's shoulder, obscuring the side of his face as she leans into him. Meg watches, breath held as Cal digs salt from his pouch. The doe doesn't wait for him to offer it, forcing her nose into his palm with a snort.

Cal lifts his head, a delighted grin stretching his lips. He looks for Meg, and his eyes glisten. Meg's throat grows thick with emotion she doesn't understand. Joss murmurs something in another language, and Rilke sighs.

Snorting and licking her nose, the doe steps toward the others, taking a wide berth around Meg.

Disappointment winds her.

"Fallon," Rilke murmurs, bowing her head where she sits cross-legged on the ground. *Fallon*. The doe nips the shoulder of her coat, dips her snout in the girl's palm, and licks her ear in one fluid movement. She swings her head toward Joss, and he bows too. Meg lowers her head, terrified and hopeful all at once. She feels rather than sees Joss's encounter with the deer, his chuckle and the shift of his shoulders. *Please*, Meg thinks. *Please.*

There's a long pause when Fallon's hooves come into Meg's direct line of sight. She shivers. Fallon is big, much taller than Meg at full height. She can only imagine the damage she could do with those hooves or the nip of her sharp teeth, and Meg would like to keep her fingers. She can't stop trembling. A rush of warm air hits the top of Meg's head, making her whole body clench. The deer nudges her gently, and a warm vibration begins in the back of her skull.

The vibration grows into a living hum, and Meg is shaken, awareness prickling her skin. The vibration is filled with intent, intelligence, attention, a thousand eyes peering into her mind all at once without the slightest sense of violation. Meg looks up slowly, afraid to lose the connection. Nostrils flaring like soft, black patina leather, Fallon scents the air. Scents Meg. Recognition rumbles in the back of Meg's mind: Fallon recognizes her. The collective consciousness of the Old Herd recognizes her. The hum is warm with welcome.

Meg's eyes fill with tears. The hum feels like . . . home . . . her own name . . . a song in her bones, the Voice of the Herd.

The hair around Fallon's nose and eyes is almost white, and long streaks of pale silver run down her neck from behind her ears. She looks ancient and beautiful, as though plucked from a poem, plucked from some medieval tapestry or mythic scroll. Meg feels she is seeing something out of time. She feels fallen out of time herself, as though she has entered a bubble separate from the real world.

The look in the doe's eyes is so knowing and sad, an ache cinches Meg's throat; she is both irresistible and frightening. Her beauty made intimidating by the aura of age and otherness, by the intelligence in her fathomless gaze.

The doe slowly cocks her head. This, Meg knows for sure, cannot be natural. Fallon isn't simply looking. She's assessing her. The brown eyes take in the details of Meg's face, and her nostrils flare. An image blurs Meg's vision, but it's not the fish-eye lens effect she experiences with Reeva. It's clearer, more detailed, rich in color and depth. Cal. His face, his body, positioned exactly as it was moments ago. The image is filled with urgency and want. Meg's skin heats, a full body blush. Can the deer detect her feelings? Are the others seeing what she's seeing?

The image changes. Sargent, his face, his eyes alert, his head turned, a scene from another day. The feeling changes too, awareness and recognition, then a different kind of longing laced with grief, bitterness, and regret. Unwitting tears spill down Meg's cheeks, her throat agonizingly tight. In that moment, Meg feels entirely seen but without shame or a sense of being exposed. Her hidden self, the archives, wounds, and severed dreams. Her subterranean brokenness, acknowledged and somehow eased by being seen. Not healed. Not erased. She is not fixed by this moment. It is simply made more bearable, the burden shared. The ache in her throat eases, the flurry of her pulse. Unexpected peace.

Finally she blinks, and the image fades, leaving Meg startled by what she sees. The forest is altered—or her perspective has altered. As though a film layers her eyes, the world looks superimposed. Everything is different. Fallon is surrounded by a shimmering aura, like a silver mist, hovering around her body. When she lifts her head, the aura shifts with it, pearling like smoke in the cold air. The forest is alive with blue eyes and silver shimmers. The Old Herd, silent and watchful. The trees shimmer; creatures sleeping in and below the boughs show up like thermal radar. Living things. Joss shifts next to her, and she does a double take. The aura glowing around him and Rilke appears silver one moment, then it shifts and the color shifts with it, like oil on water, shot with lighter streaks.

She rubs her eyes, and Fallon turns away, as though the interview is over and she has learned all she needs to know.

"What's wrong?" Cal calls softly, rising from his seat.

"I think my eyes are acting up." She wipes her tears away and suppresses a gasp—his aura is silver-blue, billowing as he walks. She gulps. "It's like I'm seeing double, and everything is glowing, and I can hear them. It. The Voice."

Cal's lips part, but nothing comes out.

"Are you *kidding* me?" Rilke says. "Now *she* has Rift Sight?"

"Wild," Joss whispers.

Rilke groans. *"There's no justice."*

BLACK MOUTH

Cal's head spins, watching Meg blinking, long deliberate sweeps. He knew she was sharing an intense moment with Fallon by the bowing of her back and the trembling of her shoulders. He was almost overcome by the irrational urge to rush to her side and gather her in his arms and—well, there would be no gathering—but this . . . *Rift Sight?*

Did Fallon give it to her? *Can* Fallon give it, like a gift? He's never heard of it. Perhaps her presence unlocked the dormant power, like Sargent had hoped. It reminds him this *is* the first time Meg has been on the island since the attack—she's never been in an environment where the effects could reveal themselves. If she has Rift Sight . . . does she have gifts?

A thrill rushes through him. How can the master rangers deny her claim to join their ranks if she hears the Voice of the Herd *and* has Rift Sight? Wait till Sargent hears. He wants to grab her by the shoulders and shout, *This is it! You can have everything you've ever wanted!* But then he remembers the calculated manner in which Sargent spoke about Meg's potential.

"Meg . . ." he begins cautiously.

She frowns, a shadow flashing behind her eyes at the same time he feels the shadow in his mind. Awareness storms his brain with the touch of Reeva's presence. Fear. Warning. The flap of heavy wings, clapping through leaves and branches — a hectic dive. She doesn't caw. She doesn't need to. They all duck. Thunder erupts: Fallon and the other deer scattering, their hooves pounding the earth.

Cal sees instantly what Reeva sees, and his gut knots tight.

Meg says it first: "It's coming from the east. Fast and — and huge — just huge."

Realization solidifies in a split second to wallop him in the face. He locks eyes with Meg, shock and understanding firing between them. Meg can see Reeva's sendings.

"What is going on?" Joss is on his feet, machete drawn. Rilke cocks her rifle, scanning the dark.

"Boar," Cal says.

Joss swears.

"Great," Rilke snaps.

Meg drops her gloves. "I don't have a weapon."

"Up," Cal says, swinging his crossbow off his back and into his arms. "Now. Move!"

"Up?" Meg swivels back and forth, eyes wide.

Joss pivots, searching the trees for leverage.

"There." Cal points at a beech tree. "Go, Meg. Now!"

Crashing awakens the wood. Meg doesn't hesitate. She runs at the tree and jumps for the "V" dividing the trunk, but it's eight feet from the ground, and she can't get a grip. She shakes her hands out. "Damn."

The ground rumbles beneath Cal's feet. "Now! Joss, help her!"

Joss rushes toward her, grabs her legs, and thrusts her upward with so much force, she lands on her stomach between the branches. That's all Cal sees before a mountain with tusks bursts through the undergrowth. Tall as Cal's chest, it charges, squealing like a rusty nail on tin. Cal's too slow to unlock the trigger. The animal is so huge, Cal produces an involuntary yelp as he lunges out of its path—not fast enough. Fire rips through his thigh, and the pig's granite flank collides with his torso. He hits the mud-packed track, winded. The crossbow digs hard into his side, scraping his rib cage as he tumbles. He gasps for breath, and a chemical waft hits him.

Jackson Spear. The man's been here?

Eyes watering, Cal scrambles to one knee, catching sight of the giant pig pelting toward Joss. The boy only just manages to turn and lift his machete but not in time to swing. The boar catches the blade in its tusks and barges at Joss, lifting him off his feet, driving him into the trunk of Meg's tree. An ominous crunch and Joss screams. The pig reels away, and the boy collapses, clutching his arm. Skidding on its trotters, the boar makes a drunken U-turn. That's when Cal sees the black ooze smeared all over its snout, dripping from its tusks.

"Hey! Hey!" Rilke roars. She yanks at the bolt of her rifle

again and again, but it won't budge. Swearing, she grabs the barrel of the gun and waves it over her head. "Come at me!"

Glistening tusks drip with saliva and black ooze, and the pig wrinkles its snout, sniffing fear and blood on the air. It paws the dirt, winding up for another charge, ignoring Rilke in favor of an easy kill. Cal swings his crossbow up before his chest, rips an arrow from the holster on the back of his thigh, then loads and primes the trigger with detached certainty.

His heart thrums like a motorcycle engine, a deep whir in his chest. Inevitability, repulsion, determination. He tastes the cost already. Rift Sight layers his vision. The creature's aura is wrong, like a red-hot signature pulsing in the air. Joss struggles to get himself upright and out of the way, dragging his useless arm. Rilke leaps and shouts and waves her arms. The boar's pink eyes fix on the injured boy; its squealing drills Cal's inner ear. The charge is hard, fast, and short. The boar crashes, shaking the ground like a felled tree, skidding tusks first into Joss's boots, an arrow buried deep in its eye socket.

There's a moment of relief that Cal can count in seconds on one hand before the shadow of death blankets his senses. The forest and his friends disappear. Darkness like a cold black mouth swallows all. His body vibrates as though gripped by a vice-tight fist. The boar's animus winks into comprehension. Rift Sight reveals it like nothing he's ever seen before, a writhing red smoke, reeking of spite, before lifting away.

Cal curls in on himself, squeezing his eyes tightly shut, though it makes no difference. He is not a spectator. He pulled the trigger. He is an ally. Death needs no words to remind him of this. Nausea boils his guts, and the purge comes hot and hard, and when there is nothing left inside him, he crawls away, unwilling to collapse in his own mess. He doesn't get far before his arms and legs give out, and he falls on his side, rolls on his back, and tumbles into darkness, ice chilling his lungs.

UNSEEN NEGOTIATION

Meg makes an awkward landing, pulse roaring in her ears. She almost keels to the right before steadying herself against the tree. The double vision has lifted, and there's no vibration in the back of her head. The world looks dimmed without glowing auras. Joss groans and swears and struggles to his feet, his arm hanging limp at his side. Sweating and pale as milk, he gestures at the boar, a huge mass even lying on its side, as though assuring her she's safe. The arrow is impossible not to look at with half the shaft deep in the animal's skull; there must be eight or nine inches buried in there. Right through its brain.

Surprisingly, there's very little blood; one red teardrop dribbles from the eye socket. Worse is the black ooze smearing the creature's snout and dripping from its tusks. "Was it dead already? Is that Nutris poison?" She shivers. It seems impossible for something that had moved with such fierce speed, mere seconds ago, to be instantly and absolutely dead.

"Damn it!" Rilke roars, wrestling with her rifle bolt. *Boom!* Meg yells and ducks.

"Watch it!" Joss shouts.

Rilke dumps it on the ground and kicks it away. "Useless!"

Joss retrieves his machete and without warning drives the blade into the animal's neck. Meg claps a hand over her mouth—the blood is red. Joss bares his teeth. "I'd say it's fed on one of Nutris's poisoned carcasses."

Meg groans.

"Pigs aren't picky," Rilke says as she joins them, her breathing labored. They're all panting, Meg realizes, like they've been running uphill. They turn at the same time, looking for Cal. His legs stick out across the track, twitching slightly in the leaf mold. Dread plunges through her, and she rushes toward his body.

"Wait," Joss calls.

She hesitates. Did she miss something? Is Cal badly injured? She takes slow steps past the brush to find Cal flat on his back, eyes open, staring sightless at the forest canopy, his body rigid, except for the irregular tremor moving through his limbs. She sinks slowly to her knees beside him. "Cal?"

A rip in his pants midway up his thigh reveals a bright red gash. Deep and bloody with a black smear at the edges. "The tusks—" Her voice cuts out, unable to articulate the rest—they can see for themselves. They're thinking it already. *Is he poisoned? Infected? Could it kill him?* She scans the rest of his body, but there's no clear evidence of injury, unless he banged his head or broke his neck, but would his arms and legs

243

be twitching if that were the case? She goes to touch him, and Rilke's hand falls on her shoulder. "Don't."

"You think he's contagious?" She looks helplessly from Rilke to Joss.

"No." Joss sags, supporting his injured arm. He raises his eyebrows, as though Meg should have figured it out already. "He doesn't like to be touched."

She stares at nothing, letting the words settle inside her. It makes sense. All the avoidance, distance, and silence, the careful coordinating to ensure Joss and Rilke were the ones to help her traverse difficult spots in the track. The flinch in the woods. Her throat gets thick. "But if he's having a seizure, we're supposed to turn him on his side. He could swallow his tongue. And shouldn't we clean the wound? That black stuff can't be good."

Joss crouches beside her, grimacing with the effort. "Just . . . give him a few minutes."

"I don't think this is that kind of situation," Rilke says. "It was a direct kill. He pulled the trigger."

Meg looks at her sharply. "What do you mean?"

Rilke screws up her lips. "We might be here awhile."

"I don't understand."

Rilke looks to Joss.

"I want to help," Meg says.

"I don't think you can," Joss says, his worried blue eyes glassy with pain.

Meg balls her hands into fists, hating the bareness of her own skin. Cal's unseeing eyes unnerve her. His hair has fallen back from his face, and she should feel guilty for staring. He wouldn't like it, not with his scar exposed like this, but she can't look away. Not because he's beautiful to look at, though he is—more than she even suspected. It's the sense that something dark and important is happening, an unseen negotiation with forces beyond a dead pig.

"Cal?" she murmurs, leaning closer. "Can you hear me?" Her breath mists the air over his face. She freezes. The temperature is icy—as though the cold is coming from him. She reaches her hand out over his chest, and Joss makes a warning sound in his throat. Meg doesn't touch, but there's no denying the chill is radiating from his body. "Why is he so cold?"

Joss swallows. "It's just something that happens."

"This is normal? His lips are turning blue."

"Normal's a bit of a reach. It's just . . . something that happens when . . . Look, it's really not my place to explain."

"When *what* happens?"

"Cal's a private person," Joss says. "It's not *my* business to be sharing *his* business with outsiders."

"Outsiders?"

"I'm not trying to be a prick."

"Tell her," Rilke snaps, hand on her hip, the other in the air. "She's one of us. More than he is. She should know what we're dealing with."

Joss glowers.

"Please," Meg whispers.

When Joss says nothing, Rilke releases a gust of air and folds her arms. "Cal senses death. It makes him cold.

245

Sometimes he passes out. It's worse when he does the killing. Which makes him a useless hunter. The whole thing is a total pain in the ass."

"Death?" She looks back and forth between them. Joss looks thunderous. She recalls the way Bren called on Cal to touch Sargent. *It's uncertain.* Her mouth dries. "You mean he senses when someone is about to die?"

Rilke nods. "That too."

"You mean . . . he senses death as a—a thing in itself, an entity?"

She nods again, curling her shoulders a little.

Meg shudders, and her eyes dart toward the shadows, a faint ringing in her ears. "Is the touching issue part of it?"

"I don't know," Rilke grumbles. "Guy's got issues up to his eyeballs."

"It's the flip side," Joss says, brow knotted. "He senses death by proximity, touch intensifies his awareness, and it also makes him sensitive to the life in others."

"The *life*?"

"Like energy or electricity," Joss says, gritting his teeth and clutching his shoulder. "Like a—a blast of . . . life. Apparently it's pretty intense."

"What about Reeva, or Fallon?" she demands, searching for understanding. "Touching them doesn't seem to worry him."

"Animals are different," Joss says, sighing. "I don't know how, but they are."

"All this is from his bite?"

Joss nods.

"Is it like this for everyone who's been scarred by the Hounds?"

"Only from bites and the gifts are always different," Rilke says, her voice sullen. "Some people get no gifts."

Meg stares at Cal while her brain spins like a hamster wheel, faster and faster but getting nowhere. Does she have gifts? Will her father live to find out? Will her mother believe *any* of this? How will she get to the Rift Stone if Cal and Joss are out of action? Would Rilke take her? She has to get to her father. Who will find the injured deer if Cal can't and the Hounds come? What if they come anyway and they're all up here, too damaged to defend themselves? She digs her knuckles into her knees and grits her teeth. "Cal's turning blue, and we're sitting here doing nothing."

Joss looks near passing out, himself. He shakes his head, uncertainty warring behind his eyes while Rilke watches on, stone-faced.

"People *die* from hypothermia," Meg snaps. "What if death is sitting here waiting for us to let that happen?"

"Meg," Joss says, warning in his voice.

"We have to stop the bleeding and warm him up." She shifts an inch closer, and the grass and leaves beneath her knees crackle and snap. Frost. Not wasting another second, Meg slips her fingers inside the ripped hole of his pants and yanks, tearing a wide strip of fabric all the way down to his boot. The seam at the bottom resists, but Rilke offers her knife, and Meg takes it with a grateful glance.

"Careful," Joss whispers. "Try not to . . ." He trails off as

Meg cuts the fabric free and slips it under Cal's thigh.

She ties the binding, flinching at the cold emanating from Cal's twitching body, panicking at his nonresponsiveness. She sits back, hot-faced. "Nothing."

"Give him a minute."

Cal stops twitching. His eyes roll back, and his hands relax.

"That's not good," Rilke says.

"No." Meg shoves up Cal's poncho and yanks open his shirt. His chest is icy. She lays her ear on his heart. Nothing. She tells herself she's overreacting. He'll wake any moment, and she'll be red with humiliation, mauling Cal without his consent in front of his friends. Her breath hitches, and a small sob escapes. He's so cold—he's freezing. She can't feel his heartbeat. *Cal. Please wake up.*

Nothing happens. No one speaks.

She jerks upright and shifts closer, blocking out Joss and Rilke. Supporting Cal's neck, she tilts his head, her thumb brushing the indent of his scar. She depresses his chin, pinches his nose, and seals her mouth to his, exhaling forcefully. His chest rises, and she positions herself, hands crossed on his heart, ready to begin compressions. Eyes closed. Head bowed. The taste of him in her mouth.

Bump, against her palm. "Oh."

She turns to find Joss's frightened eyes, knuckles white where he clutches his damaged arm. Rilke looks shaken.

"I think . . . " she says, then flattens herself on Cal's chest, pressing her ear to his heart once more. *Four, five, six, seven . . .* then *bump.* She squeezes her eyes closed and wills another. *Three, four, five ... bump.* "There's a beat," she whispers, tears swimming before her eyes. "It's slow, but it's there." She fans her fingers and presses a little harder, her tears spilling to wet his skin. *"Please."*

Cal jolts, his chest arching off the ground with a violent gasp. Meg yelps and scrambles off him. Hazel eyes blaze at her in the gloom, and Cal clamps his hands on his chest where her face and hands had been only moments before, as though reclaiming his territory.

She buries her fists beneath her armpits and wills the earth to swallow her.

"Cal." Joss shifts beside her. "I'm sorry. I told her not to."

Rilke scowls. "She saved his life."

Cal's chest rises and falls like it's being pumped by an aggressive bellows, his eyes wide and fierce and terrifying. "Spear," he says, his voice raw. "Jackson Spear."

"We know," Joss says. "We saw the black goop on the tusks."

Cal rasps. "He went to Fallon's Landing."

"How can you tell?" Meg asks.

"He caught his scent," Rilke says, frowning.

"Are you sure?" Joss grimaces. "I opened the boar's neck. It looks like it fed on one of the carcasses, then wandered up here."

"You're missing the point." Cal struggles up onto his elbow, letting his hair cover the side of his face. "He broke the treaty. He crossed the border. We have to get a message to Bren."

ADDER'S BREATH

The rain has set in, and Burntwood is no longer empty. Smoke curls from the chimney, lighter than the coal-dark sky, and a lantern glows in the window. The stink of kerosene muddies Cal's sense of smell. Whoever it is, they're not rangers; rangers wouldn't waste lantern oil when they have fire. He stops walking and grits his teeth, the pain in his thigh amplified by aggravation. If it's Spear and it turns into a confrontation, then what? He can barely hold himself upright. His eyes stray to Meg.

She pauses a few feet to his right, her gloves back in place. She's been avoiding him since he came to. He knows he frightened her, passing out. He hasn't killed anything that big in a long time; he has no clue what would have happened if he'd been by himself. Meg's touch dragged him from the pit. Fire to combat the frost. Life to push back death. He can still taste her. He wishes they could have five minutes alone so he could thank her, explain, apologize, but she won't meet his eye.

She hasn't mentioned seeing double or any trouble with her vision since he woke. They haven't talked about Rift Sight or Reeva's sendings and what it means that she has access to the Voice of the Herd. She must be boiling with questions and frantic with worry about her dad, and now their plans are in ruins.

"Who do you think it is?" she murmurs.

"They're not ours." Joss nods at the lantern in the window. "Not rangers."

She gives him a narrow look. *"Outsiders."*

"Not going to let that go, are you?"

Cal frowns, realizing he's missing something. "It could be Spear."

Rilke frowns. "You can't *tell*?"

"All I can smell is kerosene."

"Meg, hold Joss," Rilke says, grumbling as she unsheathes her machete.

Meg takes her place supporting him, her mouth falling open. *"You're not going to kill them?"*

"No one is killing anyone." Cal hobbles forward. "Not unless you want a repeat performance of Cal's Amazing Frost Coma."

Rilke and Joss perform a double take, and Cal blushes behind his hair; he never refers to his "sensitivity"—not directly. After Meg's intervention, it strikes him as a significant oversight on his part. If they're to survive the dangers on the mountain, it's his duty to be up front about risks and liabilities. "We keep things civil."

"Also, killing people is bad," Joss says, his voice husky with pain.

Cal flattens his lips and slices a look at his friend, but he guesses it's a good sign Joss is still cracking jokes.

Rilke shakes her head. "I wasn't going to *kill* anyone."

"You pulled out your machete," Meg says.

"For *protection*, Meg."

"It could be Spear," she whispers. She told them in the barn about what she saw on the dock—Jackson Spear dragging the desperate father behind the shipping containers.

"Good point," Rilke says. "Happy to kill *him*."

"Spear is the master rangers' problem," Cal says. "Ours is staying alive and getting Meg back to the village."

She balks. "What?"

"I can't track like this." Cal gestures at his thigh. "I can't get you to the Rift Stone. Neither can Joss."

"Rilke could take me."

Rilke nods.

"I can't get Joss back to camp without Rilke," Cal says, fighting to keep his voice calm. "Besides, once we get a message to her dad, let him know what's going on—Bren will have to turn around . . . I'm so sorry, Meg."

Rilke casts a grim look at Meg.

Meg gapes. "Sargent won't survive without the Rift Stone. Joss told me about how powerful it is. He said it was the—the strongest source of the ley lines' power."

Cal can't look at her and speaks to his boots. "There's no way I can track the injured deer, Meg. Even with Actaeon's

Bane, that would put us hours behind. It's nearly full moon, and if the deer's not dealt with, the threat isn't one or two Hounds that might break through—it could be the whole pack. You don't want your dad near the Rift if that happens."

"You're not the only ranger on the mountain," she says, her voice swinging up. "You're not the only tracker."

"It's about *speed*, Meg. Not skill. It's about getting it done quickly. The master rangers won't reach the summit till tomorrow night. Even if they sent trackers ahead from their side of the mountain, they'd never get there in time to kill the deer and end the distress signal. That was our job. Me to find it, Joss to put it down and close the Rift."

Meg stares into the middle distance, realization growing behind her eyes.

"Can we get inside?" Joss moans.

Cal nods at Rilke. "Remember, we come in peace."

"For now," Rilke says, leading the way to the longhouse, clomping loudly up the porch to give warning before opening the door. A cloud of greenish smoke billows out, engulfing her. She ducks and covers her mouth. "What the hell?"

"Wait here." Cal limps up the steps, hackles rising at the alarming waft of toxic fumes. Three men sprawl before the hearth, and a too-big log smokes in the fireplace, blue flames spitting around it. They've tipped solvent on the wood to keep it burning, and while it smells terrible, it's not the main cause for concern.

"What *is* that?" Meg calls.

"Stay there." Cal edges past Rilke, his head already

swimming with the fumes. Heavy bodies stir on the floor; he recognizes them as the Nutris Fortune Hunters.

One of them struggles to his feet and rocks dangerously before the hearth. "Spear said there would be no one up here."

Cal spots the incriminating little tablet smoking in an enamel dish in the middle of the floor. He stomps on it, grinding it beneath the heel of his boot.

"Adder's Breath?" Rilke leans heavily in the open doorway, coughing. "Where on earth did they get *Adder's Breath*?"

"We're legal," the young Fortune Hunter says, pupils blown out, the whites of his eyes veined red. He raises his hand as though delivering a valid defense. "We're ... legal. This is—this is legal research and development ..."

Cal swipes the smoldering Adder's Breath from the floor.

"Hey!" the Fortune Hunter cries.

Cal kicks equipment out of the way to a chorus of complaints as hard objects collide with soft limbs. Carrying the offending dish outside, he holds it away from his body and tries not to breathe. Meg and Joss recoil and cover their faces. He flings it over the lip of the ravine, and on his way back inside, he grabs the hatchet from the woodpile, fantasizing about driving it through each of their thick skulls.

"Cal!" Meg calls after him.

When he reappears, the men flinch at the sight of the ax. Rilke pauses in her efforts to force open the rusty cabin windows, eyes wide. Cal limps to the hearth and swings at the log with a grunt, part exertion and part disgust. Sparks shower the room, and the men shout and scrabble away, slapping their legs to keep the embers from catching. Cal lifts the still-burning log from the hearth, reeking of kerosene, the ax-head buried deep in the fuming wood. He shakes it at them. "You're Hunters and you don't know how to light a goddamn fire?"

The young Hunter raises his hands, wobbling on his feet. "Thought we could mask the smell."

"Honestly." Rilke scowls, forcing open another window with a crack of rusty hinges.

Cal swears and shakes his head. "Mainlanders."

"There's no need to be like that." The Fortune Hunter sways beside the hearth and pats Cal's shoulder. He doesn't survive the second pat. *Crunch.* Cal punches him in the face, and he collapses backward across his companions' legs. There's a lot of shouting and flailing. Stalking outside with the flaming log on the end of his ax, Cal knocks it into a barrel of stagnant rainwater, jerking his face back from the rush of putrid steam.

"Way to keep things civil," Rilke says.

Cal blows through his lips and digs his hands up into his hair, blood roaring in his ears. His leg burns like it's on fire, the fabric of his pants wet with blood and clinging to his skin. He balls his fists. The enormity of all his mistakes hits him anew like an avalanche. How did he let this happen? He should never have taken Meg to see the Old Herd. He wanted to give her a beautiful moment, share the wonder. It's her birthday. Now he's ruined everything, and the distress signal won't be stopped, and the Hounds will come, and Sargent will die, and he will be responsible . . . again. *This proves everything they've ever said about you—you worthless piece of—*

"Shit," he mutters.

No more punches.

He needs to send word.

Bren will know what to do.

He barely turns his thoughts to Reeva, and she lands heavily on the roof of the cabin. She doesn't squawk or caw or grumble; she just looks at him with a steady unblinking gaze. She shows him Meg kneeling beside his seizing body, the blueness of his lips, the frost on his cheek, the stillness. Meg shoving her hands up inside his shirt, her hair falling forward. The images are saturated with grief and fear. "I'm okay." He strokes her beak. She leans into his touch.

He wonders if Meg is picking up on Reeva's sendings, and he glances over his shoulder. She's helping Joss sit on the porch. She doesn't look at him.

"Find Bren. Find his scout. Show them everything." He pictures the wound on his leg, Joss's broken arm. The dead boar. Jackson Spear. The Nutris Fortune Hunters on the cabin floor. "Don't let him see Meg."

She produces a soft grumble, and Cal fishes a mint leaf from his pocket. Nipping it in her beak, she holds his gaze, and he feels her fear. "I'll be fine," he murmurs. "We're safe here."

Reeva lifts off, swooping low over Meg before rising above the trees and out of sight.

BLACK VEINS

"Hold still." Meg feeds the bandage under Joss's shoulder where he lies groaning on the longhouse cot. Cal has the Fortune Hunters herded by the hearth while he checks their belongings for contraband. Rilke digs through her kit and groans about the medical supplies she should have packed but didn't. Struggling to concentrate, Meg fumbles the bandage, her hands shaking with fatigue or fear, an argument raging in her head.

What are all those orienteering medals for, if not for this?

She doesn't have a map or a compass. Even if she did, a compass wouldn't work here.

You have a natural sense of direction and distance.

She doesn't know the Upper Slopes.

Take Reeva.

Reeva isn't here. She has no idea when the raven will return. Besides, how could she take Reeva? She's Cal's scout.

She likes you. Connects with you. She'd help you find the injured deer. You know she would.

Then what? She almost shouts it. She has no idea how to close the Rift. Would killing the deer be enough? Are there words to recite? An incantation? How will she know if it worked?

Joss's bare chest is clammy, and she's practically hugging him as she winds the bandage around his back. He groans and twists, pulling it from her grip. "You're making it worse," she says.

"*You're* making it worse." He screws up his face and groans. *"I'm trying to help."*

Rilke looks up. "Nice bedside manner."

She's about to retort when a loud screech makes them all jump. A jumble of ragged feathers tumbles through the window and off the sill to make an untidy landing on the flagstone floor. Joss lifts his head from the cot, glassy eyes filled with wonder. *"Otho?"*

The tawny little owl staggers drunkenly, balding wings held out from its side. Rilke scoops him up, eliciting shrieks of outrage, and settles him gently on the wooden rail that forms the head of the cot. Otho snaps his beak.

"I thought he was blind?" Rilke says, sucking a nipped finger.

"Mostly." Joss reaches to stroke the bird's belly. Otho coos and shuffles from foot to foot, the long feathers at his ankles like an old man's tattered slippers. "He doesn't leave camp much these days."

"He came all this way?" Meg says. "How did he know where to find you?"

"Reeva," Cal says, his raspy voice catching Meg's immediate attention. He looks almost as gray as Joss, his face sheened in sweat.

"Cal," she says. "You need to lie down."

"I'm nearly done." Confiscated Nutris products and weapons lie piled on the floor at his feet next to the sawed antlers of the Lower Herd zombie deer. The Fortune Hunters sit herded in the corner looking on with bleary eyes, rubbing their sore heads and muttering at Cal's rough treatment of their gear. The toxic fumes have cleared with the windows and door flung wide, and Meg can't stop shivering.

"Here." Rilke nudges her aside and finishes the job of bandaging Joss without a single murmur of protest from the patient, who gives her a look that says, *See?* Rilke takes a cloth from her pack and spills water over it, mopping Joss's face with no-nonsense efficiency. Otho snaps his beak again and tips too far forward, overbalancing and face-planting onto Joss's forehead. "Honestly," Rilke mutters.

Joss grunts, scrunching his face as the bird hoots and flaps and slides onto the narrow bed. A pained chuckle rumbles from his throat. "Silly old thing." The bird settles in the corner of the cot by the cabin wall, burrowing into the crook of Joss's neck. Joss leans his cheek on Otho's feathered head and closes his eyes, agony etched on his face. Meg's chest aches, and she thinks of Reeva, praying she's safe.

"There's nothing else in there," one of the Fortune Hunters

says, gesturing at the pack in Cal's hands. "We only had the Nutris paste and Adder's Breath."

"How did Spear get his hands on Adder's Breath?" Rilke demands. "We stopped making it years ago."

"Rangers made it?" Meg pulls herself up on the cot opposite Joss.

"Used to bait thermal fissures when the Ministry for Primary Industries tested for toxic emissions."

"What on earth for?"

"Feral dogs *appear* like mutant hellhounds to those who breathe the toxic fumes." Rilke bounces her eyebrows. "It's hallucinogenic."

"Really?"

"No, 'course not. Just gets people high."

Meg shakes her head. These were the lies she grew up on. No hiking on the Upper Slopes without a ranger and a ventilator. Rare stories of Fortune Hunters' close encounters with hellhounds were explained away as the mistakes of novices who failed to wear a ventilator and didn't recognize a feral dog. The stories were rare because few survived.

"Spear says Adder's Breath lets you see their true form," the Fortune Hunter says. "He says regular exposure to Adder's Breath increases your sensitivity to their approach, improving your chances of escape and survival. We have orders to audit the Upper Slopes, and we didn't want to go into Rift Hound territory disadvantaged."

"Sounds like Spear wants you dead," Cal says. "And there's

no way you're going anywhere near the Upper Slopes."

"We have orders."

Cal shakes the pack and hears clinking. He unzips the front pocket and feels a collection of glass vials and thickly folded paper. He pulls out three vials of blood and a map. "What is this?"

"Test samples, taken from the deer before we applied the R and D paste. The lab likes to contrast the data."

Cal frowns at the vials, sniffing as though something about the scent confuses him. After dumping them back in the pocket, he opens the map. Meg glimpses the main tracks to the summit, all the way to the Rift. Three red crosses indicate points of significance, but she can't make out what. Cal, however, looks outraged. "Where did you get this? Who gave this to you?"

"We were told the Old Herd likes to graze near those sites. We're trying to be efficient."

"These are sacred sites. You're not going anywhere near them." He turns to the fireplace, intending to burn the map, but loses balance and staggers sideways.

Meg jerks to her feet, and Rilke is there too, both of them with their hands out but neither prepared to touch Cal. Rilke drops her hands first. "Sit your ass down before you knock yourself out on the hearth." Rilke spears her finger at the remaining cot.

More frighteningly, Cal doesn't argue. He drops the pack and the map and limps to the bed, gritting his teeth. He lowers himself like a woman in labor, huffing and baring his teeth, unwilling to bend his leg. Through the tear in his pants, his thigh is red and swollen to his knee, and black veins snake beneath his skin from the site of the wound. "Cal," Meg murmurs. "That looks bad."

"It's too hot. I feel like I'm burning from the inside."

"Can you take some of this off?" she asks, too afraid to touch him. He wrestles the poncho up and nearly crashes against the wall. She grabs the hem of the fabric and pulls it up over his head. His thick shirt hangs open from where she tore the buttons, and she keeps her eyes on his face, blushing at the memory of lying on his chest. He struggles to get his arms free of the sleeves, his face growing pale. She catches the edge of the shirt and helps him shuck it off over his head. It's more of a collapse than a lying down.

Rilke unlaces Cal's boots, touching only the cord and the rubber sole without flinch or complaint. Cal gets his good leg on the cot with an agonized groan, and Meg lifts the other using the torn pant leg as a sling. He lies with an arm flung over his face. His torso glistening with sweat, his chest rising and falling hard and fast as he pants through pale lips.

Rilke scowls at the mess of Cal's leg.

"You seem to have enough to deal with here," a Fortune Hunter says, getting slowly to his feet. "We might as well be on our way and out of your hair."

The other two Hunters reach for their packs and the antlers. Rilke moves fast, sweeping her rifle from its prop by the door. "Stop right there."

"We've done nothing wrong."

"One of your zombie deer has jeopardized the life of our head ranger. Another broke free of its tether and nearly trampled us on the Ridgeway. Cal here was gored by a deranged boar that had been feeding on one of the carcasses you left out on the mountain. Now his leg is infected. You deliberately expose yourself to hallucinogenic drugs and expect to be released onto the mountain with weapons?"

"Accidents happen."

"These aren't accidents," Rilke spits. "It's reckless endangerment. That alone puts you in breach of Black Water law. No way we're letting you cross the ravine."

The Fortune Hunter snarls, "We've been nothing but reasonable."

"Sit down." Rilke yanks the rifle bolt to punctuate her point, but it doesn't shift. Her moment of hesitation is all the Fortune Hunters need. The man closest grabs the rifle and yanks it toward him, Rilke with it. He slams his forehead into her face with a horrific crunch and spray of blood, breaking her nose.

Joss and Cal shout. Cal tries to get back to his feet but crashes into the wall. Meg ducks and scrambles for the confiscated weapons. Too slow. Another Fortune Hunter gets there before her. He swipes a rifle from the corner and rams the butt into the back of her shoulder, driving her into the flagstone floor, dislocating the joint. Lightning fills the socket, and Meg screams. Her vision turns black for a moment, and she struggles onto her side. Rilke is on the floor, cupping her face, blood streaming between her fingers. Joss is screaming abuse from his cot. The Fortune Hunters move fast, gathering their belongings.

"The map," one of them hisses. "Get the map."

"What about the blood?"

"It's in the pocket. Hurry."

"He took the Adder's Breath."

"Doesn't matter. We'll make do. We're running out of time anyway."

"I think it's working. Everything's glowing."

"Move."

They scramble out the door, leaving Meg and the apprentice rangers groaning in pain.

SILVER MIST

The cabin flashes in and out. Inky shadows, sliced with angry reds and toxic yellows. Fire in his wrists and ankles. Fire in his thigh. Color and light burn his eyes. Everything aches. His body shakes and shakes. A desert strips his throat, and in the far distance comes the sound of someone screaming and screaming. He can't bear to hear their pain, and he backs away, ducking low through the mouth of the cave.

A hot pool bubbles beneath an icy fall of fresh water. Reeva waits on a rock, watching him with her head cocked. He plunges his head beneath the flow, drinking, gulping, then gasping for air before drinking again. Then he slips into the deep liquid heat of the spring. He doesn't even have to tread water. The mineral properties so buoyant they hold him up. He becomes blissfully weightless, and the pain ebbs. He could sleep here in this pool and never drown.

"Cal," Meg calls from the shore. In his peripheral vision the moonlight casts her limbs in silver. He catches the sensuous curves of her arms and legs and the soft brush of fabric slipping to the ground. She's a silver mist in the corner of his eye, wading toward him, sending ripples to kiss his face. He just has to turn his head and he'll see her coming to him. Anticipation sends little rockets of pleasure through his skin. He'll wrap her in his arms, pull her against his chest, taste her mouth.

"Cal."

If he can just turn his head.

"Cal," she whispers, her breath on his face. "Rilke needs to treat your wound. She has Actaeon's Bane."

Meg?

Did he say it? He can't tell if he said it. It's hard to swallow.

Meg?

"We've got to tie you down. Sorry, but this is going to hurt."

Rilke?

The silver mist evaporates. The pool goes. The waterfall. The cave. Reeva too. Gone. His throat is a desert again, and everything aches. Pressure on his wrists and ankles . . .

DO SOMETHING

Meg wakes to the spit and hiss of damp wood on the fire, the fug of unwashed bodies, and a catalog of pain. Her shoulder aches, tight and tender from the resetting, an experience she hopes never to repeat for the rest of her life even with Rilke's firm yet gentle care. Coaxing her eyelids open, she winces with the effort, confused by the fading light at the window and a shadow looming over her.

"Hey," Rilke whispers, touching her elbow. "Can you keep watch? I have to get some shut-eye before I pass out."

"What time is it?" It was dawn when she lay down; she only meant to close her eyes for a minute, but it looks like dusk outside.

"Maybe sixish?" Rilke gestures at the fireplace, where a pot of something simmers on the hearth. "Try to eat. Wake me if . . . I dunno, the cabin catches fire or the mountain implodes. Actually, don't bother."

"Rilke, I'm so sorry. You should have woken me. Now we've lost the whole day."

"Can't carry these two by ourselves. Might as well rest up till the cavalry comes." She pats her swollen nose gingerly. Her eyes are bruised and puffy. Meg feels terrible for leaving her to take care of things by herself.

Movement attracts her eyes to Cal's cot. Reeva preens on the rail above his head, her wing extended, nibbling delicately at her feathers. "She's back. Did Bren send a message? Have they turned back to camp?"

Rilke shrugs, unfolding a bedroll. "Not my scout."

Meg looks to Cal, but Rilke shakes her head.

"His fever broke a couple of hours ago. He'll be out for a while yet."

She nods and bites her lip, her heart contracting with relief to see the slow rise and fall of Cal's chest. The arm slung across his stomach is raw at the wrist, the bindings now loose on the floor. Her ears ring with the memory of Cal's agonized cries. It seemed to go on for hours, his powerful body convulsing and writhing, his face contorted and mottled red. His color seems almost normal now except for deep shadows beneath his eyes. She knew he was going through something far worse than she experienced as the poison in his wound warred with the healing work of Actaeon's Bane.

Rilke lies down between her patients' cots, her dark skin almost gray with fatigue. She tugs her oilskin coat up over her shoulder and offers Meg a rare weary smile. "You make a good ranger, Meg."

Surprised, Meg can't think of what to say.

"You keep calm, use your head." Rilke's eyes fall closed as she speaks, soft and slurred. "You've got good instincts. I see why he likes you. Personally, I think you could do better."

Goose bumps flash across Meg's skin, and something flutters in her chest. "He what?"

But Rilke starts to snore gently, and Meg sighs.

Reeva drops onto the flagstones. Two hops, a flap, and she arrives on the peak of Meg's raised knee. Meg presses her skull back against the wall and holds her breath, the prick of Reeva's talons poking through the fabric of her pants. Reeva watches Meg, and Meg's vision blurs with the picture of her own face. Not a flattering mirror. Meg's bangs are matted into spider legs, her eyelids are puffy, and she generally looks like she hasn't slept in a month. Reeva rubs the edge of her beak on Meg's knee, one side then the other, before settling in to stare at her intently. Meg sits very still, enjoying the weight and warmth of the bird. Like when Fallon touched her, looked at her, licked salt from her hand, she feels frightened yet seen, picked for the team.

A picture of Cal fills her mind, a bird's-eye view of him sleeping on his cot.

"I know," Meg whispers, recognizing Reeva's sending. "He's sleeping. He's getting better."

Reeva shows her Cal's face again, filling the image with impatience.

"We can't wake him," she whispers. "He needs to recover."

Reeva switches her weight from one foot to the other and

pecks Meg's knee, making her jerk a little with the sharpness of her beak.

"Hey," Meg warns.

A new image fills Meg's thoughts: Bren's troubled face staring intently at a sleek brown bird, perched on a boulder. A falcon. Understanding makes her breath come quickly. Bonded scouts can't communicate with other rangers, but they can convey their sendings to other scouts. This must be when Reeva reached the master rangers and shared Cal's warning with Bren's scout. "That's right. Good girl. You showed Bren. They'll turn back to camp. They'll be safe."

The raven produces a creaky door sound and shuffles again from foot to foot. The image pans out, and she sees more clearly now, Bren pointing up the mountain, men picking up her father's stretcher and continuing on the path.

"Wait," Meg gasps. "They didn't turn back?"

Reeva shows her again: Bren pointing up the mountain.

"Rilke," she calls softly. "Rilke . . ." But the young ranger doesn't stir, her snoring growing louder. Meg's breathing comes a little shorter, and she cranes her neck to see if Joss is awake. He's lying with his face pressed into Otho's chest, his deep breaths fluttering the owl's tawny feathers. The rising tide of urgency makes Meg's hands shake. The master rangers aren't turning back. They're still heading to the Rift Stone despite the risk. It's unthinkable to imagine her father prone and unable to defend himself.

"Reeva," she groans. "What am I supposed to do?"

Instinct keeps her from waking the others and telling

them what Reeva has shown her. She knows they won't agree to her tracking the injured deer alone, and she can't ask Rilke to come with her. The girl hasn't slept, and she'd never leave her patients alone. The prospect of hiking up the mountain in the fading light makes her tremble. Cal might use the Voice of the Herd to track the deer's location, but it's his sense of smell that gives him speed and accuracy. What if Meg just gets lost in the dark and the Hounds come and tear her to pieces? What if she falls in a crevasse and breaks her neck? The counterargument surges up inside her. Sargent is going up there. Her father. And Rilke's father, Bren. All their friends. They're willing to risk everything for her father's survival.

"If I found the deer and put it out of its misery," she whispers to the raven, in a desperate rush, "that would kill the distress signal and neutralize the Rift, right?"

The bird cocks her head and flashes an image of Meg's own face back at her. Is that a reply? Does the bird understand her?

She could barely bring herself to leave the longhouse when Cal suggested exploring Fallon's Landing. But knowing Bren and the master rangers are still headed to the Rift Stone makes her pulse frantic with the need to *do something*. Not because of the deed to the house or the money or the overdue rent—all of which strikes her as hopeless and irrelevant. They'd never make a sales agreement with Jackson Spear. The *do something* is specific to her and Sargent.

"Reeva, I need your help."

SPILL SHADOWS

Everything is black except for a pinprick of color in Cal's mind. His leg feels huge and heavy, a beached whale swelling in the heat at low tide. He saw one on the east coast of the island when he was a child. His father took him and Meg to see it in his trawler. The carcass was so swollen and taut beneath the midday sun, Cal had been afraid it would burst. It did, days later, Meg said, like the split seam of an overcooked sausage. Sargent told her off for making him cry.

He wishes he could find his way back to the cave with the waterfall and Meg wading toward him from the shore with possibly no clothes on, but there is no water anywhere. None in his body. None in the world. It occurs to him that this might be hell. Darkness. Heat. Thirst. Pain. What is he paying for? Fergus Welsh. Sargent. Meg and her losses. It strikes him as fair except he is a coward and he gives all his focus to the pinprick and the flicker of light, longing for escape. When the aperture widens from pinhead to peephole, he thinks of Reeva. Is this Reeva? Is she sending . . . ?

Reaching for her in his thoughts is like leaning on a closed door that suddenly gives, sending him tumbling forward, away from the heat and the dark into light and color. His pain is gone and so is the heaviness in his body, even his thirst. Stretching his arms, he forgets the burning sensation in his wrists and finds his muscles tired yet elastic, light and expansive. A blue-black shimmer in the firelight. Wings. He has wings. He lifts his shoulder, and his feathers catch and spill shadows. The room is warped at the edges, a fish-eye lens perspective, stretching and contracting. He looks down at his own face frowning in sleep on the longhouse cot. A rush to his head leaves him woozy; he goes cross-eyed taking in the sharp length of his beak. Reeva's beak. Reeva's wings. He touches the feathers, running his beak through the splendid filaments.

Movement by the hearth attracts his attention. Meg sitting up against the wall of the cabin. A magnetic urge tips him toward her, and he drops to the floor, talons clicking on the flagstone. Without pausing to consider the mechanics, he hops past Rilke snoring softly beneath her oilskin coat, Joss breathing deeply on his cot, Otho tucked like a ball of feathers against his neck. Stretching his arms, he flaps once and lands on Meg's knee. She catches her breath and stares at him — at Reeva — in shocked wonder. Firelight flickers in her yellow-green irises. Her pale cheeks are flushed, and shadows track beneath her eyes. Her dark hair has come loose from her braid, her long bangs slightly matted from sleep and sweat and rain.

It occurs to him that he is touching Meg. Touching her without pain or torment, no electric jolt of life. He wants to curl up against her neck like Otho, but while she looks delighted, she also looks wary.

Pain and heat and darkness tug at the back of his thoughts, but he gives all his attention to the sensations in Reeva's body, the urgency coursing through her delicate bones, determined to remain in the moment. He sees Reeva's sendings, Bren with his falcon, their decision to continue on their mission to carry Sargent to the Rift.

Tension ripples through Meg, her eyes widen, and her lips part. She darts panicked looks at the others and blinks rapidly until she comes to a decision and looks at him with pleading in her eyes. She shifts her weight, attempting to rise. With a momentary hesitation, she presents her arm to him, and he hops on as she rises to her feet, swaying slightly. Biting her lip, she holds him away from her body and presents him with the rail of Cal's cot, but he doesn't want to leave her. Instead he turns and picks his way up her sleeve to her shoulder.

Meg makes a soft strangled noise of surprise yet doesn't try to dislodge him as she moves quickly and quietly about the room collecting supplies and stuffing them in the front pocket of her waterproof poncho. Finally, she turns for the door, slipping out into the early evening light. The chill air ruffles his feathers, and Meg mutters quick, urgent words. Sargent blooms in his thoughts, her father's face, his bandaged head, his closed eyes. The image too is saturated in urgency, fear, longing. This is Meg. Meg is sending this to Reeva. There's a question in it. A *help me. Please.*

Panic courses through Cal's body, and he flings his wings open with a caw of protest, flapping up and away. He finds a landing on the edge of the roof. He peers down at her desperate face. *No.* He wants to shout it at her, but his throat produces a harsh, rasping noise like a rusty saw. *No.* Her lips pull and squeeze, making small, sharp shapes with angry whispers. She bunches her fists and raises her eyebrows and shakes her head and sends Sargent's image again. If a picture could sear a hole through his head, it would be this one, like a hot poker. *Please,* her whole body begs.

The wind breathes a warning, a chemical waft caught on the breeze, more chilling than mountain air. Jackson Spear. His throat rumbles, and he pushes back at Meg with an image of the Fortune Hunter's face. The white teeth, the humorless smile, an image from the campfire meeting. She stiffens and looks sharply over her shoulder. He wants to shout at her to hide, but his voice is a hacksaw. *The woods. Not the cabin. Hide. Meg, hide.* He can't form a picture to send, but she's moving anyway. She darts to the porch and grabs her bow where it leans in the corner. She takes Joss's machete too. Her quiver. He lifts off the roof, gathering air beneath his body with great claps of his wings. Rising quickly above the tree line, he directs his gaze toward the scent. Spear is crossing the ravine.

Meg sprints across the plateau toward a thicket of shrubs, ducking out of sight. Cal shrieks warning, and it reverberates across the mountain. Jackson Spear climbs the rise from the bridge and strides toward the cabin with his rifle at his side. Cal thinks of his body, lying prone on the cot—his friends sleeping unaware—but he can't bring himself to leave Meg.

When Spear passes Meg's hiding place, she doesn't hesitate, disappearing down the slope to the swing bridge. Cal throws himself after her, the scent of Jackson Spear gnawing in the back of his head. She's halfway across the ravine, running so hard the bridge bounces beneath her feet. As soon as he passes the boundary of the cliff, the ravine yawning beneath him, an electric sting ripples over his feathers, wrenching him from Reeva's body. Whiplash. Suspended by nothing, he is momentarily lost in space. He watches Meg reach Fallon's Landing, Reeva swooping above her, then an invisible force yanks him backward. Like a fishing line reeled back and back, light, color, shadow.

Slam.

He lands in his body, in the heat and the thirst and the pain, his chest bouncing up from the cot with a dry gasp. The door thumps open, and Jackson Spear fills the entrance, rifle raised before him. Rilke lurches upright, but there's no weapon in reach. Joss groans, cracking open bleary eyes.

Otho hisses like a cat.

Jackson Spear presents his teeth with the slow shake of his head. "And I thought *I* was having a bad day." He turns to eye Cal and sneers at his injured leg. "Yours is about to get worse."

LIGHTNING BUG

Meg runs until her legs shake, until her knees seem to slip in their sockets and she loses feeling in her feet. Can lungs cramp? The pain in her chest is sharper than glass. She stumbles to a halt, dropping the coat and weapons she's carried—too afraid to waste any time to even swing the strap of her quiver over her shoulder. Panting, she leans against the rough trunk of a pine tree, bent double as stars implode in her peripheral vision. She is far deeper into Fallon's Landing than they came last night. She guesses she's been running for at least as long as they walked. That must be three or four times the distance.

The light has almost disappeared, and her depth perception is shaky. She sinks to the ground, thick and springy with damp pine needles, and shakes out her stolen stash from the pouch in her poncho. A pocketknife and flint tumble into her lap followed by Rilke's tin of Yarra leaves. She doesn't hesitate to unscrew the lid and slip a prickly leaf on her tongue. She licks her fingers, wipes them across her eyelids, and blinks hungrily, almost sobbing as the shadows separate and details grow clearer. She has four thick strips of beef jerky, two apples, a stale half loaf of bread, and the last wedge of cheese.

After she refills the pouch, she leans against the tree and closes her eyes. She feels Reeva close by. The bird doesn't squawk or make any effort to communicate with Meg, but she feels seen, and knowing the raven is there makes sitting in the dark forest a notch less terrifying than it is. She can't hear past the clamor of her pulse or her panting to detect the approach of danger. She tells herself she can have the amount of time it takes her to eat a single strip of jerky before she needs to get back on her feet and figure out what the hell she's doing.

It's tough and salty and pretty horrible, but it's protein and it's safe, and she is so hungry she's sure it's half the reason she has the shakes. Eventually her pulse settles and her breathing evens out. She could drink a river, and when the salt kicks in, she's going to be crying for water. For better or worse, she's fairly sure it won't be long till the sky opens and she'll be cursing the rain.

If only she hadn't slept so long. If only she'd asked more questions about hearing the Voice of the Herd, controlling her Rift Sight, or how to ensure the closing of the Rift. If only she'd been able to grab her pack and a drinking pouch and more food from their supplies. She's exactly where she was afraid to be, on the mountain at night. Alone. *Except for Reeva,* she tells herself. She wonders what Jackson Spear is saying or doing right now, how Rilke and the others will respond, and whether Cal has woken up.

She can't help imagining confrontation. Every interaction with Jackson Spear has left her feeling threatened, from the moment he stepped in to "help" them on the dock to the bald display on the deck of the ferry when he emptied the desperate father's wallet. In Bertrum's kill yard. Even watching him speak at the rangers' camp when he didn't know she was there felt threatening. She cannot fathom why Sargent would enter into any sort of agreement with a man so ruthless and unscrupulous.

An uncomfortable thought niggles in the back of her head: *Maybe because Sargent is also ruthless and unscrupulous?*

"Reeva," she whispers. The raven's presence in her mind grows clearer, and the bird drops from overhead and lands by her feet. An image of Cal flashes in Meg's mind's eye, his unconscious body on the longhouse cot. The image is filled with question and worry. "I know—you want Cal. I'm sorry. Please stay with me. Please help me." Her voice hitches, and her eyes prickle. She's begging a *bird* for help? Does she really believe this can work? "The deer. Reeva, where is the injured deer?"

Her thoughts flash with an image she recognizes. A memory from her meeting with Fallon, seen from above. Meg's bowed head. The ancient doe licking her hand. "Not that deer," she whispers. "The injured deer, the one Cal was supposed to track."

She sees Fallon again but with more urgency, the image like a shout.

A question forms in the back of her thoughts. "You mean . . . the Voice?"

Reeva digs her beak in the pine needles, tossing her head up to flick the dead foliage at her leg. Yes? Yes. A shiver rattles Meg's exhausted body, but she tries to focus and quiet her mind. She doesn't know what to focus on; her mind is a three-ring circus. Then a weight grows at the back of her head like someone pressing warm hands to her skull. A vibration that makes her shiver again, a vibration that builds to a hum. She is filled with the sense of being seen, her ears fill with a sound like white noise, and she hunches a little. *Help me,* she thinks. The vibration intensifies. Instinct tells her this isn't the time to articulate in words what she wants, so instead she tries to relax, ignore the circus of panic, and open herself to the Voice.

Awareness fills her. She pictures herself like a pinprick of light. She is as small as a star seen from light-years away. A lightning bug on the mountain. That's when the image forms, the island seen from above. She is a pinprick of light pulsating softly in the landscape, but she isn't the only pinprick. Her mind fills with pinpricks pulsating back at her. Fallon, the Old Herd. She is seen. Then she hears it, a discordant thread in the Voice. Distress.

Scrambling to her feet, she tugs the poncho over her head and jams her gloves in the pocket. No one is going to see her hands out here. Reeva lifts off. The raven stays below the leaf canopy, winging ahead, landing in the low branch of a tree where she looks back at Meg and waits. Meg slings the quiver over her head and settles the strap across her chest, just as thunder rumbles above her and the first drops of rain pat the top of her head. She grabs her bow, draws a deep breath, and walks on.

FIERCE GLANCES

Cal glares at Jackson Spear, wishing he was sitting up, wearing a shirt, and not nauseous with pain and the aftermath of fever. His leg throbs; his head throbs. His throat is so dry it hurts to swallow. He searches for Reeva in his mind, but there's no sign of her. He can't make out Meg anywhere in the room. Spear fills the entranceway, damp air rushing in around him. Rain patters the roof, and Cal shivers with the charge of adrenaline. The Fortune Hunter swings the barrel of his rifle in a long arc, taking in each of the apprentice rangers. He settles on Cal.

"Where is the girl going?"

Cal looks to Joss and Rilke. *What's happening? Where's Meg?* They look at him with blank shock. "What girl?" Cal croaks.

Spear makes a sound of irritation at the back of his throat. "Sargent's daughter."

"She went back to camp," Rilke says, her body poised to spring where she crouches by Joss's cot.

"Hours ago," Joss says, groaning as he tries to sit up, exchanging a look with Rilke that makes Cal want to shout, *No!* It's the same poised intent. They think they can take Spear.

"Really?" Spear says. "Then who did I just see running toward the ravine?"

"What do you want with Meg?" Cal rasps.

"I would like to do my job without any more interference from children." Spear tips the barrel of the gun toward him. "You detained my men illegally. I'm here to remind you that we have a right to defend ourselves. So if you pull that kind of stunt again, there *will* be repercussions. Now, get up. You're coming with me."

Rilke rises to a crouch and then stalls when Spear cocks his rifle. She lifts her hands. "Take it easy."

"Stay where you are," Spear warns.

"His wound is barely closed."

"I don't need him to be healthy, just alive and on his feet."

"For what?" Cal demands.

"You're the kid with the scar? I need a guide on the mountain."

"You've already trespassed," Rilke says. "That won't happen again."

"I signed a contract with your head ranger that says otherwise." Spear digs in his pocket, not dropping his aim, and tosses a folded piece of paper on the flagstones at Rilke's feet. Cal struggles up onto his elbow, his head spinning.

A scowl deepens on Rilke's face as her eyes scan the document. "I thought my father tore this up."

"I have copies."

Joss snatches the paper from Rilke's hands, and Otho almost falls off the bed with the jostling. "Full access to protected territories?"

"What?" Cal shakes his head. "That's not—"

"Your dad signed it," Joss says to Rilke. "So did my mother and the other master rangers."

"Get up and get dressed."

"*I* know the mountain," Rilke says. "Take me."

Spear narrows his eyes at her. "You have Rift Sight?"

A muscle bulges in Rilke's jaw.

"Didn't think so." Spear swings his barrel around the room. "You?"

Joss scowls.

"You destroyed my supply of Adder's Breath," Spear snaps, his full attention landing on Cal again. "Now you get to be my Rift Sight."

When he doesn't move, Spear points his rifle at the wall above Cal's head and pulls the trigger. Joss shouts and Otho tumbles down the back of the cot with a shriek. Rilke ducks and Cal flinches.

"Now!" Spear shouts.

Dressing is slow and painful. The wound is closed but tender and pink. Rilke helps him bandage his leg and find spare pants and a dry shirt in Joss's pack. All of it is accomplished in silence except for Cal's rasping breath and Otho's distressed squawk. Rilke darts fierce glances, and he wills her to read his mind. *No. Don't fight.* But doing nothing isn't Rilke's style.

She fills his drinking pouch with infused water and puts all the spare food in his pack. "Thanks," he murmurs.

Spear opens the door with his foot and waits for Cal to pass him. That's when the violence comes. The scuffle and grunt of Rilke's attack, punctuated by Joss's shouts, Otho's hoots of alarm. Cal almost stumbles off the porch, turning too fast, woozy-headed and weak-limbed. Rilke struggles to wrestle Spear's rifle from his grip. Joss lunges awkwardly for another weapon. They're too slow. Spear strikes, boot to hip, buckling Rilke, and a head butt sends Joss staggering backward against the wall. Before Rilke can fully right herself, Spear smashes the butt of his rifle into the side of her head. Cal shouts as she collapses, shuffling toward her. Spear slams the door closed behind him and spits, "I'm running low on patience, boy. Don't be the reason I kill them both."

* * *

Spear keeps his distance, rifle trained on the back of Cal's head, but that's not the cause of Cal's plunging dread as they cross the ravine and hike deeper into Fallon's Landing. Meg's scent, though fading in the rain, is fresh enough that he can differentiate between today's venture and the faint trail of last night's visit to the sacred forest. She's headed for the Rift. He thought he was dreaming, hallucinating about being inside Reeva's body, but his scout is nowhere to be found. He can't feel her in his mind. The thought of Meg on the mountain alone makes his chest tight. At least Reeva will warn her if . . .

He shudders and reaches for the Voice of the Herd, and the vibration thrums through his skull, an active noise, focused. Their attention centers on the distress signal coming from the injured deer. Almost as though they anticipate his search. They know relief is coming. Meg intends to finish his job; they're guiding her.

The moon will reach its fullness tonight, and he should have killed the deer by now; they're out of time. She won't make it. The desire to turn around and club Spear with his own rifle ignites hot sparks in his skin. This is Spear's fault — Cal wouldn't have lost an entire day of tracking to injury if it wasn't for Nutris greed. The injustice of it makes him want to scream. "If we die tonight, it will be your fault."

Spear grunts. A cold laugh escapes, grabbing Cal's attention. Spear swings his pack under his arm. He pulls a small foil package from the front pocket. He taps two tablets into his palm and presents them to Cal. "Neural blockers to suppress pain and a hybrid stimulant developed by Nutris to support the central nervous system."

"Why should I trust you?"

"You're no use to me unconscious. Look, I have a job to do, and I'd prefer not to die in the process. You're my guide to the Rift and my eyes if the Hounds come."

"Coming up here isn't part of the audit. Why jeopardize the treaty? Risk your life?"

The man purses his lips, considering. Finally he says, "We have an agreement with your head ranger that will benefit

Nutris *and* your community, but we're on a tight schedule. So take the bloody pills and get moving."

"How does breaching the treaty benefit anyone? This is protected territory for a reason. Blood shed on sacred ground makes the Rift unstable. You could draw the whole pack. How does that help Nutris? How does that help the Lower Herd or the cull? More than half of the ranger community is up on this mountain tonight; Sargent wouldn't agree to anything that would endanger their lives or the Old Herd."

Spear gives him a long, assessing look, and Cal knows there's something the man isn't telling him.

"Sargent understands that ensuring one's legacy comes at a price."

Cal shakes his head. "At the price of people's lives?"

"Move."

BLUE PINPRICKS

Meg's thighs burn, and the threat of cramp nips at her calves. It's been hours since she ran from Burntwood; she must be getting close. It's not just desperate hope that makes her think this. It's the vibration in her mind and the tingling in her chest. The intensity level of connection and awareness has been steadily growing, like she can feel the life of the mountain beneath her feet.

This is what anchors rangers to Black Water. Despite the danger and the promise of horrors, this is what makes walking down the mountain, climbing in a boat, and sailing away so unlikely. She's not sure if it mollifies her feelings about Sargent abandoning her to the mainland, but exhausted and terrified as she is, she *feels* the magnetic pull.

Gritting her teeth, she trudges on, keeping her eyes on the narrow track, so steep in places the bedrock has been carved into steps. Sweat lathers her throat and chest, and her shirt clings to her back. She shed her raincoat an hour ago and tied it around her waist. She's grateful now for the cooling drizzle falling on her head.

Finally, the track curves left, and the close face of the mountain retreats before a broad and thickly forested plateau. She groans as she crests the lip of the track—flat ground—and then collapses on the dirt, her bones heavy as lead, muscles weak as rice paper. She blinks at Reeva, perched in the tree above her. The bird stares into the forest, beak slightly lifted as though scenting the air or listening for something. Meg closes her eyes, rain pats her face, and the Voice of the Herd hums in the back of her head. She wonders if the rangers carrying her father have made it to the Rift, if the power in that place can mend what Actaeon's Bane can't.

Reeva sends Meg an image of the surrounding landscape. Meg hears the thick flap of the raven's wings but stays in the vision, watching the earth tip and turn as the perspective rises high above the forest. Catching her breath, she digs her fingers into the dirt to remind herself she is anchored to the ground. The vast plateau is carved from a crooked lower tooth of the mountain. The trees hem a huge grassy basin three quarters of the way around the bowl of the tooth, giving the impression of an irregular amphitheater set against the rock face with one large stone formation laid out like an off-center stage. Meg feels the significance of the place through the image, and her skin flashes with goose bumps. Though she sees nothing that resembles a magical portal—or what she imagines a magical portal might look like—she knows in her skin, it's here.

Movement at the eastern edge of the basin makes her sit bolt upright. Rangers. Somehow she holds the connection with Reeva, though her heart belts hard in her chest. They made it. There's a sense of military urgency about their approach, rifles ready, knees slightly bent, caution and high alert. Bren directs the rangers to fan out around the edges of the forest; some train their weapons toward the off-center stone, others aim into the forest. Bearers carry Sargent's stretcher, and the image tilts counterclockwise, keeping her father as the focal point. Meg wishes Reeva would land. She's so dizzy she has to draw her knees up, prop her elbows, and hold her head.

The vision cuts out, and Meg gasps at the ground beneath her boots, waiting for her body to find its center of gravity. She stalls for the sound of Reeva's return, the announcement of her wings, but nothing comes. *Reeva?* An image blasts back at her: Cal, unconscious on the cot at Burntwood. Meg scrambles to her knees with a strangled cry. "No, Reeva, don't go!" The bird fires the image at her again, filling it with such longing Meg sinks back onto her heels in despair. She's going. She's delivered Meg to the Rift, and she's going back.

The rush of anxiety is almost as giddy-making as the raven's aerial visions. Meg staggers to her feet, awareness of Reeva fading as quickly as her dread rises and she realizes to what extent the bird's presence in her mind had been warding off fear. Instinct compels her to dig her gloves from the pouch of her poncho, and she fumbles them over her dirty fingers. She curls one hand inside the other and presses them tightly to her chest. A prayer? An affirmation? She grabs her quiver and bow and turns in the direction she hopes leads to Bren and the grassy basin. The Voice of the Herd shrills in the back of her head like a fire alarm.

West. West. Her feet defy reason, following the signal away from the rangers to the right. Instinct tells her to arm herself, and she reaches over her head to pull an arrow free from the quiver. Catching the shaft below the fletching, she holds it with her bow, jogging now down a gradual incline, watching the uneven footing. Shadows whip at the edges of her sight, a monochromatic blur as her footsteps vibrate up into her skull, pound, pound, pound, heart and feet.

Quiet thunder rumbles beneath her boots, and she almost stumbles with the echo of hooves ahead. *Not Rift Hounds,* she tells herself. There's no howling. A strange metallic smell hits her a split second before her foot hits something soft yet heavy and she falls, smacking into the dirt. Her bow bounces out of her grasp, and arrows clatter from the quiver, spilling around her head. Winded, she rolls and clutches her chest, the earth rumbling beneath her. She blinks her eyes open, but her vision is warped with a second layer. A blur of heat signatures and silvery auras stream through the trees. The Old Herd, fleeing.

Close beside her a man lies on the ground staring at her, his mouth slack with surprise, but his outline makes no sense. He has no aura, no silver glow. His eyes are blank, and his face is bleeding. His neck. His back, ribbons of fabric and flesh, and Meg clamps her eyes closed, pushing herself away, crawling, scrabbling backward until her hip collides with the trunk of a tree.

The metallic tang is blood. The man is dead. His blood is on her clothes, her gloves. Oh God, she touched her face. Her hands shake violently, and she dabs at her cheek with the back of her wrist—is it wet? She can't tell if it's blood or sweat on her glove; the stink is too much. The man isn't wearing an oilskin coat or a ranger's standard-issue poncho. A black baseball cap lies a few feet from the body. Realization slices through her: one of Spear's Fortune Hunters. All the way up here? Trespassing. Dead.

She blinks furiously, trying to clear her eyes, then stops. Losing Rift Sight right now would be bad. Very bad. The Old Herd are slipping away through the trees, but the Voice of the Herd is still a blaring alarm in her head. Her mind can't face the obvious conclusion—what else could cause injuries like that? What else?

A light winks among the trees, a bluish pinprick amid thick shadows, bobbing slowly toward her. Her bow is several feet away. Her arrows are scattered across the ground. To her right, the Fortune Hunter's rifle lies abandoned in a tangle of weeds. Warning blares through her nervous system, *boom, boom* in time with the thrashing of her heart. She can't seem to find her legs. Instead she lunges on her side, slipping a finger over the nylon strap, yanking the weapon to her chest. It's heavy, and there are side bolts and catches that she doesn't recognize. Rolling up to sitting, her spine grinding against the rough trunk of the tree, she holds the weapon up before her and tries to find the blue pinpricks in her sights.

Stench floods in like molasses, slow and heavy and thick,

obliterating every other smell, almost suffocating. A whimper drags up her throat, her eyes dry from staring. It's the smell that triggers sense memory. She is eight years old again, in the cave and completely unprepared. A massive shadow ushers the blue lights through the break in the trees, with it the harsh sound of wet breathing, rattling in its throat. The shadow swarms, forming hulking shoulders, a barrel chest, tapering to narrow hips, and the tail swings like a whip. The massive head lowers to the ground, lips rolling back to reveal black fangs.

A growl rumbles up from the deep chest, growing thick in its throat before grinding through its teeth. The stench rolls over her like a hot wave, erasing Meg's senses. Fear siphons strength from her arms, shakes it from her marrow, leaving the rifle limp in her lap. Meg is lost in old nightmares come back to life. The Rift Hound tips its head back and howls. A star shaker, if there were any stars to see. A slick, upward hurtling note, carving its way across the mountain. She squeezes her whole body to keep the sound out.

The Voice of the Herd shrills through her skull. The Rift Hound paces toward her, stopping to sniff at the torn body of the Fortune Hunter. Something wakens inside her, and she fumbles the rifle back into place, pulls the trigger. Nothing happens. Panting through her nose, she yanks the bolt back and forth. In answer to Meg's agitation, the Hound clamps its jaws around the fallen Hunter's shoulder and tosses the body like a chew toy out of its path. Meg pulls the trigger, and again nothing happens.

A high-pitched keening rises, and her brain is slow to

register the noise is coming from her. She produces a strangled sob, and her numb fingers paw at the catches on the side of the gun. Her gloves, her goddamn gloves. Something clicks, and with a dry gasp, she yanks the bolt once more, and it shifts, slipping into place. She pulls the trigger, and the sound is hard as a punch to the face. The Hound shrieks, and its shoulder buckles, the skin shimmering like a bruise, absorbing the wound and smoothing again like liquid.

A short scream sears her throat, and she yanks the bolt and fires again, yanks the bolt and fires again, yanks the bolt and fires again. Each shot enrages the Hound, sending it stumbling back a step, but each wound closes, and Meg screams and sobs and scrambles to her knees, ready to swing the rifle like a club. The heavy thud of boots heralds a rush of bodies into the little clearing. Rangers. Three of them, their auras shimmering, machetes swinging. One, a woman with a crossbow, fires almost six feet in the wrong direction, and the men swing in wide arcs, with the precision of a ballet dance, yet they don't seem to even face the direction of the slavering beast.

A horrific realization skewers her back to the tree. They have no idea where the Rift Hound is, but they can hear it . . . and they must be able to smell it. "Left!" she screams. "It's right there! Three feet to the left, by the log! Ten o'clock. Ten o'clock!"

The woman fires exactly where Meg directs, and the arrow lodges in the animal's neck, eliciting a furious roar that makes Meg light-headed. Somehow the arrow holds, and the shimmering skin contracts around it, but it doesn't dislodge the bolt. The ranger in the center of the swinging machetes lunges forward, using the arrow as his guide. The blade connects like an ax hitting wood, hard and deep. The Hound produces a strangled scream, and black ooze bubbles from its mouth, slashing the air with its paw. A second woman steps forward, swinging her machete in the same place, severing the beast's head from its neck. Shadow explodes from the wound, a gobbling black smoke, dissolving the enormous shoulders, buckling the barrel chest, billowing inward, until nothing is left but a lingering reek.

The woman with the crossbow turns and offers a hand, hauling Meg to her feet, but Meg stumbles, her knees too weak to hold her. She leans back against the tree, panting.

The woman ducks her head to make eye contact. "We need to get back through the ley line."

Meg can't find words; the whole forest seems like it's on a lean, the air charged with electricity. The Voice of the Herd hasn't calmed. The distress signal is a full-scale red alert blaring in the back of her skull. She stares past the rangers gathered staring at her, wiping their blades in the brush. Beyond them, deep in the trees, blue pinpricks wink in the darkness, and she jerks backward, slamming her spine into the tree.

The rangers whirl, machetes raised.

"How many?" the woman demands and squeezes Meg's forearm.

"I—uh . . . two," Meg rasps. "Two."

"Run," the woman commands. "Now."

Meg's legs work a miracle, and she runs. Her lungs heave

air in and out of her aching windpipe. She has no sense of direction, relying completely on the rangers to direct her path. When the stench folds around her, she begins to sob, and the running becomes a sprint, dodging branches, leaping over sudden rocks and hollows. A sound like boulders tumbling together rumbles behind her, the Rift Hound's throaty growls, and the thump of heavy paws.

The clearing opens through the trees, and Meg and the rangers burst into the basin, the grass sloping quickly. The air distorts before her face, resistance like passing through an invisible film. A sting flashes across her skin, making her catch her breath, and she stumbles, hitting the ground in a painful clap of limbs as she flips from stomach to back. She rolls to try to haul herself upright, gagging as she gasps for air, the stench filling her lungs. All around her cries go up, and she knows her death is coming.

Above her the Rift Hound skids to a halt, its claws gouging the grass. Meg can't look away, her muscles frozen in terror. The creature extends its neck toward her and growls, its breath making the air warp. She waits for it to lunge and tear, but it paces back and forth before releasing a roar that turns her bones to milk, and a black fog swallows her vision. Her face hits the dirt.

BLOOD-SOAKED

Cal feels the ley line coming and picks up his tired feet. He knows this place well. The lodestone that marks the final leg of the hike to the Rift. It juts into the path, an intersection of two lines, like a wedge of living power. Exhaustion and pain make him dizzy; he needs to recharge. Plug in. Spear pauses on the track below him, but Cal doesn't wait, almost running the final few yards, despite his limp, and collapsing against the boulder with a groan.

The relief is instant, the hum rumbling into his arms and chest, down into his legs. He closes his eyes, soaking it in, willing life into his bones. He never would have made it this far without the Nutris meds, but they're nothing on this—this is life. His moment of relief is undermined by a collision of senses: a chill seeping up his legs, something wet and sticky beneath his palm, the scent of blood on the air.

He draws back slowly and examines his hand, finding his

skin smeared red. "There's blood on the lodestone," Cal growls, holding his palm up for Spear to see.

The Fortune Hunter barely glances at the evidence, his rifle poised as he scans the trees. He knows as well as Cal what it means and what may be stalking the mountain.

Turning on the spot, Cal searches for signs of struggle before he finds exactly what he feared. A few yards farther on, legs stick out across the path. His gut shrivels until his brain grasps the details: the scent isn't Meg's, they aren't her boots, they aren't even ranger boots, but this is bad. Very bad. "There's a body."

"One of yours?"

Cal won't go any closer, not while he's this weak. The last thing he needs is to pass out in the presence of death with Rift Hounds on the loose. He leans as far as his muscles will let him, craning his neck for a glimpse of the blood-soaked black fatigues and Nutris puffer vest. Shredded. He shudders and looks away. "One of yours."

"Was he shot?"

"Torn apart." Cal sniffs at his palm. "But . . . this isn't his blood on the lodestone . . ." He sniffs again, and he turns slowly to face Spear. "This is Sargent's blood."

Spear raises his eyebrows and lowers his gun. "He said you were good."

Cal inhales again. Blood smells like blood, yet the identifying scent, the signature details, are missing. Sargent's scent has always been a confusing absence, like the man's been erased in some way. "How is this here?"

Spear draws a long breath, exhaling as he comes to a decision. "Sargent gave me his blood and a map to the three lodestones; his efforts to open the Rift and keep it open long enough were unsuccessful. My men are taking care of that while I take care of my responsibilities."

"You expect me to believe that Sargent tried to open the Rift?" Cal remembers finding the vials in the Fortune Hunter's pack, the confusing lack of scent. The map. But this ... Sargent, complicit? It's impossible to accept.

"We had an agreement."

"To test your products on the Lower Slopes, not to threaten the lives of the people on this island. One of *your* men is dead. Half my community is up here tonight."

"He knew the risks," Spear says.

"Do the master rangers?"

"Aren't they your best people?"

Cal gapes. He shudders to think of the wealth of knowledge, lore, and wisdom at risk on the mountain, the lives that will be snuffed out.

"Sargent is fully aware that the potency of Actaeon's Bane has dropped progressively over the last few decades," Spear says, as though irritated at having to explain himself. "When he saw our new product could dramatically increase the potency and compensate for lost profits, he saw an opportunity for a mutually beneficial solution. Open the Rift, induce chemical panic in the Herd, and the greatest threat to our investment becomes our greatest asset."

Cal's breathing grows short and shallow, and pinpricks of

299

light flare and die in the corners of his eyes. "You don't care who dies, as long as your profit margins rise."

"This is about long-term sustainability, not only for Nutris but for your community."

Cal clenches his fists. "Sargent would *never* allow this."

Spear lunges at Cal, clamping a hand around his throat, driving him back against the lodestone. Cal is momentarily stunned by the bolt of the man's life force roaring through his consciousness, but the moment his back hits the stone, something changes. The roar of life defuses, and the shock of not being overwhelmed delays Cal's instinct to fight the man off.

"Sargent trapped the buck on the Northwest Loop," Spear spits the words in Cal's face, like he's held his tongue for as long as he could stand and he's had enough. "The buck you carried down the mountain."

He's interrupted by a black cannonball falling from the sky; Reeva dives at Spear with an eardrum-splitting shriek.

RIFT STONE

Meg loses consciousness for only a moment. The subterranean hum brings her back, the hum of life in the bedrock. Rangers rush around her, auras shimmering, the sounds of struggle, human pain, and animal rage echoing back and forth across the basin. She pushes back onto her hands and knees, and her gaze slides past the battle with the Rift Hound to the slab of rock sitting slightly right of center. Her father lies on top of the slab. All around him the air ripples and glimmers, and if she couldn't feel the pulse of electric energy humming through her body, she'd think she was hallucinating.

Her skin remembers the sting of passing through the film of invisible energy, and she hugs her arms. That's the distortion in the air, force fields of energy like upended glass bowls sitting domelike across the basin. Not one dome but many, some large and small, intersecting like the flipped cross section of a drunken Venn diagram. The slab of rock sits where multiple domes intersect. The Rift Stone. Meg finds her body tipping toward it, and she catches herself, hands on thighs to keep from falling again.

A final bloodthirsty growl rips the air and cuts short. Meg looks back as black smoke pours from the Hound's severed neck, that gobbling shadow, imploding inward, rippling across the surface of the invisible dome until it disappears before a trio of rangers and their machetes. She staggers to her feet and lets the gradual slope and the magnetic pull guide her across the grass to the rock. Behind her, voices rise in urgent discussion about what to do next. Meg doesn't care. All she can see is her father, his face gray, his body unmoving, oblivious to the chaos around him.

He has no aura—not like the others with their shimmering second skin—and it makes her heart clench, and she hunches her shoulders forward. Above his face a ribbon of air flutters silver, gray, black, and blue, shifting, shimmering, and changing like oil on water. Though her father's chest barely rises and falls, with each gentle exhalation the ribbon flutters. Curiosity, wonder, and alarm war inside her. No aura, just a ribbon of . . . what? Life? Spirit? A thread of life, threatening to slip free and leave his shell empty? She wants to grab that fluttering thing and jam it down his throat, then clamp one hand over his mouth and slap him awake with the other. *You don't get to die. You don't get to slip away and not make things right. You don't get to abandon me here.* She also wants to fall on his chest, cling to him, and cry like a baby.

The air distorts directly before her face, and she holds her breath passing through another wall of energy, gritting her teeth against the brief snapping sting on her skin. The slab is almost twelve by fifteen feet across at its widest points, and just over four feet high, so when she stands at the edge, it reaches her navel. The vibration is strongest here, pulsing and humming. She was expecting some kind of magic portal, a swirling vortex or black hole to another dimension like in the movies. She isn't exactly disappointed, given there's quite a bit going on, force fields, Rift Hounds, and aura-wise.

The magnetic pull brings her hands up from her sides, and she spreads her fingers on the rock with a deep sigh. Just as she felt it in the hot spring when she lay upon the rock, the hum of living energy rumbles through her palms, up her arms, down her spine, through her belly and legs to her feet. She is entirely plugged in. *Home.* Her eyes grow wet, and she closes them. *Home.* Even with the calamitous uproar in the Voice of the Herd, the thrumming is filled with life, and her bones hum, a battery recharging. The aches in her body begin to fade, her fatigue begins to fade, and a hand clamps her wrist.

Her eyes spring open. Sargent appears unconscious, unmoved, except for his extended arm and his fingers like a vice around the bones of her wrist. The fluttering ribbon of shifting light and shadow ripples toward her, one end still centered above his mouth and nose, the other reaching toward her like a wriggling eel. Her breath hitches, and she looks for Bren or anyone to tell her what it means. None of the rangers are looking her way; they're rushing toward the edges of the forest, and the ground is rumbling again beneath her feet.

"Sargent?" she whispers, but he doesn't open his eyes. "Dad?"

A sound like rolling thunder fills her ears, distant at first, then crashing in, loud and harsh. She closes her eyes again, hunching against the noise—not yet ready to pull from her father's grip. The darkness behind her eyelids bursts with color . . .

* * *

She clings to Cal in the mouth of the cave as an unearthly howl sweeps the mountain, answered by another closer, louder, longer howl. Fergus Welsh, the head ranger, crouches before them, his eyes black and hard. "Of all the places to be on a night like this," he says, panting and wiping his brow. "You kids don't move, you hear me? You don't move."

She and Cal nod in unison, his chin banging against her temple, his fingers digging into her back as he clutches her sweatshirt. She must be bruising his shoulders, she's holding on so tight.

Sargent drops into the little hollow, panting hard. His brown eyes wild with love and terror. "Meg, Cal," he whispers, grabbing them both to his chest. "My god."

"Dad, I'm sorry," Meg chokes. "I thought it was safe. It's not full moon."

"It's my fault," Cal says. "I didn't want them to take me. Meg was trying to help."

Sargent makes a strangled sound of exasperation. He hugs them so fiercely his whole body shakes, and Meg's little bow grinds against the inside of her elbow. With a watery sniff, Sargent kisses the top of her head and ruffles Cal's hair. "It's all right. I've got you. We'll worry about Social Services later."

"Sargent," Fergus whispers, his voice sharp with warning.

Sargent releases them. He cups their chins. "I want you to get right back against the rock. Stay low. Don't move. Don't make a sound."

Cal nods and tugs her away. Meg can't feel her feet. "Dad . . ."

"It's all right," he says, unsheathing his machete, the waft of dried rue scenting the air. "We have four rangers on this ridge, and Fergus has signaled his falcon. They'll find us."

Fergus kicks dirt over Meg's campfire, sending up a small billow of smoke and plunging the cave into darkness. The pitch black is so intense she can't tell if her eyes are open or closed. She drops her bow, useless in the dark, and squats to run her hands in the dirt, searching for a rock—some kind of weapon. Her fingers close over a stone the size of a baseball. Cal hauls her up and pushes her behind him.

A putrid reek fills her nostrils, worse than a rotting animal carcass—worse than the dead whale on the beach, baking in the hot sun. The sound of heavy paws padding the ground above the cave entrance, a low guttural growl that makes Meg squeeze her legs together. Her fear is bigger than her body, bigger than the cave. The cave is too small. She's trapped. They're all trapped. Cal, Fergus, her father. They're trapped because of her, and death is coming. Death is here.

A growl rips around the cave walls, her father's shout explodes, and Fergus produces a war cry. Chaos in the dark, heavy bodies moving hard and fast. Sounds of pain and violence. Sparks rise, and the campfire flares to life, disturbed by a boot or paw turning the earth. All Meg can see is her father swinging his machete, Fergus splayed on the cave floor, blood glistening at his throat, eyes wide open. The rest is formless shadow, but her father is there swinging and screaming and driving at . . . something.

Dust swirls in the red light of the flickering campfire. The reek is in her mouth. Something huge and heavy paws the ground and blasts the bowl of the cave with a roar. She can't see it; there's nothing but shadow. Her father stops midswing, his chest suddenly exposed, the fabric of his shirt rent, the lapels of his oilskin shredded, his skin from throat to navel made into red ribbons.

Meg screams.

Sargent falls.

Cal yells and barges her back against the rock before lunging for her father's fallen weapon. It's big and heavy, and he has to use his legs to get momentum as he lifts the machete and swings wildly. A roar pushes his hair from his face, and he staggers back. Meg throws her rock with a hate-filled shout. It ricochets off empty space, producing a thud and eliciting a vicious growl. The reek sweeps toward her, cutting all light from the campfire. A hot, wet weight drives her face-first into the dirt, putting such pressure on her back she has no air to scream. Cal is screaming. The weight clamps at the nape of her neck, a stab of pain and something pierces her skin, and then all her body weight is hanging from the point of pain as she is tossed in the air. She flails her arms and legs, the last embers of the campfire racing up to meet her.

She turns her face away, landing hands-first in the sputtering fire. The burn is instant agony. Momentum throws her sideways, and she rolls onto her back screaming, cradling her hands, her melted skin. Her vision is skewed. Cal has a shimmering outline that blurs as he bounds across the cave to skid to his knees before her. Looming above him, breathing putrid air, the enormous head of a hideous black dog. She comprehends this for a split second before it strikes, lunging for Cal, knocking the machete from his hands. Its jaws clamp on the side of Cal's face, lifting him from the ground, shaking him like a dead rabbit, tossing him against the wall.

An icy howl winds up the mountain, and the beast pauses, cocking its head, snorting blood and saliva over Meg before turning away and bounding up and out through the entrance hole.

Meg shakes uncontrollably, lost in pain. She struggles to turn her head, to spot Cal. He lies in the far corner of the cave, the shimmering outline of his body throbbing in the darkness. Below the mouth of the cave Fergus Welsh lies still. He has no weird glowing outline except for a gray streak of light fluttering above his mouth.

Sargent's outline flickers in and out like candlelight fighting a strong wind.

"Dad," she croaks. "Dad . . ."

The shimmering glow flares suddenly, coalescing above his chest like a silver globe of living light, pulsating once, twice, three times, and then it slips away from his body, twisting, fading, up and out the mouth of the cave. The breath stops in her throat.

The fluttering ribbon of gray light above Fergus Welsh breaks free of its invisible tether, dipping and twisting on a breeze she can't feel. It loops, twisting straight at Sargent. There is no resistance. The ribbon snakes between his lips and disappears down his throat. Sargent's chest arches off the floor with a phlegmy gasp.

The earth quakes, and she opens her eyes. Sargent lies still as stone on the slab, his hand resting at his side, not clamped on her wrist—did she imagine it? The questing ribbon of blue and gray light no longer reaches toward her but lingers, fluttering above her father's mouth. Meg staggers away from the stone, from her father—the *thing* that's been *using* her father's body—awareness crashing in unforgiving waves. Her father died nine years ago. She watched his spirit leave his body, watched it slip away through the mouth of the cave. She didn't know what she was seeing—didn't know what was real or imagined. The pain and nightmares that followed, she'd explained it all away.

The earth shakes again, knocking her from her feet. Above her, the arcing distortions that dome the air wink in and out, like a bad television signal.

The air suddenly clears, all the distortions gone, but this doesn't bring her comfort. She knows the electromagnetic ley lines were the only thing keeping the Hounds at bay. This fear is erased from her mind by an impossibility. High above her father's body the air tears along an uneven seam, as though ripped by giant unseen hands. The edges flap like torn fabric, fluttering in the night sky. The air above the mountain is close and heavy with thick rain clouds. The air beyond the Rift is a starry vault, and a warm wind blows.

Meg couldn't stand even if the earth wasn't shaking, the cold damp grass soaking up through her clothes. The vibration hums from the bedrock to her bones, detaching her from reason, comprehension, or instinct. She cannot make her brain translate what her eyes are seeing; it is so beyond, so outside of her known universe. She couldn't even dream this thing.

A colossal mist-wreathed beast, silvered and shimmering even without the moonlight, steps into the world, antlers breaking between the folds of space and time. Its hoof lands inches from the side of her face. The weight of its step makes the earth bounce beneath her. She turns her head to find a deep divot of bruised grass as it steps away and the rear hooves follow. A blast of sound shatters the quiet. A stag's roar, magnified in the basin.

FRESH BLOOD

Spear shoves Cal painfully against the lodestone and stumbles back with a shout, batting the air as Reeva attacks his face. Talons and beak tear at the man's flesh. Cal's heart lurches to his throat as Spear swipes viciously, knocking her away. Reeva tumbles to the forest floor with a squawk of pain. Cal cries out and lunges for the man with his bare hands but not fast enough, as Spear kicks Reeva away through the trees.

"No!" Cal punches any part of Spear he can land his fist on. The Fortune Hunter grunts and gasps as Cal forces air from his lungs, but away from the lodestone, the impact of physical touch takes its toll. Spear's life force grows to a lightning strike, obliterating Cal's senses, the blast of it overwhelming his mind. When Cal fumbles, the Fortune Hunter seizes the advantage, driving his fist into Cal's ribs, hitting his knee with a rough knock. Cal sprawls on his back, but Spear rolls him, pinning the side of his face with his knee.

Overcome by the relentless roar of the Fortune Hunter's life force, Cal struggles to make sense of the man's words. He speaks roughly, panting as he crushes Cal's skull. "Sargent trapped the deer," he spits. "The distress signal was supposed to bring the Hounds while supplying Nutris with its first Old Herd deer to test Limited Reanimation in the wild."

"You're lying," Cal chokes. Despite the chaos in his body, a jarring thought slips through his defenses: there was no identifiable scent at the snare site. He couldn't understand it at the time, thinking the rain must have washed the scent of poachers away. Sargent had punished him, humiliated him in front of the whole community . . . but he'd also reinstated him the next day, acted like nothing had happened. More telling is the clarity of Spear's scent now. Lies smell sour. Cal groans, "He wouldn't . . ."

"It wasn't enough to keep the Rift open," Spear says, pushing upward suddenly and stepping away.

Cal gasps with relief, the horrific noise clearing from his head. He lies agonized and shaking on the muddy ground, waiting to come back to himself.

Spear stands over him, panting, rifle poised. "He supplied his blood as a backup with a map to the lodestones. He went that night to the summit and injured another deer to draw the Hounds and provide you with a tracking mission. He wants you at the Rift."

Cringing at the pain in his body, Cal frowns up at the man, unable to comprehend the implications. Joss's mother nearly died that night. *Cal* nearly died. Deliberate sabotage would be unthinkable. "That doesn't make sense," he rasps, trying to calm himself and get air into his lungs. "Sargent wouldn't need to invent a scenario to send me to the Rift. He could have simply ordered me to go. I would have obeyed him without question."

"He felt a tracking scenario, requiring your unique gifts, would circumvent questions from the community." Spear turns his head and spits blood on the ground, wiping his mouth on the back of his wrist. "Only senior rangers are permitted to attend an endowment rite. Sargent's injury was an unexpected deviation from the plan."

"Endowment rite?" Reeling, Cal grips his head, struggling to comprehend what he's hearing. The endowment rite hasn't happened in years. The last head ranger to be appointed in an endowment rite was Selene Anders, Bren and Antonia's grandmother. The details of the rite are cloaked in mystery. The only thing he knows for sure is that it happens at the Rift Stone, the seat of power where the ley lines converge. "Sargent was going to hand over the leadership?"

Spear draws a steadying breath, and Cal notes the scent of fear receding. The man's self-control is impressive, but the shift only amplifies the whiff of aggression, and Cal is certain that if he gives the Fortune Hunter any more trouble, there will be vicious consequences. His heart squeezes as he thinks of Reeva. He reaches for her in his mind but struggles to focus.

"He *is* going to hand over the leadership," Spear says. "To you."

Cal shakes his head. "They're taking him to the Rift Stone

for *healing*. That's where the ley lines converge. This can't be the endowment rite; Sargent's unconscious. He could die. He could be dead already if there's a Rift Hound on the loose."

Spear takes a step back, gesturing with the rifle for Cal to get up. "Sargent believes his lack of Rift Sight is detrimental to the role of head ranger. That is why he has chosen you to replace him. He believes the rite will be more powerful if the Rift is open to its fullest extent. He wishes to draw the Old One."

Cal's head swims as he pushes upright, his heart hammering at Spear's words. "*What?* You draw him, you draw the whole pack."

"He wishes for more rangers to have the opportunity to possess Rift Sight."

A wave of nausea hits Cal. "Deliberately expose half the community to Rift Hounds in the hope that some of them will survive the attack? There's no way Bren would agree to that." He rubs his face with shaking hands. "There's a reason I'm the only member of the community with Rift Sight. I didn't survive because I was strong or smart. I was eight years old. I survived by a bloody fluke."

"A good leader makes hard decisions for the long-term benefit of the community."

"Hard decisions?" Cal spits, rolling onto his knees. "Well, you're out of luck. I sent Bren a message to turn back. They won't risk going to the Rift Stone with the injured deer still roaming the summit."

"Boy, they won't turn back. Sargent was explicit that the

rite must go ahead and you must be present. Bren knows that it is my responsibility to ensure you make it to the summit, tracking or not."

Cal staggers to his feet, leaning his hands on his thighs as he pants, "You expect me to believe Bren is part of this?"

Spear's eyes glimmer coldly. "I'm beyond caring what you believe, boy."

Cal shakes his head. "I'm a kid. Worse, I'm a fisherman's son. *No one* wants me to be head ranger."

Spear narrows his eyes, thinking, then gestures with his rifle toward the Lower Slopes. "You know what makes the Lower Herd so successful? Fresh blood. The potency of Actaeon's Bane might be diminished, but their breeding rates, their resistance to disease and environmental challenges makes them far more resilient than the Old Herd that you coddle and fuss over."

"What does that have to do with . . . ?" Cal feels sick.

"Fresh blood," Spear says, his voice devoid of emotion; he's laying out the facts. "That is what Sargent wants. You are fresh blood. Were you to produce offspring with a Rift-Sighted lineage member of the community, you would produce the most capable and gifted rangers the community has seen in generations and a natural line of succession."

"Offspring?" Cal chokes.

"I believe Sargent has been encouraging your connection with his daughter."

Cal leans back against the lodestone, his disbelief in freefall.

"Stronger, more capable rangers ensure the survival of the Old Herd and the Lower Herd. Everybody wins."

Cal moans, closing his eyes. "Everybody dies."

"Not everybody," Rilke says, appearing behind Spear, rifle held before her. Spear spins to face her, lifting his weapon, but she fires first. The sound booms across the mountain. Cal watches a red hole widen on the back of Spear's jacket, just above his right shoulder blade. The Fortune Hunter drops his weapon and sinks to his knees. "Just you." She aims again, this time for his head.

Cal gasps, half collapsed on the lodestone. "No! Rilke, don't kill him!"

"Our people will die tonight because of him."

Spear struggles on his side, scraping the ground with his feet trying to get away from her.

"If you kill him . . . I'm not strong enough. I'll . . ." Cal gestures at the ground where he knows he'll end up passed out. Even being this close to the body farther up the track is turning the air in his lungs to ice. "We need to get to the summit and warn your dad. We have to find Meg. She has no idea what's coming."

The earth kicks beneath their feet with a subterranean growl, nearly shaking them to their knees. The Voice of the Herd rumbles straight into Cal's skull, and Rilke flinches, gripping her forehead in one hand while gripping her rifle with the other. Spear looks back and forth between them, scrabbling at the pocket on the side of his pants.

Closing his mind to the tide of panic sweeping through the Old Herd, Cal launches himself at the fallen man, kicking the handgun from his blood-soaked grip. Spear grunts and grapples for his weapon, but Cal lands his boot on the Fortune Hunter's jaw, and his body falls slack beneath him.

"Did you hear," Cal pants, his pulse drumming like fury in his ears, "what he said? The lodestones."

Rilke nods, breathing hard, her battered face screwed up in a tight scowl. "You think Sargent really planned all this?"

Shaking his head, Cal mutters, "I don't want to believe it, but they had his blood, the map. The Voice of the Herd is in chaos — the Rift must be fully open."

She pants through her nose, jaw hardened, eyes glinting. "My dad's up there. My brother."

Cal gives a grim nod. "Where's Joss?"

She cringes and covers her face with a trembling hand. "I left him at Burntwood, told him to bar the door. I couldn't sit there and wait."

"Joss will understand," Cal says. "I'm glad you came."

The tightness in Rilke's jaw loosens a fraction, and she manages a shaky nod.

The mountain groans, and a howl rises, cutting through the night with the promise of death. Cal takes Spear's rifle, and Rilke lifts a strap from her shoulder and swings the crossbow toward him. "You'll need as many weapons as you can carry."

He takes it without question, the weight of it on his back a relief. "Reeva's here somewhere. She's injured." He ducks to peer through the trees, his throat tight with grief at the thought of her in pain, at the thought of her gone.

"Can you feel her?" Rilke asks cautiously.

He tries to concentrate and reach her with his thoughts,

but there's nothing, and he hangs his head, tears stinging his eyes.

"If she died," Rilke says, her voice catching, "you would have felt it, here, like a tearing."

Cal lifts his head, struggling to hold it together. Rilke taps her fingers to her sternum, her eyes welling with the memory of her own recent loss. He swallows and shakes his head. "There was nothing like that."

She presses her lips together, a bolstering attempt at a smile. "That's a good sign, Cal. She's probably taken herself somewhere safe. To heal."

He releases a shaky breath.

"What about Spear?" Rilke says, hardening her voice, pulling him back into the urgency of the moment. "Let him rot?"

"The Hounds will find him," he says bitterly.

"Good."

"Rilke . . ."

She swears and swings her pack off her shoulder and digs out her jar of Actaeon's Bane. "He doesn't deserve this."

"I didn't say you should be gentle."

ACTAEON'S BANE

The pounding of boots behind Meg. Rough hands grasping her arms, propelling her upward, her head snapping back on her shoulders with the impact. Rangers: two, three, more? They almost lift her from the ground as they run. She tries to shout, to cry out, but all that comes is a strangled yelp. The slab where her father lies grows up quickly before her. They stop short and push her down. A broad back wearing an oilskin coat shields her. The ground shakes, and subterranean thunder makes her want to lift her feet off the ground as deer stampede the basin.

Meg peers over large shoulders. So many deer. But with her vision distorted, it's a stampede of ghosts. Huge and gray, beautiful and terrifying, each with a silver mist trailing, blue eyes flashing in the dark. Struggling against one another, half climbing each other's backs, they follow the Great Stag, fleeing what comes behind. A Hound breaks from the forest as another leaps from the Rift above them.

Meg doesn't know whether to cover her head or her nose and mouth. Bren yells orders, but the rangers look agonized, covering their heads as though the sound is causing them physical pain. Meg realizes what's afflicting them—the Voice of the Herd—yet somehow she resists the tidal wave of suffering. Bracing against the undertow, she leans her head back against the slab.

Instantly she is aware of the presence of her father . . . or the *thing* that has claimed her father's body. It reaches toward her in her mind, and when she looks up, she sees with Rift Sight the fluttering ribbon of blue-gray light questing the air above her head, and instinctively she ducks away.

Bren barks another command. "Hold! Hold!"

Squealing rises from the thundering Herd, wiping out all sound of the rangers' voices. From east to west it travels in waves. Chaos spreads and multiplies. Deer begin to leap higher, twisting, colliding, falling beneath one another's hooves. The screams now mix terror with agony. The inkblot shape of a massive Hound, darker than the night itself, leaps into the middle of the Herd, sending a wall of deer flesh careening toward the rock where they huddle.

Cries of alarm and she is shunted to the left as bodies barge sideways, taking her with them. The Herd is thinning as they bolt, bawling and screaming, but a Hound cuts them off. Taller than a man, slavering fangs flashing in the darkness. It moves so fast she doesn't see the strike, yet three deer fall. Two does with chests gouged open and one young buck, his neck clamped in the Hound's slavering jaws. Even with its mouth

319

full, it produces a deep and ominous growl in the back of its throat. It doesn't pause, shaking the buck with a vicious toss of its head, until it stops fighting. The rest of the deer clear the glade, following the Great Stag into the forest, leaving behind several deer badly wounded, legs broken.

Terrible cries of distress break from the rangers, and several of them retrieve their rifles, aiming at the fallen. They shoot, releasing the injured deer from agony. Small relief with the Hound still before them. "Where?" shouts one ranger, swinging back and forth with his crossbow. "Where?"

"Watch the dirt for tracks," Bren calls, but the ground is torn up.

"It's right there!" Meg shouts. "It's right there!" She turns to the woman beside her and gestures for her crossbow. The woman surrenders the weapon, already loaded. It's heavy, and her arms shake, yet she holds it before her and shoots, landing an arrow in the Hound's chest. It screams and leaps toward them, but the arrow gives the rangers its location, and they swing into action.

There is no reprieve. The ground shakes again, not from the pounding hooves but the bones of the mountain trembling in horror. Meg looks up, and the rangers around her duck and turn to watch the impossible seam in the sky disgorge Hound after Hound. Three, then four. The stench is a tsunami, suffocating and oppressive as they spread out across the basin. Two bound after the stampeding Herd and the Great Stag while the other two turn on the rangers, half of whom are already engaged with the Hound marked by Meg's arrow.

"Two more!" Meg screams, and cries of dismay rise in the chaos.

"Where?" Bren demands, the back of his wrist pressed to his nose. He gestures for Meg to come forward. "Show us!"

Fumbling another arrow into the crossbow, she works the lever until the line is taut. She wastes no time lining up the shot, and while the ground trembles and the world crumbles, Meg finds a quiet place in her mind where the Voice of the Herd can't infect her with fear. She steadies her sights. Exhales. Fires. The Hound staggers and howls outrage. Incredibly, three master rangers run toward it, machetes swinging, ready to strike the invisible monster. Their courage astounds her, and she stares, mouth hanging open until Bren drops his hand on her shoulder. "Again, Meg! Where's the other one?"

The third Hound rampages back and forth across the basin, crazed with the smell of blood and the flailing terror of the injured deer and the call of the stampede. Unfortunately, its attention falls on the rangers closing in on its injured pack member, and it begins to stalk toward the fray, muscled shoulders rippling flesh like an indigo bruise. Meg reloads and lifts her crossbow. Steady. Exhale. An arrow skewers the beast behind the ear, but she didn't pull the trigger.

"Go! Go!" Bren shouts.

Meg follows the trajectory of the arrow back to the edge of the forest where Cal collapses to his knees, his crossbow clattering to the ground before him. Rilke races toward the dancing arrow, where the roars of the Rift Hound blunt the air. Meg holds her breath, torn between the sight of Cal struggling and failing to find his feet and Rilke's bold charge.

"Cal," Meg shouts and waves her arms, but there is death all around him, two fallen deer and a ranger facedown on the grass. "Cal!"

"Cal?" Bren peers across the plateau, and she points just as the boy falls, passed out at the edge of the basin.

"Abbot, Leif! Bring him to the Rift Stone. We're running out of time."

As the younger men weave through the carnage, hunched low to the ground, yards away the Rift Hound encircled by Rilke and three other rangers isn't backing down. Meg cries out as the beast swipes its massive paw, wiping out one woman halfway through an elaborate maneuver. Rilke swings, but she doesn't see the beast twisting sideways. Like a bear trap, the Hound's jaws clamp on Rilke's shoulder. Meg screams as it lifts the girl in the air and whips her back and forth before tossing her away to face the fury of the remaining rangers. Rilke lands limp on the grass and lies unmoving.

Bren cries out and runs toward his daughter. Meg barely notices the rangers dispatch the first Hound, her full attention on Rilke and the red, raw wound of her torn shoulder. The master ranger gathers the girl in his arms, hoisting her up to his chest, and staggers back to the Rift Stone, converging just as Abbot and Leif return with Cal's unconscious body.

Bren lays his daughter on the slab to Sargent's right, and the boys lay Cal on the left. Abbot looks at his sister in dismay. Leif clutches his arm, his blue eyes tortured, pressing his hand to Abbot's chest, right over his heart. Meg trembles where she stands; the earth trembles beneath her. Bren packs his daughter's shoulder with medical gauze from his pack, his hands shaking.

"What can I do?" Meg calls. "What does she need?"

"Stay, baby," he murmurs over his daughter, ripping the lid off a tub of paste Meg recognizes as Actaeon's Bane. "This needs pressure. Put your hands here."

Her joints seem frozen at first, but she forces herself to move, rounding the slab, clambering up above Rilke's and Sargent's heads. Bren guides her hands into place, and she cringes at the wet warmth seeping through the gauze.

Bren digs a finger full of paste from the tub and forces it into Rilke's slack mouth. Meg widens her eyes; she has never seen it used like that before. Bren digs another bit from the tub and brushes her hands away to daub it directly on the wound. Meg turns her head, unwilling to look. That's when she notices Cal.

"Bren," she whispers. "Bren, look at Cal . . ."

"Give me a second."

Meg blinks, Rift Sight blurring her vision. Cal's aura is silver-blue, pulsing slowly, flickering in and out like a bad connection. Next to him the ribbon of grayish light whips the air above Sargent's nose and mouth, as though the presence of so many bodies on the slab has stirred it. Meg ducks as it flicks the air above her head, distaste pulling her lips back from her teeth. Rilke too is fading. Her silver aura pulses, flares, disappears, and bursts back into sight. Meg feels as though she is watching life on the brink.

"Here," Bren says, grabbing her wrist. "Apply pressure."

Meg clamps her hands back on the wound. "Bren," she whimpers. "Cal is . . . look at him."

Bren lifts his head and groans. "This was supposed to be an endowment rite, not a funeral."

"Endowment rite?"

He shakes his head, rubs his face, and casts his gaze over the carnage in the basin. "This isn't what your father wanted."

"My father is dead." Her voice breaks, a painful sob tearing her throat. "He died nine years ago. I saw. I don't know what that thing is inside him."

Bren's eyes widen. "No. No, Meg, he didn't die. The head ranger carries the spark of the first ranger. A remnant."

"A what?" She recoils.

"It passes from head ranger to head ranger. It's what gives them their connection to the Old Herd. It's what gives them authority to command the—"

"It takes over," she chokes. "Like a parasite."

Bren blanches. "No. Nothing like that, Meg. It's a—a blessing. A sacred impartation."

"No," she says, her eyes streaming. "Sargent died. That *thing* has been using his body. You knew what he was like before. People don't just change like that."

Bren shakes his head sadly, like she's hysterical and confused. He speaks softly, as if pleading with her to be rational. "His heart was broken when your mother took you to the mainland. He was suffering. He was under so much pressure taking over from Fergus Welsh."

"You're not listening to me," she cries. "I'm telling you. That's not my father—" She cuts short, noticing frost creeping up Cal's cheekbone like tiny diamonds. The air turns white above his nose and mouth, and his aura flickers out. "Bren! Cal's light—his light went out!"

"His what?"

"His light! The—the glowing aura thing! It's gone!" She rises on her knees. "Abbot! Take my place!"

Rilke's brother rushes to her side and clamps his hands over his sister's wound. Meg clambers to her feet, ducking away from that twisting ribbon of gray light snaking through the air above Sargent's face. She scrambles over the bodies, treading on her father's arm, pinching Cal's thigh with her boot before straddling his hips, forcing a puff of white air from his lungs. His aura flickers again, a silver-blue flare, and then blinks out. *"Cal."*

A cry goes up. The trees shake at the eastern edge of the basin. Meg and Bren turn just as the colossal stag reappears. The remaining Rift Hounds pause midstruggle, the rangers too, all eyes fixed on the Old One. She can't tear her eyes from the creature, tossing its head, roaring like it might dismantle the world, a sound so filled with ancient rage and longing it breaks her heart. Across the basin a tall doe emerges through the trees. Meg recognizes her immediately and the collective gasp from the rangers confirms it is Fallon. She paces across the torn-up grass as though magnetized, her brown eyes unblinking, focused on the stag. He lifts his head, chest proud and full, snorting and pawing the earth.

The two Rift Hounds who remain in the basin howl wildly and leap forward, eyes rolling, consumed with madness, teeth bared and slavering. Their paws churn up the dirt as they race toward the stag. He doesn't move to defend himself, gaze locked on the doe. When the Hounds leap, one for his throat, the other for his shoulder, he braces his legs for impact, then roars and tosses his head, antlers sweeping the air, catching one Hound in the neck. The screams of agony make Meg duck over Cal's freezing body. The doe cries out, a blast of despair, and gallops toward her mate. The ground trembles, and the air above the Rift Stone sucks inward like an endless gasp, whipping everyone's hair and clothes toward the ripped seam.

The Old One and the raging Hounds begin to lose definition. Meg squints, trying to bring them back into focus. Their edges dissolve, imploding, billowing smoke and mist, black and silver, twisting into a column that stains the air, funneling up and away through the Rift. Something snaps at the corner of Meg's eye, and she turns her head sharply. The ribbon of gray-blue light fluttering above Sargent's nose and mouth whips and buckles and twists madly, reaching toward Meg and Cal. Meg ducks, blinking at the flying dust and the flapping of her hair in her eyes.

It reaches for Cal, flicking above his face, detaching from Sargent. Meg lunges, clamping one hand over Cal's mouth, the other wrenching his shoulder. She throws her weight off the edge of the Rift Stone, pulling Cal down on top of her as she falls. When her back hits the ground, his weight crushes her chest, punching air from her lungs. The impact coincides with the bright silver flare of his aura and the gasp of his breath in her ear. Over his shoulder, Meg watches the last of the stag and Rift Hound vapor trails disappear through the Rift, and the air seals with a ripple like water. The earth gives a short sharp quake, and the quiet that follows is smothering.

Around the basin, the voices of the rangers sound, calling to one another, some in pain, some offering comfort. From above them on the Rift Stone comes a great gasp and Abbot's cry of joy. Bren calls his daughter's name with such relief, his voice breaks. Rilke is alive. A shudder moves through Meg as she thinks of the questing ribbon of gray light that detached from Sargent's body. Where did it go? This disquieting thought is dislodged by another sensation: warmth. Cal's breath heats her neck, and the weight of his body pinning her chest, stomach, and hips no longer chills her.

Groaning, he struggles to lift his head, bracing himself on his elbow. "Meg?" he croaks, grimacing like he's hungover, his hair falling in her face. "You're alive."

"Sort of," she pants, her hands drifting up, settling somewhere on his ribs, her eyes spilling tears as she sobs with relief beneath him. He's alive, and she's covered in mud, and her father is dead and she just watched a giant stag turn to vapor and get sucked through a hole in space.

He tilts his head, pushing his hair back. "Are you hurt?"

She laughs shakily, dazed by the nearness of his face and the concern darkening those intense hazel eyes. "You're kind of suffocating me."

He shifts his weight, gasping as he tumbles against the

base of the slab, her arm still trapped beneath his body. His gaze sweeps past her, taking in the wreck of the basin and the rock at his back, his eyes widening. "The Rift Stone."

"I'm so sorry," Meg whispers, waiting for him to cringe and shove her away. Her touch must be making him horribly uncomfortable, but she can feel the life-giving vibration of the ley lines, humming down the length of his body and into her. "I didn't mean to touch you. I thought you were dying again, and now my arm is stuck."

His gaze slips back to hers, lingering on her mouth. "Meg, the ley line . . ."

BLANK SPACE

The Rift Stone vibrates through Cal's spine, the power of the ley lines humming life into his body, chasing away the chill of death, though death lies all around him, carnage in the basin that should have filled his lungs with ice. The wonder of it is only matched by Meg, half pinned beneath his side. Her life force sings through his bones but somehow doesn't overwhelm him.

He waits for a moment, body-shocked by proximity, mesmerized by the flecks of gold and green in her irises, the redness of her lips. God, he's *still* touching her, and neither his brain nor his bones have exploded. Yet.

"Meg, it's the Rift Stone. The ley lines, I think . . . it feels different . . . defused somehow." He pauses, listening to his body to see if the intensity will overwhelm him, but it stays steady. It stays incredible. He's not dying, and her life is in his bones. He swallows, rising on his elbow, his eyes riveted to hers, finding grief and longing churning deep in her gaze. A switch flicks inside him, and his hands take over, like they did when she collapsed in Bertrum's kill yard, like they know what to do, like it's all been hardwired. Sliding his fingers up behind her neck, he cups the base of her skull, filling his chest to meet hers. As their breath mingles, her eyelids flutter closed, her chin lifts, and her lips part.

She fans her fingers over his ribs, and for a moment, it's the next and newest most incredible sensation he's ever experienced, eclipsed only when her lips brush his. Her mouth lights the fuses on a thousand tiny rockets, sending arcs of exquisite fireworks through his skin, and he keeps himself very still, willing the ley line or whatever miracle's at work to hold.

She kisses him again. A question.

Let it hold.

An invitation.

Let it hold.

A demand.

With a shiver, he sinks into her kiss, instinct and hunger carving his answers one by one, until she's twisting her fingers in his shirt. For Cal, it can't get any better. What is happening in this moment is the best thing that has ever happened to him in nearly eighteen years. Then her tongue seeks his, and he is proved instantly and irrevocably wrong, confirming that he knows nothing. At all. About anything. Ever.

"Meg!" a distant voice calls across the basin, tugging them out of their bubble, landing them firmly in the mud and bloody reality of their circumstances. Meg looks almost drunk, her eyelids sweeping slowly, pupils blown out to full aperture, her lips swollen. She looks so utterly blissed out, Cal decides this is basically what he wants to dedicate the rest of his life to—kissing Meg.

"Meg!" There's a desperation to the call that turns both their heads. At the edge of the trees, two figures stagger onto the grass. One holds a lantern and rifle, the other leans heavily on a cane.

Meg starts to wriggle out from his side, her mouth dropping open. "Is that . . . ?" she says, her voice hoarse. "That's my mother." Then she's scrambling up on her knees and struggling to her feet with a choked cry. Cal hauls himself upright, his body like a sack of broken bricks. Meg's detachment from his side makes him feel momentarily lost in space, and he finds himself moving to follow her.

He doesn't get far before the impact of the surrounding carnage hits him—a dozen dead deer, four fallen rangers. The cold smacks him right in the chest, that icy sensation feathering up his spine and behind his ears. He stumbles back to the Rift Stone, collapsing against the slab, willing himself to stay upright and conscious. His head spins, and the cold nips at his legs, at his spine, but the life in the stone hums into his chest, and he almost sobs in relief.

"Cal," Bren calls, looking up from his work on Rilke's bloodied shoulder. "Don't leave the Stone. You can't lose consciousness again, not so soon. Stay where you are."

"She's all right?" Cal winces at the sight of Rilke's gray face. Her eyes roll, and her chest rises and falls rapidly. Abbot stands close at the head of the Rift Stone, his hands stained red, passing his father gauze swabs and instruments from Bren's medical kit. His eyes are red and his nose swollen. Leif stays close beside him, stroking his arm and shoulder.

"She's awake," Bren says, his eyes on the work, his face set with grim determination. "You tell me."

Cal leans on his forearms, willing strength from the Stone, and blinks, bringing the film of Rift Sight into place. Rilke's aura is a bluish blaze, flickering but so bright it almost hurts to look at her. In contrast, Sargent laid out next to her is a blank space. His body has no outline whatsoever. Cal doesn't reach for Rilke; he clamps his hand on Sargent's ankle, and there's nothing. No bolt of life. No presence of death. No pulse. He shivers and squeezes his hands together. "Sargent's dead."

Bren looks up sharply, his brow furrowing into deep lines, then he closes his eyes and sighs. "I waited too long. I should have—"

"No, Dad," Abbot says. "You did everything. You faced hell. If the Rift Stone couldn't bring him back, what could?"

"No," Bren says. "He made me promise to perform the endowment rite before he passed."

"I'm not taking his place," Cal says with bitter certainty. "Did you know? He planned all this. He opened the Rift on purpose."

Bren gives him a hard look, and Abbot's face shifts gear from sorrow to frowning disbelief. "What?" he demands.

"That can't be true," Leif says, his voice almost a whisper. "Sargent would never do that."

"Why would you suggest such a thing?" Bren demands.

"Spear told me." Cal rushes over the details.

Bren's dark skin develops a sickly pallor. "Spear must be lying. I knew Sargent had asked him to ensure you made it to the Rift Stone," he says, unable to meet Cal's eye. "But the rest ... he must be lying."

"I would have smelled lies. I saw the blood on the lodestone. Sargent injured the deer to draw the Hounds, and when that didn't work, he gave them vials of his own blood and a map to the lodestones. I saw them in their pack. Spear says Sargent wanted to *strengthen the community*. He planned for all the senior rangers to be on the Upper Slopes to increase the numbers with Rift Sight. He wanted people to get bitten. It was Sargent's idea to taint the Herd with chemical panic so Nutris can use their Limited Reanimation product and increase their profits."

Abbot recoils. Bren's mouth falls open, his eyes casting back and forth across the Rift Stone before settling on Sargent with cold comprehension. "My daughter nearly died tonight because of his obsession with Rift Sight," he rasps. "He's never been satisfied. How many have we lost?"

"Four," Cal says with a heavy sigh. "I could feel four out here. More are fighting to stay alive, but that's just here in the basin. There were rangers in the forest too, and three Rift Hounds followed the Old One and the Herd in the stampede. Who knows how many others."

The overwhelming horror of such a deliberate act strikes Bren silent for another moment or two, and he leans on his hands, his mouth opening and closing before he gathers himself. "Where is Spear?"

"Rilke shot him. She saved me. She wanted to execute him, but I stopped her."

"You shouldn't have," Abbot snarls. Leif squeezes his shoulder, yet his expression is one of grim agreement.

"There was already a dead Fortune Hunter in the vicinity," Cal explains. "I was struggling to stay conscious. I didn't want Rilke to have to keep watch over my body in case of Rift Hounds. Besides, we needed to find Meg."

"How is she up here?" Bren asks.

"Long story." Cal sighs. "But once I was injured, she decided to try to track the deer herself."

"What?" Bren shakes his head.

"She's good," Cal says. "She saved our lives near Burntwood."

"She's coming," Leif warns, nodding past Cal's shoulder.

Cal turns and marvels at the sight of Meg propping Cora's arm over her shoulder, making their way slowly across the basin. The woman is covered in mud, her clothes torn, blood on her hands, cuts on her face. She leans heavily on a cane, and Antonia follows close behind, just as disheveled, carrying a lantern and rifle.

Antonia rushes around the Rift Stone to hug her nephew and embrace her brother. Her eyes fall on Rilke, and she gives a shuddering sob. "What happened? Is she going to make it?"

Bren lets his sister wrap her arm around his shoulders and gives a shaky nod.

"The stampede nearly took us out," Cora says, her voice

334

hoarse as she talks to Meg. "I don't understand what I saw, Meg. There were shadows mowing through the deer. . . ." Her voice cuts out. "Is he . . . is Sargent . . . ?"

Cora comes to the top of the Rift Stone, near Sargent's head. Reaching trembling fingers, she brushes the hair back from his face. Meg supports her mother, a hard frown creasing her brow as she eyes her father's body. Cal's stomach shrivels. He did this.

"I'm sorry, Cora," Bren murmurs. "He's gone."

She shakes her head, her face contorting. A small sob breaks from her throat. "We could have put him on the ferry. Taken him to the mainland for proper medical care."

"No, we couldn't," Meg says softly.

Cora ignores her. "But you drag him all the way up here, through all this, for a magic rock?" She flings her hand at the carnage in the basin and slaps it back on the Rift Stone. "And my daughter . . ."

Meg sighs. "Bren had no idea. I forced Rilke and Joss to let me join them on the western track. Cal tried to stop me. He only relented because he knew I would have come by myself anyway."

Cora sobs. "*This* is why I took you to the mainland. This place. These people. It's like a sickness. An obsession. For what? Nutris has Black Water by the throat, and there's nothing any of you can do to change it."

No one says anything. Cal leans against the Rift Stone, its living energy sustaining him in the middle of death and misery. Could he begin to explain to Cora what the island means to him? That despite the terror and the mayhem the island's pull is undeniable; the sense of home and belonging thrums in his blood. Maybe she's right. Maybe it's a sickness, but he felt like this when he was a kid, before he knew about the Rift and the ley lines, before he was bitten and the pull intensified. He can't explain it.

He feels Meg's eyes on him, and despite the wretched weight of guilt when he meets her gaze, the connection produces a tingling rush through his stomach. She looks exhausted and sad, yet there's a boldness in the way she holds his gaze, a knowing that makes him feel seen in a way he hasn't felt seen before. He doesn't deserve it but senses in their connection a commonality; she feels it too, the island thrumming in her bones. Her sadness is for her loss, her mother's grief, and knowing that she cannot convince Cora of why this place is worth fighting for.

"You should have stayed in the village," Abbot says to his aunt, his face screwed up with worry. "So dangerous to come all this way."

"I couldn't stop her," Antonia says, nodding at Cora now bent over the Rift Stone, her face in her hands. "She was frantic about Meg and I couldn't let her come alone."

"Antonia," Bren says, sighing heavily. "Spear caused all of this. He's still on the mountain. He can't be trusted. What if you had stumbled across him?"

"Nutris can kiss my ass," Antonia says, raising her rifle. "I know the tracks up here as well as you all. I may not have joined the community, but I'm not an empty-headed mainlander."

Rilke stirs, her eyes fluttering open. "Fallon." Her throat

produces a low guttural sound. Cal shivers, his Rift Sight blurring as Rilke's aura flares in and out. "Fallon."

"She's safe," Bren murmurs. "She returned to the forest, baby. You're okay. Just relax. I've got you."

Cal catches Meg's look of alarm and a confrontational glance exchanged with Bren, who hardens his jaw in warning. Something is going on. It occurs to him that things have been said while he was out under the grip of death. What does Meg know or think she knows? An uncomfortable idea cuts through his muddy thoughts. Does she know Sargent had him in his sights as replacement head ranger?

Rilke coughs, and whimpers with the effort, her voice clearing, softening. "Dad?" Her normal voice seems to provoke a sigh of relief around the Rift Stone. "Dad?"

"I'm here, sweetheart." He brushes her cheek, and she screws up her face, tears spilling down.

With a steadying breath, Bren looks up, his gaze moving slowly over the basin. He lifts his voice. "Bring the injured to the Stone. Then I want the fallen moved to the eastern edge of the forest. I need volunteers to scout the woods. We have men and women out there; we have to find them. We set up camp here for the night. Those able to travel will return to camp at first light and gather the apprentices. We need help getting the injured down the mountain." He pauses, frowning as he considers what else needs to be dealt with. "As for Jackson Spear and any remaining Fortune Hunters, we cannot allow execution-style justice. They must be detained and their weapons confiscated."

Around the basin, the rangers still on their feet listen

attentively before dispersing to follow orders. Cal wishes he could step away from the Rift Stone and make a meaningful contribution and grits his teeth at his own uselessness.

"Tomorrow we get a message to the village," Bren says. "Have someone contact the Ministry for Primary Industries on the mainland. We are declaring a state of emergency."

"State of emergency?" Abbot asks.

"It's our only legal recourse to delay Nutris. The cull must be put on hold until we investigate what happened tonight. We have enough evidence to charge Nutris with breaching the treaty. But"—he pauses, his weary gaze landing on Cal— "there may have been collusion, and we'll need Antonia to handle the legal details."

"Nutris won't like being shut out," Abbot warns. "They'll send reinforcements."

"That is why we must notify the Ministry for Primary Industries. They are obligated to protect our borders. The coast guard too."

Cora straightens up, wiping her tear-stained face. "What about Sargent?"

"We'll take his body back to camp and prepare him for burial."

"We'll need his will," Antonia says. "He may have stipulated how he would like his remains to be . . . dealt with."

Meg closes her eyes tightly, and Cal wishes he could go to her side and wrap his arms around her.

"Of course," Bren says. "Cora and Meg, you may wish to sort through Sargent's belongings in the head ranger's cabin."

"It can't be safe up here," Cora says. "What about the dogs?"

Bren's jaw tightens. "The danger has passed."

Cal catches his look, and he clears his throat. "It's safe. The dogs are gone." Though he feels the grief and distress of the Old Herd, the Rift Stone confirms the gate is closed. There is none of the feeling of instability that alarmed him for days leading up to the Rift opening.

Cora, however, doesn't look placated. She looks tired and sore and brokenhearted. "I need to sit down," she says.

Antonia grimaces and settles her lantern on the Rift Stone. "Bring your mother over here, Meg. We'll get things figured out." She moves away, and with a glance from Bren, Abbot follows to help his aunt.

Meg gives Sargent and Rilke a curious parting look before leading her mother away, some mixture of grief and worry, resentment and fear. Cal again feels the magnetic pull in his core to follow her, but instead he stays where he is, glued uselessly to the Rift Stone. "Spear won't be the last," Cal says roughly.

Bren looks up.

"If Sargent planned this with help from Nutris, Spear won't be the last Fortune Hunter they send to induce chemical panic. Now they know they can boost their profits, they'll do everything in their power to make it happen again."

Bren's face hardens. "Then we cull the Lower Slopes before they get here."

Cal swallows. "Can we do that?"

Bren gives him a look filled with meaning. "Head ranger makes the call."

THE PYRE

A rare break in the clouds filters tepid morning sunlight over the summer barracks. Meg takes a wide berth around the cluster of buildings, still feeling the stiffness in her shoulders and lower back. She slept almost a full twelve hours once they made it back to the rangers' camp. Bren offered her and her mother Sargent's cabin, but Meg made do with a spare cot in the women's barracks. Cora wouldn't stay in the camp at all, still furious with the rangers for their stubborn refusal to allow Sargent conventional hospital care.

In the end, Cora let Antonia lead her back to Nero's Palace with the copy of Sargent's will found in his filing cabinet. There had been a brief blistering argument when Meg refused to return to the village with her mother, but she wanted to stay close to Cal and the conversation circling about the community's next steps. She wanted to see Rilke when she woke. Talk to her. Hear her voice. Bren did the best he could on the mountain, but back at camp, he gave her strong sedatives to ensure rest while her shoulder healed. Meg hasn't brought up her suspicions with anyone. Bren hasn't mentioned her outburst at the Rift Stone, her declaration that Sargent was a shell, a vessel for whatever that thing was . . . or is.

When Rilke woke on the Rift Stone, moaning in that deep guttural voice, all the hair on Meg's body prickled. She can't stop picturing that ribbon of gray light breaking free from Sargent, reaching for Cal. Her instinct to clamp her hand over his mouth and drag him off the Stone still strikes her as right. The Rift Stone unlocked her childhood memory. She saw Sargent's aura flicker and lift from his body. In her heart she believes that's when he died, and she realizes now, she's been grieving ever since.

She makes her way to the barn, and despite the weight of sorrow and worry, her pulse kicks up a notch. This will be the first time she's seen Cal since they made it back to camp. The first time she's seen him after a shower and a fresh set of clothes. She cringes to think of the state she was in when they kissed by the Rift Stone. However, the memory of that kiss has been on constant replay in her waking and sleeping thoughts since their lips parted.

A soft, deep laugh rises beyond the barn door, and Meg hesitates. It's Cal, laughing. A rare, marvelous sound that warms her inside. Someone is laughing with him—Joss, she thinks—and she can't decide if she's relieved or mortified that he's here. Has Cal told him about her, about the kiss? A sneaky desire to eavesdrop keeps her from nudging the door open.

"Well," Joss says, sounding extremely pleased with himself. "This makes up for abandoning me at Burntwood while you and Rilke ran off to have the adventure of a lifetime."

"How are *abandonment* or *adventure* even *remotely* the appropriate words for what went down on the mountain?"

"Says the glorious hero."

"Glorious?" Cal snorts. "Rilke saved my ass from Spear. I barely managed to fire one arrow up at the Rift Stone before I passed out and Meg brought me back from a frost coma. Again. *They* were incredible."

Meg smiles and bites her lips, straining to hear more.

"Master rangers still want you for head ranger."

A heavy sigh. "I'm seventeen, Joss. I've spent almost half my life trying to prove to this community that I belong here —"

"You don't have to prove anything to me," Joss interjects. "Or Ma or Abbot, Leif, Rilke, Bren. You have friends. You don't have to be so . . . isolated."

"I appreciate that," Cal says softly. "But there are plenty of others who don't feel the same way, and the thought of spending the rest of my life trying to prove I'm worthy of being head ranger sounds pretty tedious, to be honest. I'm not interested. Besides, there are now two master rangers about to develop Rift Sight besides Rilke. They have options."

Meg's shock distracts her and she doesn't hear Joss's reply. The master rangers had wanted Cal to replace her father. She doesn't know what to do with that information.

Joss's voice breaks back into her consciousness.

"At least you got the girl."

"Give it a rest," Cal mutters.

"I *told* you to be creative and look what happens."

"How can you possibly take credit . . . *shhh*."

"I'm a believer."

"*Shhh*," Cal warns again. Then, lifting his voice, "Meg?"

She cringes, and her face heats, but she lifts her chin and steps into the barn, giddy and hyperaware. "Busted."

Cal stands in a pen, his back to the door, his body half turned toward her, caught in a photo-perfect shaft of light streaming through the high window, golden dust motes gilding the air. He's feeding two young deer by hand, and the stampede survivors lift their heads timidly from nuzzling his palm. He's wearing clean khaki pants and a long-sleeved T-shirt, the soft gray cotton clinging to his shoulders and broad chest. She almost wishes she wasn't wearing gloves. His brown hair, slightly damp from a recent shower, is tucked behind his right ear, and that single hazel eye moving over her face and down her body confirms it: she definitely wishes Joss wasn't here.

Joss sits on the edge of the pen, his broken arm supported by a sling. Otho sleeps in the crook of his elbow, his beak buried in his tawny chest. The sound of a creaky door signals Reeva perched on a barrel, her injured wing folded close to her body. She performs an enthusiastic shuffle, and Meg rips a corner off the cold toast she brought with her from the summer barracks. Leaning on the gate, she tosses the toast onto the barrel, and Reeva clamps it down with a talon and stabs it with her beak like it's live prey.

"She'll be too fat to fly by the time she recovers," Joss says.

Cal snorts. "She's earned it."

Meg tears another piece off the crust. "What's Joss taking credit for?"

"You *were* eavesdropping," Joss says, eyes sparkling with mischief.

"Not very successfully with Detective Nose on the case."

"I almost didn't recognize you," Cal says. "You smell so clean."

"You can roll me around in the pen if you like," Meg says, ignoring the bloom of heat in her cheeks.

Cal dips his head, letting his hair swing past his face, biting back a smile.

Joss widens his eyes, a broad grin on his face. "My work here is done."

"Is anyone going to explain?" Meg asks innocently.

Cal levels a lethal stare at Joss, who clears his throat, swings his legs out of the pen, and hops down. "I believe I'm expected at the summer barracks. I'm on setup for the wake."

The tone immediately grows somber and Joss gives Meg's shoulder a gentle squeeze. "I'm sorry about your dad. I know things were . . . complicated . . . but he was a great man."

Meg nods and swallows, but there's a stone in her throat that won't go down.

Neither she nor Cal speak while Joss walks away, Cal with his attention on the deer, Meg with her eyes on Reeva. When Joss's steps fade, Cal says, "The master rangers found Spear."

She tosses the rest of the toast to Reeva and brushes the crumbs from her gloves. "He survived?"

Cal nods, scattering the last of the deer feed on the ground. He scuffs his palms together and wipes them on his thighs before turning to face her. Meg catches a heady waft of his warm, soap-clean skin and the hint of mint. She wants to reach out and pull him against the gate. "Him and only one other Fortune Hunter. They're being held in the old lockup in the village. The Ministry for Primary Industries is holding them until they can send an investigator."

"What about the cull?"

"Well, Bren is acting head of the community until the master rangers convene and make a call about the position of head ranger, and he's requesting a postponement on the cull. He wants the rangers to deal with the Lower Slopes and keep Nutris out of it."

"Will Nutris go for that?"

"They'll have to if the ministry finds in our favor."

Meg grips the top rail of the gate. "Will they?"

"Bren thinks so; there was a lot of shady stuff going down. Spear said . . ." He hesitates and rubs his hand along his jaw. "Meg, he said some things about your dad . . ."

A watery sensation weakens her joints, and she braces herself against the gate. "Tell me."

Cal draws closer, resting his hands on the gate. She wants to lean and rest her head on his shoulder, but something about his posture, his caution, warns her to keep her distance. He begins to speak, detailing Sargent's plan to assist Nutris in opening the Rift to induce mass chemical panic among the Herds. This is shocking enough, but the flip side of the agreement, to expose half the community to Rift Hounds in the hopes of increasing the number of Rift-Sighted rangers makes Meg want to lie down. He explains Sargent's failed intention to perform an endowment rite and pass on the leadership, but he looks away, not explaining what that means or who Sargent intended to replace him.

Her thoughts swerve straight to Rilke and the ribbon of gray light. She dips her face into her hands and digs her fingers into her forehead. "What if it's already happened?"

Cal looks up sharply, his hazel eyes searching her face. "What do you mean?"

"I saw something at the Rift Stone," she says. "I remembered what happened the night we were bitten, when Fergus Welsh died and Sargent was injured. I saw this . . . thing."

Cal listens intently, never once showing doubt. It gives her courage to tell it all, what she saw on the Rift Stone when he and Rilke lay on either side of her father and the moment the ribbon of gray light reached for Cal and she panicked, pulling him off the Stone. A shudder ripples through Cal, and his knuckles grow white on the gate.

"That's how we wound up on the ground?"

She nods. "Listen, I sort of heard what Joss said about the master rangers wanting you for head ranger. Did I do the right thing?"

He expels a gust of air, half choked as he says, "Yes.

Absolutely, yes. Did you hear me tell him I'm not interested?"

"What if Rilke . . . what if it . . . got inside her?"

"You didn't see?"

"I heard her gasp, seconds later, and Abbot and Bren, happy she'd come to."

Cal frowns intently. "Then we go back to Bren and the master rangers. Tonight. After the service and the wake and everything. We tell them again what you saw. I'll back you up."

"What if they won't listen?"

"We *make* them listen, and we talk to Rilke when she wakes, and if she feels even the slightest bit different or she's unhappy or starts acting weird . . ." He heaves a sigh of frustration. "I don't know . . . but we *don't* shut up or look the other way or pretend like everything's normal for nine years. We make some noise."

She shivers, part relief to have Cal so fiercely on her side and part nervousness at the thought of bringing it all up again.

He presses the side of his fist to his lips, his eyes casting back and forth. "It must . . . explain a few things for you? About your dad? It explains a few things for me."

She curls in her shoulders. "I thought he hated me for leaving. I thought he blamed me for what happened to Fergus, that he would never forgive me, that he punished me with nine years of silence, but really . . . he wasn't thinking about me at all. It wasn't even him."

"Meg." He hesitates, then rushes on. "I'm so sorry. None of this would have happened if I hadn't freaked out. If I'd just shut my mouth and gone with Social Services . . ."

"Don't say that." Her windpipe is so constricted she can barely speak. "We were kids. We made a terrible mistake."

Cal clamps his teeth together, blinking rapidly. "You must want to get on that ferry and never come back."

"You know that's not true," she says softly. The memory of the power in the ley lines throbbing through her bones makes it impossible to walk away. "This place is inside me, like it's inside you."

He rubs his face, and she glimpses the scar arcing across his jaw before his hair falls back into place. "Your mother won't let you stay."

She sighs and licks her lips, her eyes drifting to Reeva preening her good wing. The raven lifts her head, and Meg's vision blurs with the image of her standing close to Cal, him watching her intently. The image is filled with such contentment it soothes the tightness in her throat. She blinks the vision away and focuses on Cal, a soft smile lifting the corner of his mouth—he saw Reeva's sending too. "I'm eighteen."

He stares at her, then his eyebrows slowly rise. "You're going to stay?"

"Antonia came early this morning. Sargent left me the post office, his savings, and some assets. I don't know. I'll have to talk it through with Cora. Sort out the debts. But I can afford to stay. I can study by correspondence."

His face lights up, then he suppresses it just as quickly. "Things could go bad if Nutris pushes back. It might not be safe. I mean, it's *never* safe. The Rift will open again. And you have a—a life on the mainland. Your mother will . . ."

"Cal," she murmurs. "Don't you want me to stay?"

His chest expands, and he leans close, his eyes filled with intent. "Meg, I'm trying very hard not to be a selfish jerk."

"I want you to be a selfish jerk."

"Yes," he moans. "I want you to stay."

"You couldn't stop me anyway."

He snorts softly. "As I am well aware."

She leans closer, her chest almost brushing his arm, her face so close their breath mingles. "Am I allowed to kiss you?"

"Meg." His voice drops low, and he reaches tentatively to brush her long bangs back from her eyes. His fingers barely touch the skin of her cheek, sparking a delicious rush of tingling down her neck. He catches his breath and pulls his hand away, swallowing thickly. "Permission has nothing to do with it. Do you remember what I said about the ley lines?"

She screws up her nose. "Vaguely."

His gaze traces the details of her face like a caress, lingering on her lips, as he explains his theory about the lodestones defusing whatever makes physical touch so difficult for him. "I'm sorry," he finishes. "Not much use, am I?"

"Don't say that." She teases her bottom lip through her teeth. "We just have to be a little . . . creative."

"Excuse me?"

"You must know all the secret spots."

"Uh . . ." He blinks. "I . . . um."

"I don't mind a bit of hiking . . ." She cuts off, a smile spreading across her face. "There's a boulder in the hot springs. Where I first connected with Reeva."

An answering smile curves his mouth. "I think I know the one."

A bell chimes from the training yard, and their humor fades. The service for Sargent and the fallen rangers is about to begin.

* * *

Seven bodies lie shrouded in ranger burial cloth, a thick muslin embroidered with symbols that Meg knows nothing about. Laid out on wooden platforms, the fallen have been arranged around the fire pit like the rays of the sun. Sargent lies at the bottom of the circle. Above his head, flames blaze white and yellow, sparks crackling in the updraft. Bren and the remaining master rangers form a semicircle on the porch of Sargent's cabin. Meg stands with her mother, holding hands near Sargent's feet, tears slipping freely down their faces. Antonia and Leira stand on Cora's left. Cal and Joss and Joss's mother, who insisted on leaving her bed, stand on Meg's right. The rest of the community gather around the fallen in concentric semicircles fanning back across the training yard.

As Bren leads the service through a series of readings from ancient texts, Meg's gaze shifts to the master rangers' cabin. There are only three bite survivors. Rilke and two women, recovering in the makeshift infirmary. Their bites range from neck to shoulder to leg. Her stomach twists in knots thinking of the waste of lives before her, and for what? Sargent's obsession with Rift Sight? Or the thing that used his body for the past nine years. She can't tell what she's crying for, this loss or the loss of her childhood, or the men and women who were sacrificed in the pursuit of power and strength.

Her mother releases her hand, hitches a breath, and fumbles for tissues. She blows her nose, and Antonia wraps an arm around Cora's shoulders, gathering her close. Meg stretches her fingers, hot and uncomfortable in the now clean and patched gloves. She stares at her palms, and her chest tightens. Yak fur gloves. A gift from her father. *Not* her father. What then? A lie. A lure. A false promise.

She doesn't know if she's ready to live with bare fingers, but suddenly the thought of wearing these gloves a moment longer makes her skin crawl. Biting hard on the inside of her cheek, she peels the fabric free. She briefly fantasizes about tossing them on the pyre, but that would be melodramatic. People would look, and she doesn't want the attention.

Instead she jams them in the pockets of her jacket. Cal shifts next to her, catching her movement. She looks up at his concerned eyes, and her heart swells. His gaze flicks to her hands, a question creasing his brow. The intensity of his gaze communicates, more loudly than words, his desire to take her hand in his. He doesn't, of course, for his own reasons and for hers.

She wets her lips and brushes her fingers over the back of her knuckles, slowly, deliberately, inviting him to look. The gesture feels bold, intimate, and while his gaze is directed at her hands, she holds her breath, turns one palm over, and runs her thumb across the scars. Breath held, she forces herself to look up and meet his gaze. A tremor moves through his body. Slowly, not taking his eyes from hers, he reaches and tucks his hair back behind his left ear, revealing the fullness of his face.

In that moment, the uncertainty that lies ahead, the tough decisions, even the painful conversation she'll have to face with her mother, seem less impossible. She smiles gently and folds her hands together. He lowers his head and lets his hair fall again across his jaw. They each release a soft shuddering breath and turn to face the pyre.

ACKNOWLEDGMENTS

Thank you to my Heavenly Papa, my source, my joy, and my rock for surrounding me with the support that makes this journey possible. Thank you to the stalwart and generous loves of my life, Ian, Sophie, Isabelle, and Evangeline. Four books and the band's still together!

My heartfelt thanks to publisher Linsay Knight and the stellar team at Walker Books Australia for not merely nodding politely, or backing away and making a note to change the locks on the doors, when I proposed this peculiar story. I'm so grateful for Mary Very (Verney) rushing the opening chapters to Linsay's office with a great gushing "We need to publish this book." How super to have editors and a publisher who love mythology and dimensional rifts and mutant space hounds as much as I do!

Thank you to the ever-encouraging and supportive Nicola Santilli, whose sharp instinct and editorial vision, working alongside Linsay, helped me pull this story into shape. Working with a pantser author requires faith, patience, and courage. Nicola and Linsay have these qualities in spades.

Thank you to my agent, Chris Else, whose calm, good sense keeps me on an even keel. I so appreciate your ongoing support and belief in me and my work.

Thank you to Jessica Walton for many wonderful Twitter DMs, links to online resources, and articles around disability, facial difference, and living with scars. I treasure our long Skype sessions about *The Rift* and so much more: life and love and being. Thank you for encouraging me to grow in awareness as I sought to make this work more inclusive and accessible. You are compassionate, fierce, and wise, and I so appreciate you.

I am the grateful beneficiary of yet another incredible cover design by the brilliant Amy Daoud, who just gets me. Thank you, Amy, for the way you embrace my words and my eclectic writing-music playlists as you capture the atmosphere of the story so beautifully in art. I am so proud of this cover. I love it.

My appreciation to copyeditor Virginia Grant for making the text shine, and to Jebraun Clifford for providing the perfect name for Nellie's hummingbird, Flint.

Thank you to the marketing team at Walker Books Australia, Simon Panagaris and Steve Spargo, and the dedicated sales reps who put my books into the right hands and onto the best shelves. Thank you to my former and current publicists Anna Abignano and Maraya Bell, digital wizards Bethany Nevile and Stephanie Ryan, and publishing assistant Sarah Ambrose for all their hard work, support, and creative flair. Thank you Stella Chrysostomou and Thomas Koed of Volume Books for their kindness and support. Thank you to all booksellers, librarians, and teachers who value young readers and local authors.

I cannot express the giddy thrill of receiving Isobelle Carmody's support of this book. Pinch me, I must be dreaming! Then Alison Goodman and Michael Pryor joined the endorsement party, and I needed a cup of tea and a lie-down. My heartfelt gratitude to these three legends of the craft.

Thank you to Hayley George for being so keen on my zombie-deer adventures and for your unflagging love and support. All of my generous and enduring friends who answer my desperate text messages with kind words, loving prayers, and timely good humor, Ann Ridden, Audra Given, Tracey George, Jo Roche, Miriam Fisher, and so many others, thank you.

Thank you to the YA writing community who make the journey such good fun. Fleur Ferris, Ellie Marney, Trinity Doyle, Nicole Hayes, and Gabrielle Tozer, thank you for all the laughs, love, and wisdom on the ups and downs.

My appreciation to the supportive community of Kiwi YAKers on Facebook.

Twitter YA: you are never boring, often hilarious, and always passionate about books.

Many thanks to the bloggers, reviewers, and fans (#SparkArmy!) who pour their passion into e-mails, art, Instagram, fan fiction, and events.

And to every reader who has taken a chance on one of my books, I'd like to bake you a cake.